MW00782083

THE DEVIL IS FRENCH

ALSO BY
DELILAH MARVELLE

THE DEVIL IS FRENCH

A WHIPPING SOCIETY NOVEL

DELILAH MARVELLE

My dearest Reader,

Unlike most historical romances that feature a hero and heroine whose journey and love for each other ends at a mere one book, I am extending a unique invitation for you to join in on a much bigger love story.

When Ridley and Jemdanee first appeared to me, and their pages started to go beyond what two books could hold, I realized they needed three books. This is the second book of the three in *The Whipping Society Saga*.

While I will ensure each full length book ends without dangling your hearts too far over the edge of impatience, please come to this book and those to follow as you would to an episode of your favorite TV show. Many questions will be answered, others not. Each book will be wrapped up in its own way, but obviously… for there to be more, not everything can be resolved.

Please note this is still very much a historical romance, simply done on a three book scale. It's my hope you enjoy spending an unusual amount of time with Ridley and Jemdanee as each book brings them to closer to the people they must become to embrace what awaits them: true love.

I thank you for being a reader.

Much love,
Delilah Marvelle

GLOSSARY OF TERMS

Arrey—Expression of surprise in Hindi. Like 'Hey!'

Bas—'Enough!' in Hindi.

Bête sauvage—'Wild beast' in French.

Bibi—The Hindu mistress of a house and/or a Hindu lover, usually used with respect.

Bidi—Indian cigarette made from tobacco rolled in an ebony tree leaf.

Bhang lassi—A drink made of yogurt or milk, spices, rose water and cannabis (weed).

Bhoot-nee ke—Son of a female ghost in Hindi, an offensive term for someone being mischievous or an idiot.

Bhut jolokia—Ghost pepper cultivated to India, known for its exceptionally high heat level. Jemdanee keeps a powdered form of it which she utilizes as a defense equivalent to mace.

Bonne nuit—'Good night' in French.

Capsicin/Capsaicin—Active ingredient in chili peppers that causes burning of skin/eyes. First extracted in 1816 by Christian Friedrich Bucholz, he called it 'capsicin' after the genus Capsicum. John Clough Thresh isolated it in a purer form naming it 'capsaicin' in 1876. The decision to use the spelling of 'capsicin' in this book instead of 'capsaicin' is due to it being the only word in use at the time by the scientific community.

Chakla—Although this term is for an Indian kitchen utensil (a flat circular board to roll out dough) it is ALSO a historical term for 'brothel'. Laying out dough on a board one smacks and rolls seems rather… fitting.

Challo—'Let us go' in Hindi.

Charas—A hashish form of cannabis handmade in India,

Pakistan, Nepal and Jamaica.

Coca/Limestone combination—Prior to the first known extraction and isolation of cocaine from coca leaves back in 1859, crushed limestone was used to draw out the 'high' from coca leaves. The coca leaf by itself gives the user a heightened effect of modern caffeine.

Commiphora wightii—A flowering plant known as guggul found in North Africa and Central Asia, but is most common in India. The resin, known as gum guggulu, is harvested from the plant's bark and has a scent similar to myrrh that is used in incense and/or perfumes. There is a belief it drives away evil spirits and removes the evil eye.

Dactylorhiza hatagirea—A species of orchid found in Nepali/Himalayan regions consisting of long flowering stems. A 'Panchaule' (meaning five fingered hand) arises from its root resembling fingers of a hand bearing 3-5 fingers. The plant is gathered for its medicinal tubers and roots that taste sweet.

Dhatt—A Hindi form of expression used to reprimand something inappropriate.

Diya—A clay lamp with a cotton wick dipped in vegetable oil.

Felo-de-se—Act of suicide, derived from the Latin term 'felon of himself'.

Gopika—A Sanskrit word originating from the word *gopala*, a person in charge of herding cows. In Hinduism, *gopika* is the feminine form of *gopi*, and refers to a famous group of herding girls made known for their unconditional devotion to Krishna.

Goonda—Thug or miscreant in Hindi.

Government House—A colonial mansion in Calcutta resting on 27 acres of land. It was built in 1803 by the first Marquess of Wellesley with the belief that India should be ruled from a palace, not a mere country house. It became the home and political seat for every viceroy of Calcutta. Its construction took four years and was completed at a staggering cost of £63,291 (about 4 million today!). As a result of its obnoxious expense, Lord Wellesley, who had it built, was dismissed for improperly allocating the funds of the East India Company in 1805. Although the man lost his position as Governor General over the creation of the Government House, it went on to be used by every viceroy thereafter.

Haan—'Yes' in Hindi.

Hariya—Indian beer made from rice.

Idli—A flat cake made of de-husked black lentils and rice, popular in India during breakfast.

Ittar—Hindi term for 'attar', an essential oil derived from botanical sources, used to perfume.

Phaujee—Soldier or male constable in Hindi.

Jee—A formal response to a yes or in answer to a question in Hindi.

Joie de vivre—'Exuberant enjoyment in life' in French.

Kala namak—Literal translation from Hindi is 'black salt'. A very pungent condiment salt used in South Asia, also known as 'Himalayan black salt'.

Kara bracelet—Worn by Sikhs to symbolize an eternal and unbreakable commitment to God.

Kirpan—A sword or dagger carried by Sikhs, originating of religious command that five items of faith be word by a Sikh at all times, a kirpan being one of those items.

Krishna—One of the Indian divinities worshipped as the eighth incarnation of the Hindu god Vishnu and also as a supreme god in his own right.

Lakshmi—Hindu goddess of wealth, fortune, and prosperity. She is the wife of Vishnu.

Lapis lazuli—A blue mineral consisting mostly of lazurite used for gems or pigments.

L'Appel du vide—'Call of the void' in French, meaning: a sudden urge to do wild things.

Laudanum—An alcoholic-based solution or morphine/opium used for pain.

Maa—'Mother' in Hindi.

Mon chou—'Sweetheart' in French.

Ma femme dorée—'My golden wife' in French.

Memsahib—A white foreign woman of high social status living in India.

Mohur—A gold coin formerly minted by British India, usually equivalent to 15 silver rupees.

Mon coeur—'My heart' in French.

Mon dévot—'My devotee' in French.

Murdannia striatipetala—A flowering plant from the dayflower family, found in tropical regions, including India. Petals are pale lavender/purple with dark contrasting veins, consisting of three petals to make the flower, flowering from knobby wooden stems.

Nahin—'No' in Hindi.

Pallu—The most decorative part of the sari that is draped over the right shoulder. It can be tucked, pinned or left free-flowing, and much like the language of the fan in the Victorian era, which was used to communicate, its placement can be used to communicate an expression.

Papaver somniferum—The opium poppy, a species of plant, and the principle source of opium. Latex oozes from the incisions made on its green pods, and once dried, can be utilized to create the opiate. Dried opium and laudanum are derived from this particular species.

Punkah—A massive cloth fan (sometimes soaked in water) fastened to a frame suspended by the ceiling and worked into motion by the pull of a rope to produce the movement of cooler air through a room. This was done by servants and its usage dates back to as far as 500 B.C.

Raat ki rani—Night blooming jasmine, referred to as 'Queen of the Night' given its small, white flowers only open at night.

Rara avis—'A rarity', derived from its Latin use of 'strange bird'.

Rupee—Monetary coin tracing back to ancient India in circa 6th century B.C. and one of the earliest known issuers of coins in the world. The coin remained in use during the takeover of India by the British and was silver based during much of the 19th century.

Salla—Expression of disgust, derogatory in Hindi.

Sahelii—A word for a 'female friend' in Hindi.

Sahib—An Urdu honorific as a term of respect that is the English equivalent of 'Sir'.

Semnopithecus priam thersites—Tufted, grey langur monkey, found in Southeast India.

Sepoy—An Indian soldier serving under British or European orders.

Shiva—One of the principle deities of Hinduism.

Sonti—A rice-based Indian alcoholic beverage similar to sake.

Tendu—The Coromandel or East Indian ebony is a species of a tree native to India and Sri Lanka and has a hard, dry bark. Known by its Hindi name *tendu*, the leaves are wrapped around tobacco to create the Indian *bidi*.

HISTORICAL CHARACTERS

Dr. 'Professor' Nathaniel Wallich—Born January 1786 in Copenhagen, died 28 April 1854, London. Wallich was a surgeon and botanist. After sailing to India in 1807, he worked for a period of time as an assistant botanist to the East Indian Company. He contributed to the development of the Calcutta Botanical Garden, creating a massive herbarium collection which was distributed to collections throughout all of Europe. Many of the plants he collected from expeditions were named after him. He served as a Professor of Botany in Calcutta.

FUN HISTORICAL ON DIT

In Chapter Ten, Jemdanee is awakened by a song sung by drunken soldiers and Ridley. To experience the song and melody in its time of history, go to YouTube for Henry Purcell's COME, LET US DRINK, while you read the opening chapter.

This authentic song pulled from history was playing while this chapter was being written and will put you in a jolly mood, as intended.

PROLOGUE

Pandora has a box (or a wicker basket).

O ne of seven hundred and thirty seven letters stuffed into an oversized wicker basket that is falling over from the weight of endless words.

17th of March, 1832
My little raven,
Whilst I continue to battle the stiffness of this long healed injury, boxing daily at the academy has proven helpful in strengthening its weakness. Unfortunately, my lethophobic physician only ever nags me about my overexertion and is unable to comprehend that I am a resurrected rara avis. In other words, a rarity that has risen above science in the name of a woman. My strength resides not within the muscular structure of this broken body, but within an unbreakable mind that seeks to claim what it wants most: you.

Feeling invigorated enough to work outside the house again, I have returned to working alongside Scotland Yard. Hence the silence. Aside from guiding more progressive inspectors like Parker, whom I am beginning to admire due to his tenacity, Finkle continues to amuse me by assigning my talents to 'unusual' cases. This last one involved a confectioner obsessed with cannibalism (the heart in particular). To quote this bête sauvage, he confessed to me that it was the toughest muscle to chew through and he found it sweet.

It certainly gives a new meaning to the term sweetheart.

You seem to have gone down that feral path yourself, mon chou. For you revel in devouring the beating heart of a man. This man. How does it taste? Is it really sweet or more on the side of bitter? Keep chewing at all four chambers and its two ventricles if you must, but remember I only have one heart for you to consume and I do consider it vital to my ongoing existence.

How I suffer. I am forced to stare at the copper tub you once pleasured yourself in and all too often cling to its sides, pleasuring myself alone. Moans, osculation and growls of our pleasure as we sweat and spend together overtakes every ragged breath I drag in through teeth knowing it will one day be real. The feel of your gorgeous, brown skin haunts these fingertips as I try to remember what holding you feels like. In too many breaths and very soon, I will dig out the magnificence of your soul that belongs to me whilst your cunt weeps along with you, begging I do nothing but fuck you into bliss.

Why do you not write? Have I not crawled enough? Or is it because I am too obscene in my devotion? Obscenity, my Jemdanee Kumar, defines me. That night, when I toasted to your innocence and drank laudanum to erase my breath, it was my chivalrous attempt to eradicate a mind that never rests whilst saving you from the depravity that has devoured my decency since youth.

Your ever annoying Dr. Peter Watkins has asked once again in a curt missive that I cease writing to you and enable you to embrace a future without me. Inform that mustachio of a clothesline that even if my hands were cleaved from each wrist, I would still be using this mouth to move the quill across the parchment.

As you know, I continue to be in close communication with the Field Marshal to ensure your wellbeing. He informs me of your progress there at the Government House and verifies you have, in fact, been reading all of my correspondences.

Which brings me to the point of this letter.

I have negotiated and accepted an assignment from the Field Marshal through his intelligence squadron that will take me into Bombay. Kneel to your venerated inspector knowing the contract you so fatuously bound yourself to, will be terminated in return for my services. I do this and more in your esteemed name knowing you have miraculously unleashed the man I swore I would never be to any woman. I count each breath in the hope of folding you into my arms without any further damage to anatomical or life-sustaining organs.

Your humble servant and overlord,
Evan Oswald Ridley

Postscrīptum. *Your attempt at domination is unremitting and charming. What happens next?*

CHAPTER ONE

Calcutta, India—1833
The Government House, 6:21 a.m.

Beyond the marble and mosaic domed halls of the Government House that beckoned her into believing she was amongst cultivated men, Jemdanee Kumar had seen enough unregulated behavior to evince otherwise.

As apothecarian and greenhouse custodian it kept her well-employed.

Last month, before a dining legion of upper class society, a diplomat had punched a fork into the hand of another diplomat, impaling that rattling palm to the pristine linen table they supped at. The two 'gentlemen' had been arguing over a state-commissioned contract when the subject of his philandering wife came up.

Jemdanee had been hollered upon by his lordship, the Governor General, to provide her wound-healing turmeric paste to the oozing, blood-pronged punctures as fainting women were ushered out. Fourteen men had hovered over that trembling hand to observe the anti-inflammatory effects of her turmeric paste and were so impressed by its quick deliverance of recuperation, they ordered several dozen jars for their shaving kits, earning Jemdanee an additional twenty rupees.

It had been a most excellent night.

While delegates from other countries occupied her time with

4

their incessant need for insect repellents and aloe elixirs for sun-burnt faces, Lieutenant Bradley, under whom she was formally employed, depended on her services on the hour. Sometimes as late as midnight, he rang for her to deliver a tray of restoratives into the Council Room where he oversaw most of his political work.

If only it ended there.

As mandated by her contract, Jemdanee was responsible for the production of every herbal-based curative which Dr. Harper issued to soldiers at the compound.

Despite being a female *and* a Hindu, her usefulness outweighed everyone's prejudiced snickers. In fact, once the men grew accustomed to her vivacious, chatty presence, she became incredibly popular.

Too popular.

Officers elbowed their way into Dr. Harper's office merely to watch her climb up toward the ceiling of the rolling ladder and use her sari-clad hip to skid from one shelving side of inventory to the next. Her refusal to wear slippers or a corset was whistled at and her bright blue eyes set against the deep bronze of her skin had earned her the nickname of Lapis Lazuli.

It was why she started wearing non-prescriptive spectacles.

Aside from making her look more 'sophisticated' whenever she staggered out of the government library with a stack of phytology books, the gleam of the lenses and the small-frames brass did something miraculous.

It distracted men from seeing her eyes.

Eyes that, in her not-so-humble opinion, were far too blue for a Hindu.

She hated that men noticed the shade of her eyes in the same way they noticed the shade of her skin. Whilst certain women obsessed over jewelry, she obsessed over having a collection of glasses. She had a variety of styles that ranged from Martin Margins to lorgnettes. Each represented whatever mood she was in.

Today's mood? Railway spectacles.

There was a lot to do.

Jemdanee looped the brass wire around each ear, adjusting the square lenses into place.

Still nude from the hip bath she'd taken, her bare feet squeak-

squeak-squeaked across the tiled floor of her bedchamber.

First order of business?

The Regimental Surgeon needed nine bottles of laudanum for an upcoming amputation.

Having attended eighteen surgical amputations in the past three years, she no longer fainted and/or gagged when the flesh was sectioned off by a blade like bacon, a trephine bored a hole into the cartilage, and the rest of the bone crunched off beneath the saw like toffee brittle being served to a hoard of eager children.

Gagging didn't help the poor bastard on the table who screamed for more sedatives.

"*Chunmun.*" Sweeping up a prescription ledger from the drawer of her pedestal desk, Jemdanee slid a large bowl of sliced apples across the uneven floor with her foot. "*Chunmun!*"

A scrambling sound, followed by fingers grabbing an apple, clattered the porcelain bowl against the tile at her feet. A grey langur monkey darted back across her bedchamber, climbing up the banyan trellis and past a maze of ropes woven together to uphold countless jars filled with carnivorous plants that decorated the room.

He dangled by the hemp ropes with one arm, swaying jars as he crunched on an apple with the scrape of teeth. "*Hoooowaa!*"

She pointed. "You are most welcome. I decided on a change in the menu. Bananas are boring."

Flipping through the ledger, Jemdanee noted the prescription she'd written last night had been... chewed out from the deformed binding. "*Chunmun.*" She snapped up the ledger, wagging it. "What is this? Do I not feed you enough?"

Large black eyes framed within an equally black face blinked. His grey, fringed hairy head tilted in confusion. With the smack of lips, he held out the saliva-slathered, gnawed fruit.

She tsked. "Like any man, your inability to comprehend how you complicate my life is annoying." It appeared he was getting into drawers now. "Fortunately, it is our last week here at the compound, so feel free to destroy whatever government property pleases you."

With a smirk, she set the ledger onto the pedestal desk, dipped the nib of the quill into the well, ignoring the dots of ink she flicked across the teakwood, and scratched out another cordial.

Dried opium, 9 oz. Pour upon it 9 gills of boiled water and work into mortar. Funnel equal parts into 16 oz. bottles containing alcohol of 76 percent proof, ½ pt each, adding alcohol to preparation. Requires saturation period of 24 hours before use.

She still had to leech the *papaver somniferum* plant whose stalks she had earlier cut in order to make powdered opium. She never stored it on her shelves anymore.

Officers were stupid enough to roll the opium in dried *tendu* and smoke it.

One idiot stole an entire tin from her inventory, tapped out too much and died.

She didn't feel sorry for him at all.

The tin had been labeled with the word WARNING.

Wedging the quill into the ink well, Jemdanee tore the prescription from the ledger.

The chime of the clock made her snap toward it naked. "Oyo."

Stumbling over to the cluttered dressing table, she tucked the prescription into the medicinal chest knowing she was late. Banging open the wardrobe, she grabbed a blouse and petticoat, yanking both on, while wagging out a sari from beneath the mass of tangled silk.

With the twist of exasperated lips, her fingers poked through uneven holes covering the lavender silk of the *pallu*.

It had been... chewed through by Chunmun.

She almost thudded her head against the wardrobe.

Rescuing him from the cage of a market had turned into work. She sometimes left the window open hoping he'd find himself a mate and disappear.

It never happened.

She pointed at Chunmun's head. "You and I are going to discuss your lack of manners and it will affect the sort of fruit you find in your bowl." Rifling through the stack of saris, the quivering pile toppled, sending veils and saris across the tile floor at her bare feet. "*Ayyyyy*."

Shoving them all into the wardrobe with arms and a foot, she slammed the door and frantically pleated and wrapped herself in a sari, ensuring the decorative part draped her shoulder.

Earning a wage was anything but glamorous.

Wedging out several *bidis* from a hidden stash, Jemdanee tucked them into her blouse.

The distant shouts of the regiment gathering drifted in. She quickly pushed aside the shutters of the massive window to permit a breeze to flow through. "Chunmun." She gestured toward the window. "Go visit some relatives and make turds everywhere but here."

Chunmun swung from the roped maze of potted plants down onto the floor and grabbed another apple from the bowl, crunching. He eyed her, curling his grey tail and gave her his back.

She snorted at the direct cut and patted the frame of the open window as hues of the rising sun streaked the vast morning sky beyond the tamarind trees.

Lowering her gaze to the sill, she paused.

A stunning bouquet of *murdannia striatipetala* held together by a black satin ribbon was draped on the ledge. The gathering of dew on its striped, lavender blooms hinted it had been delivered late at night.

Her heart popped as she frantically angled the missive attached to the black ribbon.

Until our breaths meet on the morrow,
I am, as ever, your servant and overlord,
-R

Awareness prickled her skin, her thighs, and her breasts.
Ridley.

The swaying creak of potted ropes from within her room fittingly announced his presence.

She knew he'd been set to arrive out of Bombay.

He'd been writing missives through military courier every other week.

Missives she... had finally responded to.

A woman couldn't be miffed forever.

Like a sepoy awaiting the first round of fire, she edged past the frame of the window and scanned the surrounding garden acreage outside the stone columns of the building. The rustling of low hanging trees basking in the bright morning light and the chirping of exotic birds as several peacocks bobbed across the lawn with tails dragging downward affirmed he was nowhere in sight.

Her fingers dragged up the knobby stems and three-leafed,

lavender blooms.

Touching its soft, oval petals adoringly to her lips, the honeyed fragrance permeated the muggy morning air, whispering of too many exotic things to come.

You are now in my land, Ridley. Not I in yours.

Heavy, approaching steps made her almost flop the flowers onto the windowsill.

A lanky but tall cadet trudged past the gravel pathway of the manicured grounds with the thud of scuffed leather boots, his musket propped on the shoulder of a yet to be decorated uniform. He glanced toward her, pecan-brown eyes capturing hers beneath a cap that matted down sweat-soaked hair.

His freckled, boyish face brightened despite a sizable bruise fingering his jaw. He perked and tapped his forehead in salute. "*Miss Kumar*! I heard from the Field Marshal it's your last week!"

Jemdanee touched two fingers to her forehead in salute. "It is and praise be *Lakshmi*. Do tell your brethren there will be no more requests for *charas* and *bangh*." She pretended to puff the cannabis most of these soldiers wanted her to roll for them.

Tucking Ridley's bouquet against the sill, she eyed Dunning. "What sort of trouble met your face this time?"

He averted his gaze. "The usual."

"Come." She waved him over. "Permit me to examine it."

He shook his head, cringing.

"There could be blood clots." Jemdanee tapped against the sill, refusing to let him dart like he always did. "Boots here, if you please. Why did you not call on the office?"

Cadet Dunning heaved out a breath.

Trudging toward her across the treed grove, he matted the grass with large boots and veered through the low-hanging tree between them. He angled his face up toward her. "If I came to you every time this happened," he grouched, "I'd never leave Dr. Harper's office."

Jemdanee examined his jaw without touching it, the sizable black and yellowing bruise curving well below the throat. There didn't appear to be any blood clots, but there were visible thumbprints within the bruise hinting at what she already knew. His superiors used their hands like weapons and their authority without remorse. "I have a jar of comfrey salve to accelerate the healing. Shall I fetch it?"

He made a face. "Half your salves make me smell like a chit, which only gets me further pummeled." He pointed to the bruise. "Unless you have an ointment to ensure this never happens again, I'll do what I always do and live with it."

She leaned toward him, gripping the sill. "I may have to crawl through a few windows at night before I leave and put molasses in their boots so the fire ants can eat their toes raw. Last time, that bruise was over your eye. It keeps moving like an arrow on a compass."

"If only I had sense of direction." He fidgeted. "Do you have any honey sticks? The dining hall was cleared this morning before I arrived."

Poor Dunning. At eighteen, he had only enlisted because his father sought to make 'a muscle-flexing man' of him. As if there was anything wrong with a lanky boy with a big heart.

The heart was still a muscle.

As a result, the boy puffed and staggered behind the regiment, sneaking books on dragons into his uniform. Over too many weeks of him calling on the medical office for gauze and witch hazel balms due to tussles he never started, she became the mother he desperately needed.

The only acquaintance Dunning had made in the entire compound was with a Hindu sepoy.

It made him a bigger target.

Officers partook in endlessly assaulting him, calling him 'Dunce Dunning', pissing on his bedding (while he slept in it), and smearing henna onto his forehead to mock his support for Indians.

The boy endured it and even tried to smile at his aggressors.

Which only made it worse.

She reached out and adjusted his cap. "A honey stick will not get you through the day, *phaujee*. Go through the service door and ask Kalpita for a stack of *idlis*. She made them this morning. Tell her I sent you."

He perked. "She wouldn't mind?"

"As long as you praise her food, your bowl will never be empty."

"I'll praise her braid for a chance at more." He hesitated. "Does Kalpita ever ask about me?"

Chunmun scrambled up past her onto the windowsill and

shoving away her arm, hopped out, darting across the garden.

One less monkey to worry about.

She tsked. "For the safety of your heart which is the only thing not getting pummeled, never show Kalpita any interest. Aside from her not-so-subtle involvement with the Field Marshal, she would only flick your freckles off. Now I really must go. Everyone is realizing I am departing and the panic has set in. The prescriptions are *four* times what they usually are."

His brows creased. "The officers were talking about you in the barracks last night."

Jemdanee lowered her hand to the ledge of the window. She expected as much given she was leaving. Captain Thornbur, she knew, would 'miss' her most.

That puffy-faced Romeo made her braid frizz.

She'd learned to ignore his incessant, amorous shouts that included, 'Tap that dot for me, Hindoo!' His attempts to engage her reminded Jemdanee of being seven and listening to Bengali boys yelling, 'Your mother sucked my father's cock!'

Vexingly, the rooster always trudged into her greenhouse, clucking for attention.

So she did what she always did and turned to her most reliable friend: nature.

After all, a machete was not an option.

To ensure Thornbur and other romantically inclined officers couldn't get into her greenhouse, she started setting sumac traps above every door. It earned her the nickname of the Lapis Lazuli *Witch* (or bitch, depending). Having military men call her a witch (or a female dog) was more of a compliment than they realized.

A witch held power and a dog had teeth.

Unfortunately, both required effort and she had no time for idiots. "I am not at all surprised given my history with some of these officers. What were they saying?"

"It had to do with Mr. Ridley."

Her breath hitched. "What about him?"

Glancing around, Dunning picked at the metal of his musket and leaned in. "He came into the barracks last night and rammed Thornbur's head into several walls. I've never seen anything like it and will admit he lives up to the dark name the government gave him."

Her lips parted. "Ridley *rammed* Thornbur's head into a wall?"

"Several, actually. There was also a very sizable table involved." There was a watchful fixity in his face. "Doesn't he scare you?"

An exasperated breath escaped her. "In truth, I prefer to ignore the gossip."

He eyed her. "Why? Have you not been apprised on the reputation he earned over in Bombay?"

"Ridley had a reputation in London, as well, but that did not keep him from being a cultivated gentleman toward me."

"*Cultivated?*" He gaped. "You clearly never heard Officer Meyer's story. Meyer stupidly backhanded a sepoy and with the flick of cuffs links, Mr. Ridley turned and... *booma cracka*! Meyer was on the dirt, blood oozing out of his leg, howling more than the Hindu he'd hit. Mr. Ridley then whirled the pistol back into his belt and strode off whilst medics scrambled over to Meyer who had already fainted from the amount of bleeding from his calf."

Jemdanee cringed. *Ridleyyyyyy.*

"The Field Marshal, who despises *everyone* for not being crazed enough, *reveres* him. What does that say?"

She puckered her lips. "The Field Marshal reveres me, as well, but I am not crazed."

"Sometimes you are." Fervent enough to be more dramatic, Dunning pointed his musket at a nearby tree with a squint. "Last night, Barker confessed that when he was stationed over at the Flagstaff Tower, your Earl of Hell rode in and beat men to stitches with a cane that eerily looks like a raven. I saw it last night. It's made of *cast iron*. It gives a whole new meaning to making a man fly given it leaves *beak marks* the size of a fist!"

She lowered her chin. Ridley had nefariously upgraded his 'title' from *The Shadow Man* to *The Earl of Hell*. Shiva save his troubled kingdom and what she was about to inherit. "None of the rumors are true. I know him."

"I pity you for that." Pushing up his military cap with a finger, Dunning peered up at her. "I've read penny novels about inspectors like him, and usually, it's the criminals they arrest that prove to be more interesting, not the actual inspector. Why is he working for the government? Did the crown hire him to be an assassin?"

Like most men on the compound, this one was overly curious.

Ever since Ridley arrived into Bombay months earlier on a high-profile squadron case, she'd been answering a very long list of questions as if she held the suitcase to Ridley's mind.

She wished she did. "Cease with the nose-twitching. He is not an assassin. Ridley gallantly erased the terms of my contract with the Government House by taking up squadron duty." She adjusted the flowers on the sill adoringly. "Working for Dr. Harper has proven to be a bit… *lumpish*."

He nodded. "So I heard. Must be grand having an iron fist on your side. I have another ten years due to what my father insisted on. Might you inform Mr. Ridley I'm willing to hand over teeth to be out of here in five? I'm halfway out of teeth anyway."

She rolled her eyes. "Are you done with this chaffering? I have no time and must go."

Dunning fidgeted. Glancing around, he lowered his voice. "Given you're leaving soon and I won't have anyone to talk to about it, I do have a few… *female-related* questions about… *the anatomical sort*. Do you have any books on the subject?" He blinked rapidly.

Why were these ignorant souls always drawn to her?

She was beginning to understand the bruises. "I will give you the only map to a woman's body you will ever need." She pointed two fingers downward and tapped at the top of the V between her knuckles. "Her pleasure resides *here* above the entrance and never below it *or in it*. May she live happily, use a condom, and we are done. Now go survive the military by being less of a gossip. I have a long day ahead of me."

Dunning surveyed her fingers, then his own. "If it rests well above, how am I supposed to—"

She leaned out the window, shoving at his head. "I am phytologist, *not* a professor and must depart. I am late!"

He made a downward V of his own two fingers and squinting, jabbed at it. "Do I poke or… is it better to ram?" He demonstrated.

She snorted. "*Dunning*." She lowered herself and knelt on the floor, setting her chin onto the sill so they were face to face. "A bit of advice. Never chew anything stronger than yourself. Now lower those fingers lest I send the gods to ram and poke *you*."

He cringed and snapped his hand down.

The clock in her room chimed.

Groaning, he stepped back. "Gate change in ten minutes."

Thank Krishna. "You, my freckled companion, make me reconsider ever wanting children." Jemdanee swept a finger right. "Go to Kalpita for breakfast or you will never survive the day."

"I will! *Thank you!*" Scuffing his large boots with a frantic backpedal, he stumbled. "I will miss you more than I miss my mother!" He saluted. "May you survive the wrath of Mr. Ridley." He made a face and sprinted down the pathway toward the main entrance.

She heaved out a breath and angled the flowers on the sill.

Edging out of the window, she scanned the surroundings for a pulsing moment. Whatever happened to the educated, cultured gentleman she fell in love with? Had he ever been that?

In a most unladylike manner, she hollered, "*Ridley! Are you and trouble about?*"

Silence pulsed.

A peacock quickly turned and bobbed its way toward her. "*Mae owww! Mae owww!*"

She gave the spread of those feathers a withering look. "Wrong peacock. I was asking for the one with more feathers." Sweeping up Ridley's flowers, whose petals she pressed into her cheek, she closed the window, latched it, and rippled the blades down.

A creak and a click from within the room made her snap toward it.

Silence pulsed as Jemdanee surveyed the bamboo-paneled room that only revealed furniture.

Unnerved, she cradled the bouquet knowing the past and the present were about to be pushed back into the arms of Mr. Evan Oswald Ridley.

CHAPTER TWO

The following morning
The Government House, 8:19 a.m.

Staggering out of Dr. Harper's office past the banyan door that kept shutting on her rear, Jemdanee turned toward the cavernous marble corridor and wobbled against the skin-pinching weight of the medicinal chest she had to deliver into the greenhouse.

She hastened down the corridor, her bare feet pattering past opulently-decorated domed halls and massive ornate rooms that were quiet and eerily empty.

The constant silence and lack of people hinted at the waste Britain was known for.

A hall clock in the distance gonged, announcing it was on the half hour of eight.

Jemdanee froze. *Bradley*. She forgot!

Groaning, she trudged back.

Despite being already late, she slowed her dragging steps even more, the glass bottles, tins and clay jars in the mahogany medicinal chest chinking in mutual protest.

The termination of her contract couldn't come soon enough.

Veering into the vast Council Room, she set the sizable chest onto a teak sideboard with a thudding clatter. The creaking of

15

ropes that sent cool, circulated air from the *punkahs* attached to the ceiling swept the alluring scent of oak moss cologne wafting toward her.

He only wore it when he tried to impress her.

Which was often.

Men were such whores. It was amusing. "I bid you and that overuse of cologne a very good morning," she offered in her best boarding school English. "It appears the clocks in this building were ever so rude and lied to me again. Am I early?"

Lieutenant Rufus Adam Bradley, who was already in full regalia of his oak-leaf embroidered collar and cuffs and shoulder cord and nine pins, finished going through piles of paperwork he was organizing at the campaign desk.

She folded her hands before herself, awaiting yet another brotherly lecture.

Overly proud, overly religious, and inflexible given his rank and level of power, Bradley always, always hovered and fussed and sermonized against her 'wild Hindu ways'.

It was the Christian way.

"Almost forty minutes late," he muttered. "I'm astounded you appeared at all." Tucking away a small key he'd been fingering on the necklace he wore beneath his collar, he glanced back at her but didn't fully turn. "Where under the guard of Gabriel were you?"

And so it began. "I was gathering items from Dr. Harper's office. It took longer than expected."

He organized his desk, stacking ledgers. "Being late expresses a sign of disrespect."

"Being early expresses a sign of eagerness I never feel on *any* morning." She eyed him and all too honestly confessed, "I overslept and have not recovered a minute since. Am I forgiven?"

Turning toward her, softening green eyes captured hers. "Every time and always. How art thou, cherub?"

This one thought he could still charm her. Pfaw.

When she had first met the man three years earlier upon arriving back into Calcutta from London, she could sinfully attest that, yes, her knees had wobbled. Much like every woman's knees did. There wasn't a daughter or a wife of any officer whose corset strings didn't twitch like a cat's whiskers when Lieutenant Bradley and all six feet of him walked into the room.

His sunlit hair streaked with gold was never out of place. His forest green eyes made promises to a woman well before they were made. His classically handsome face, which was only disrupted in its perfection by a crooked nose broken in field combat, demanded a woman look twice to ensure his magnificence wasn't an illusion. He even had a dimple when he smiled and had been blessed with the astounding talent of being an artist who could paint and sketch scenes and portraits.

If angels had armies and military tassels, he defined it.

And then she got to know him.

He became the older brother she never wanted.

For Bradley lived by the way of the bible but unlike any normal man.

She was fairly certain he even crossed himself before he pissed.

His only flaws (according to him) were drinking apple brandy straight out of a decanter (but never too much!) and putting up his sand-ridden boots on the desk (which he didn't clean anyway).

It was incredibly unsettling to meet a barrel-chested paragon who propped the bible on the bulge of a bicep whilst sketching random scenes of Calcutta with charcoal sticks on every paper.

Sometimes, she was fairly certain he wasn't human.

"It's your last week at the Government House." He attempted to hold her gaze.

She kept her gaze trained at a window to avoid offering more than words. "*Haan*. It is."

He brightened. "The viceroy left me in charge given he departed on state business to Meerut. That gives me access to the terrace for supper this evening. Might you join me?"

Him and those green eyes were trouble. "*Nahin*. You know better than to ask."

He pointed. "You do nothing but emotionally assault me." Grabbing up an uncorked decanter of apple brandy from a pile of maps, he grudgingly swigged it and swigged again, letting out an appreciative breath between straight white teeth before setting the decanter aside with a chink. He crossed himself for it.

She chewed the inside of her cheeks in an attempt not to judge.

"When do you depart again?" He angled a piece of paper and picking up a charcoal stick, started sketching.

"Friday evening at eight."

Moving the charcoal stick in sweeps, he squinted down at his sketch. "Don't think you and I are done shaking this tree merely because you are leaving."

She rolled her eyes. "There was never a tree to shake, Bradley. Now might you please sign the paperwork the Field Marshal sent this morning? It needs to be delivered into the barracks for approval by Thursday."

He released the charcoal stick with the flick of fingers, letting it roll. "You will need a place to stay while you transition into a new way of life. Permit me to arrange a room for you over at St. John's. I will cover any and all of costs for however long you are in Calcutta. There, at least, you will be well protected by the clergy at all hours. All I ask is that you to be available to meet with me in the chapel every Monday and Thursday during the hours of one and four."

Mmmm*huh*.

As always, this tassel-wearing sermonizer did nothing but try to take over her life.

She had bitten her tongue raw these past three years in an effort to keep the peace when she realized that her own guardian, Peter the troublemaker Watkins, had strategically placed her in Bradley's care in the guise of 'employment'. When, in fact, it had been an 'agreement' between two Christian gentlemen wanting to make a respectable bride out of an Indian.

Bradley had met her several times over the years prior to her leaving to London and had asked Peter for an opportunity to utilize her phytology skills. Peter heard the choir sing in approval.

Who needed a meddling mother when she had a meddling Peter?

Fortunately, she had barred *everyone* from thinking it.

Whilst life at the Government House had given her independence and expanded her knowledge in phytology, it had been no different than staying at a bloke convent. Much like everyone at the Government House, she'd been forced to abide by more commandments than what Moses had actually brought down from the hill.

No smoking.

No drinking.

No cosmetics.

No exposing of the arms or the throat or any cleavage despite the wretched heat.

That, of course, was only a small list of over forty other rules that *also* involved a nine o'clock curfew. For three years—three!—she had endured a 'Thou Shalt Not' life.

At one and twenty, she was done with it.

A woman had to start living lest she start dying.

Thank goodness for Ridley. "I thank you for the offer of St. John's, Bradley, and I am quite certain their accommodations are 'divine', but a set of rooms have already been arranged for me at… *Spence's Hotel*." She almost hit her bindi and then him so he might feel it. "Did you know they have an emporium that sells cosmetics *and* a restaurant that serves *sonti* by the bottle all on the ground floor with a full hundred rooms above it? Did you *also* know each room has its own balcony overlooking Calcutta? Posh is posh."

He jerked toward her. "The rooms there cost an obnoxious sixty four a night and there is no chapel."

That would be the best part. "Such a pity, is it not?"

He squinted. "How are you even paying for it? Does Peter know?"

Ridley was paying for it. Waggle. "Peter and I no longer converse, Bradley. Not since he dragged me into this mess you and he both call my employment."

His brows flickered. "Are you *insinuating* you and Mr. Ridley are sharing a room?"

Uff. He knew and she knew and the world knew. "I am *insinuating* no one has any further say as to who I associate with or why. If you have any concerns, feel free to contact Peter but tell him I said 'Kiss my toe'."

Bradley paused and gestured toward her throat. "One would think you were off to meet the devil. Where is the cross the bishop gave you?"

She stared him down. "You seem to forget I am not of your religion."

He stared her down, in turn. "You wore it before. Why not now?"

"I only wore it out of respect for the employment I kept here, but I leave this Friday and have no further use for it." Crosses and Ridley seemed… satanic. No, simply no.

Bradley turned and stacked several ledgers. "People might offer you more tolerance as a Hindu if you wear that cross."

What little he knew.

A cross didn't stop people from spitting.

They simply nudged it out of the way.

Since arriving into his service, she had learned to choose her battles. For although, yes, Bradley was overbearing, as many of these white officers were, he did have a tassel of humor, generosity and kindness. Unfortunately, his largest tassel was that his way of thinking was as righteous as it was odd.

He often walked around Calcutta, sketching disjointed random scenes. If a Hindu woman was pouring uncooked rice into a clay pot with her frayed veil flapping in the hot wind, his charcoal stick would scratch out the woman's bare feet peering from beneath her sari, detailing the dirt between her toes.

Nothing more.

It was as if his mind worshipped things it oughtn't. She had never understood what Peter saw in him other than a shared strong belief in the Christian faith.

Apparently, that was enough.

Bradley folded several parchments, wedging them into folders. "I cannot permit you to share any form of lodging with a man you aren't married to. Peter would slash my throat."

"Peter is not as wrathful as you think."

He hesitated and softened his voice. "I am asking you to reconsider my offer of matrimony."

This man needed to be shot.

He'd been asking her for almost a year. A year! Like a whining child intent on going to the park and lingering by the window. She'd never met a man so overly polite about his pursuits.

One would think he were asking for a lump of sugar he wanted to add to his tea. "I am not interested in marrying *any* man. Not even Ridley. As a Hindu, it would eradicate more than my freedom. It would eradicate my religion."

Tossing his paperwork onto the desk beside him in agitation, Bradley glanced at her. "If that is your stance, I will send my mother to accompany you at Spence's for however long you are there."

She choked. "I would rather you send the Field Marshal. Sitting on a wicker chair listening to your mother talk about how useless her Hindu servants are whilst looking at me irks me into wanting to slap people. *Namely her*."

"This isn't about her, but my duty to you." He glared and pointed rigidly to himself. "Watkins named *me* your intended. Not Ridley. *Me*. How did I get left out of this?"

A breath escaped her. "Peter may have raised me, but that does not translate to ownership that now passes on to you. I came here this morning, not to be burdened by matrimonial advances, but to witness the signing of a certain document that enables me to leave the compound this Friday. I expect you to abide by your duty and will stand here and watch."

She pinned her gaze to his campaign desk to demonstrate.

His jaw worked. Aligning papers with several thuds, he dipped the nip of the quill into the ink well and scratched his signature with an upward sweep. "*There*." He tossed the quill, easing out a breath. "I hereby terminate your contract with the Government House."

She dared not fathom what Ridley had done to erase the terms.

She blamed herself.

After she'd stupidly signed a five-year contract, given it had offered her financial independence, she realized all too quickly she'd been duped into working for a man who Peter insisted she ought to 'seriously consider' after the 'scandalous debacle' back in London.

It was a mess.

Fortunately, Ridley had been in close contact with the Field Marshal all along and had rolled up his sleeves to remove the terms. That alone made her forgive Ridley everything for it spared her from disappearing into the night and getting arrested.

Desertion and its list of punishments were written into every government employee's contract.

As a Hindu she should have known better. "I have a long day ahead of me." She jabbed a finger toward the doorway of the Council Room. "Might I depart?"

"No. No, no, no. We are far from done. You will stand there and do something you never do: *listen*." Bradley angled toward her. "Other female employees under contract are now taking it into their heads that they can break every last rule the Governor General has set because of how lenient I have been toward you. That falls to me and I have to answer to the viceroy. Did you know Kalpita was out on the verandah openly smoking before a visiting guest? She never used to smoke at all."

Jemdanee cringed. "That one could take paintings off the wall and *still* not be dismissed. You do realize she and the Field Marshal are…" She popped a finger against her cheek.

He muttered. "Unlike the Governor General who never notices the trouble he employs, I see it all. Only that *bidi* she was smoking wasn't given to her by the Field Marshal, but you." He pointed. "You, Jemdanee, have been procuring tobacco to her, to others and yourself all paid for by *me* given I provide *you* a three acre greenhouse that grows the leaves. The only reason I *never* report you for the violation of our policies is because if I don't protect you from the wrath of the Governor General, *no one will*."

She bit back a smile. "Though you annoy me, I appreciate having an accomplice."

He sighed. "Understand that the bible insists on abstaining from such impurities."

It was her last week living in this weed-infested Garden of Eden.

What did she care if she miffed everyone off by eating a bushel of apples?

It was time she return to who she'd always been.

A Hindu paying homage to Krishna who was exemplary in defeating demons whilst playing chicanery, flirting with *gopikas*, and stealing butter.

Holding his gaze, she slid her fingers into the blouse beneath her sari and plucked out a *bidi*. She tucked it between her lips and said whilst wagging it with her mouth, "I have read your bible, Bradley, and nowhere does it say in *any* verse or even on the binding that I cannot smoke. Where does it say, *Thou Shalt Not Imbibe in Tobacco*? Show me that verse in that exact language and I will not only marry you but give you fourteen children."

He said nothing.

"Point made." She tugged the *bidi* from her lips and held it up, chanting to herself not to throw it at him. "*This* is part of being human, Bradley. I enjoy having flaws for it reminds me that I will never take the place of the gods I seek to worship. For *that* is true blasphemy. We are here to be human, not to be gods. We are here to live, not to die. Let me live."

He picked up the bible, gripping it. "Given the way you seek to live, you *will* die. I do nothing but worry. *I worry.*"

This one had too many pins weighing down the wrong side of his uniform.

Breezing over to the sideboard where she knew he kept the flint, she thudded open a small box and struck a match, lighting her *bidi* with a few puffs. Turning toward him, she blew out smoke into the air and set a sari-clad hip against the sideboard. "I will find you a wife, Bradley. That will be my gift to you given you have always watched over me." She meant it. "As such, you will not be rid of me quite yet."

Muttering, Bradley closed the distance between them and snatched away the bidi, tossing it into a nearby vase. "Why must you always go against everything I say or do?"

"Because you never permit me to say or do much. There was a reason Eve darted out of Eden. *It got boring.*" Leaning past him in agitation, she turned over the vase, carefully tapping out her *bidi* which was thankfully still lit.

"You and Eve could do with a bit of boring given the company you keep." Wagging up the bible, Bradley yanked out a parchment tucked within its pages, its wax seal broken. He unfolded it, setting the bible aside, and snapped the parchment straight, reading in an overly strained voice, "*My seed will become our communion as you revel in swallowing its thickness and finger your budding cunt to bliss.*"

Jemdanee cough-choked-coughed and winced, letting the *bidi* fall back into the vase, realizing he was reading one of Ridley's letters. Glaring, she snatched the letter from his hands and folded it, still glaring. "Where did you get this?!"

"That is for me to know and for you to explain." He snatched the letter back from her hand and held it to her nose. "Obscenity hardly offends me given I serve the government, but how is this even romantic?"

She pinched her lips refusing to get riled by his righteousness.

His gaze held hers. "You're failing yourself if you think passion defines love. Passion can blind you from seeing that there is no love at all. I used to be what he is, Jemdanee. Crass. Rebellious. Lustful. But such passions ultimately lead to self-destruction. It wasn't until I came to India that I was forced to recognize my own mortality and rediscover what matters: the soul I have to carry."

Her chest tightened knowing this 'angel' had only been born *after* coming to India.

Prior to his arrival to India, he'd been what most wealthy merchant sons were: self-entitled. He raced horses, studied art in Italy that would never see income, and spent money, money, money on women, wine, coaches, boots and cravats.

And then he joined the military upon his uncle's insistence that he take more responsibility for his life. Bradley's highly placed commission brought him to India where he continued to not only whore but drink and gamble beyond his own income.

Until a revolt had seen his body tossed onto a bullock-pulled cart loaded with still bleeding corpses of other officers that had been slaughtered.

He barely survived. It changed his whoring, drinking, and gambling loving ways.

He ordered bibles to be set in every room and in every barrack and donated sizable portions of his estate to countless charities, churches and the building of Christian Hindu schools whilst attending sermons as if entering himself as a horse in his own race.

Few men ever tried to change their ways and she admired that about him.

More than she wanted to admit.

She heaved out a breath. "I do not dislike you, Bradley. In truth, I do find you to be endearing, but you are more of a brother to me, which will never translate into anything I would ever kiss."

He folded Ridley's letter. "You seem to forget I have generously permitted you to work in a field reserved for white men and have given you privileges that go beyond your station in life."

How quickly men reverted to being children. "I never asked for any privileges."

"Maybe you should." He lifted Ridley's letter and smacked it. "*This* will *never* equate to respect. He will grow bored of you once he takes what he wants and will move on."

What little he knew. "There is far more to him than you think."

"Isn't he the sole reason why you first came to the Government House? To find sanctuary outside of his suicidal tendencies? Yet you mean to embrace him? *Why*?"

Her mind burned hearing it said aloud.

It was true that all she had from Ridley was a history too dark to tell and a tipping pile of letters that were as romantic and erotic as they were arcane. But his continued devotion whispered of what she had always known. What they felt for each other was real.

It had always been.

Her voice softened. "Ridley needs me. He is alone in his head and in this world." She gently tugged the letter from his hand. "If this is the torch he still holds for me even after three years, I can only imagine the depth of his heart." She tucked the letter into her blouse to demonstrate where it belonged. Over her own heart.

Bradley said nothing.

She glanced toward the clock, easing out a disbelieving breath knowing it was almost time. "As you know, the Field Marshal arranged a greeting line for Ridley which I was asked to be part of. I have not seen him since his attempted suicide and it will be an emotional hardship for both of us. I am asking you to respect that."

He said nothing.

Jemdanee squeezed his arm. "I am grateful for the position I have held here. You have protected me from your own associates at every turn and for that alone I am beholden to you." She peered up at him and smiled. "Might we part amicably?"

Bradley gripped the key attached to a chain around his throat. "You are the first woman I have ever met who treats me like a person as opposed to a prize. Given the sort of man I used to be, I need to be reminded of that at every turn."

He knelt, swaying the tassels on his uniform and lifted his green eyes pleadingly to hers. "I no longer wish to serve this government but you." He removed the pins from the sash of his uniform, one by one, and held them all up in one hand. "Marry me knowing I will do everything within my power to ensure your happiness. Marry me knowing I have met enough women in my life to know you are the path I wish to take."

She cringed.

Ah, yes. This was the grand illusion of what every woman wanted.

A dashing wealthy officer on his knee, followed by a church wedding and glimmers of children sired in the darkness of the night without a candle lest an ankle be seen (oh my!).

Then on that glorious holiday known as 'Christmas', everyone would tither around an axed tree sipping on punch floating with fruit bearing no alcohol. Whilst she? She would sit in eighteen pounds of neck-choking lace at a piano she would never be able to play as their half-bronzed children climbed up onto the muscled lap of an Adonis officer who over-smoothed their little heads with male pride and read them the bible in between tales of wars fought in India.

It whispered of a future full of mirth, hearth and certainty, but… no passion.

It was called being humble together.

And then there was Ridley.

A dark, provocative man who had fought his passion only to have almost died trying to keep them both from feeling it. There was no offer of mirth or certainty, but who needed it when the raging tingles in her chest and in her mind erased it all?

No man would *ever* be Ridley.

She gathered the pins without meeting Bradley's gaze and pinned them respectfully back onto his sash, one by one. "We have nothing in common. Not even a religion."

"That isn't true." He quickly rose. "Think of what you could do for your people."

O that be clever. Dangle her love for India and then accuse her of abandoning her people by not marrying him. "I cannot very well save my people when I refuse to save myself. Ridley is the only chance I have of being myself in the presence of a man."

Bradley swiped his face and ushered her over to the campaign desk. "Let us discuss getting you a separate room at Spence's. I will pay for it."

She groaned. "Bradley, I have apothecary orders to oversee."

"They can wait." He grabbed the decanter of apple brandy off a stack of maps. "Much like I have fought to place you into a position every government official lambasted me for, I can and will bend to whatever freedoms you seek. I will treat you like the equal you clearly wish to be. *Here.*" He quickly brought the decanter to her lips. "Go on. No glass needed."

She snorted and shoved away the decanter.

His hold fumbled, spraying and pouring brandy everywhere, all over her sari and his coat.

They flinched in unison as he scrambled to set it back against the pile of maps and the sketch he had earlier drawn.

Seeing the charcoal sketch, her lips parted. It was... her profile.

He leaned in, shoving it beneath a ledger. He piled other ledgers onto it. "I'm pathetic, I know."

She glanced up and softened her tone. "Why not ask Miss Wimberly to a picnic? Much like every woman without a ring on her finger, she asks about you all the time."

Bradley's features wavered. "Miss Wimberly can barely say her own name without blushing."

She laughed. "Is that not what you want? A humble woman dedicated to the ways of God and respectability?"

He glared. "I want a woman capable of knowing her own mind. None of these women—Why can you not..." Jerking her into the bulk of his arms, he thudded them both against the desk. "Hold onto those glasses." His mouth swooped down on hers. The burn of apple brandy stunned her as his tongue stroked hers, his hands jumping to her face to keep her from moving.

She choked, almost too stunned to comprehend what was happening.

Glog, it was like kissing her brother!

The son of a—With a backhanded punch and a shove, she jarred him away with the thud of hands, her palm gouging into a pin on his sash She scrambled off the desk and stumbled away from him, her heart racing.

Still astounded, her fingers now dug into her mouth, the sinful taste of apple brandy overtaking her lips. Even her sari was soaked with his brandy.

The room pulsed.

Bradley's green eyes grudgingly met hers, the rise and fall of his chest faltering. "Forgive me," he finally said.

Staring him down, she swore not to pick up his bible and start beating him with it. "I will set the bishop's cross on your mother's table. You might want to tell her why." She glared, swung away and hurried toward the door that was not as close as she wanted it to be.

"*Jemdanee*. Don't—" Bounding for the desk, he snatched up the decanter of brandy from his maps. "Duck, cherub." With the swing of his tasseled shoulder, smashed it against the frame of the door, shattering glass and spraying liquid that startled her.

Pulse roaring, Jemdanee stumbled against the wall to avoid the shattered glass strewn against the floor which almost gouged her bare feet.

She skidded toward the sideboard.

Thudding open the chest, where she kept all defensive substances, she frantically glanced toward him to ensure she had time, and grabbed a jar of *bhut jolokia*, uncorking it.

Dried chili pepper capsicin was going to make more than his nose bleed.

Holding it out before her like a sword, she waited with the spread of bare feet against the marble floor, centering her mind to remain calm. "I dare you to throw something else at me. I dare you, you-you… *bhoot-nee ke*. Your eyes and skin will burn *for weeks*!"

Bradley swiped hands across his collared throat. "I wasn't… I didn't want you to leave and knew you wouldn't run past the glass in bare feet. It's the military man in me." He held his gaze. "There is something I have to tell you. Let me say it."

Jemdanee swallowed hard, lowering the open jar in her hand.

He arranged ledgers on the desk. "I did something I shouldn't have and I'm ever so sorry."

She swallowed, tightening the fingers on the jar. "What do you mean? What did you do?"

Sinking downward against the desk, his knuckles gripped the far edge tight to white. "I—" His weighing hand slipped downward against the edge of the desk in an attempt to straighten himself. He stumbled, his head cracking hard into the desk from the impact. Rolling onto the floor, he went limp, his hand unfurling as blood gushed from his forehead.

Jemdanee's eyes widened, setting aside the jar. "Bradley?"

He didn't move.

She choked. "*Bradley*!"

With the grit of teeth, she heaved up the weight of her medicine chest and hurried over to him, setting it on the floor beside his unmoving head. Yanking out a linen gauze from her chest, she folded it fast.

Remain calm. He is not dead. Not. Dead.

Uncorking a jar of turmeric paste, she swatted the gauze into it and angling down toward that oozing wound, she set it hard against the wound, compressing it into place until the paste and the blood adhered to each other.

She set her cheek to that mouth, its faint breaths announcing he was still with her.

His lids opened with a wince, revealing eyes that had shades of amber in their green. He momentarily stared up at her in anguish, searching her face. "I shouldn't have kissed you. For now it's all I will ever think about."

Still kneeling on the floor beside him, she stared him down. "I have known you for three years, Bradley. Never once have you disrespected me. Why now? What is this about?"

He averted his gaze. "Sometimes the man I used to be rises above the man I want to be." Bradley sat up, his tassel swaying against his shoulder. Stripping the gauze from his head, he glanced at the blood and tossed it as if it were a weed. "I need to tell you something. I owe it to you and I owe it to my faith."

He lowered his chin to his chest as a line of blood traced its way down his brow. "Peter had asked me to remove Ridley from your life given his concern for your safety. His concern became my concern after I had an associate in London disclose information about Ridley. He associates with incredibly vile people, Jemdanee. The worst sort. Aside from his choice of career, his former wife runs a brothel dedicated to things I dare not verbally admit to and his closest acquaintance used to be an assassin for the crown who went rogue. That man, who abides by the name of Quincy, now lends his services to the highest bidder in the criminal world."

Startled, Jemdanee tried to piece together what she knew to be true. "Ridley is a good man."

"Of sorts. In glimmers. All men try to be and too many fail, me being one of them." He was quiet for a long moment. He sighed. "Nine months ago the Field Marshal tasked me to appoint a name to an executive order for a highly classified assignment." He averted his gaze. "A war with the Sikhs was tremoring the ground and no one in the intelligence squadron was willing to take on the delegation so I recommended Ridley. It was a… *felo-de-se* assignment."

Her chest felt as if it were cracking.

She knew about *felo-de-se* assignments.

It meant a man going in and never coming out.

And if it had involved the Sikhs, that assignment involved blood. For Sikhs were all too often misunderstood by the ruling hand of the British who only saw their dark skin and armies. Sikhs were incredibly fierce warriors, yes, with their *kara* bracelets that symbolized eternity and *kirpan* daggers they wore as part of their faith, but they were also people dedicated to meditation, their God and a code of conduct and honor.

An honor to protect their land and their people and their ways until all were dead.

Her throat burned. "Why would you do that? He is an inspector, not a soldier."

Still avoiding her gaze, he confided, "His investigative skills were needed to locate and destroy stolen documents from dangerous factions. He and another highly trained officer were assigned to the millstone and completed the assignment, but were discovered and attacked in their encampment a few miles outside of safety. The officer working alongside him was grievously injured and their horses were slaughtered in the raid, stranding them. I was astounded to hear Ridley had carried that officer for six miles to deliver him to a military medical tent, saving his life. So I suppose he has earned some of my respect back."

Her lips parted. "Why are you telling me this?"

Bradley swiped his face. "Ridley had sought to erase the terms of your contract with the Field Marshal so I… recommended him for the assignment. I did it thinking he wouldn't survive."

It was like death scraping her entire spine with a nail as it hit every cord and bump.

Her eyes burned. "You wanted him to die."

He lingered and then half-nodded. "In your name, yes. I'm sorry. I wanted you to know."

This one needed far more than his halo ripped off.

Staring him down, she uncorked a jar of capsicum and swatted a piece of gauze into it, then with the grit of teeth, reached out and set it *hard* against the wound of his forehead wanting him to feel more than pain.

He choked and hissed, jerking away, while huffing out breaths against the sizzle of the capsicum she knew he was feeling. He winced and swiped away the sticking gauze, bearing his teeth against the induced pain.

She glared, unable to breathe. "Can you feel the flames of the hell you preach to? *Can you?*"

Bradley no longer met her gaze.

Awful uncertainty washed over her knowing Ridley wasn't the one dragging in a mess this time. She was. She did this.

If she hadn't left London, if she hadn't abandoned Ridley, he wouldn't have had to resort to working for a government that had almost seen him butchered.

Realizing her trembling hand was bleeding from the impact of the pin, she seethed out a riled breath. "I cannot forgive you or Peter in this. *I cannot.*" She grabbed a gauze for herself and pressed it against her palm, scrambling to her bare feet.

Bradley sat, his blond hair matting against the blood-streaked gauze. "Do not blame Peter."

It was as if she had invited more than one devil into her life. She now had two.

One born of dawn and the other vesper.

"You have cursed us all." She back away. "What am I to do now? What am I to say to him? That I permitted your lips to touch mine barely an hour before his arrival after you attempted to sentence him to death?" Her eyes burned knowing it. "I feel guilt now. *Guilt!* As if I had somehow brought this upon him. *As if I had invited this!*" She glared and swung toward the doorway to leave. She paused before all of the scattered glass and pools of amber liquid.

Bradley jumped to his booted feet. Striding up to her, he tossed her up into his arms, causing her to choke.

She slapped and slapped and slapped him, stinging her hand. "I do not want your hands on me!"

He leaned away from her strikes but quickly crunched over the glass. Veering them into the corridor, he set her down, away from the glass. "If it gives you any consolation, I'm cursed to live with more than guilt." He held her gaze. "I'm cursed to love a woman who will never love me."

She swallowed, edging back. "Let me go, Bradley. I never invited this. I never wanted this."

He untied his cravat, letting it hang, and nodded. "I know. I was playing the part of a guardian angel not realizing I was letting the man I used to be take over. Go to him. Go. Maybe one day, when you realize his path takes you to a wall, I will be there to guide you away from it." He half-nodded. Turning, he used his large boot to sweep the glass strewn on the floor back into his study.

Numb, she swung away.

Dragging her hand across her lips to replace the burning taste of apple brandy with the salt of her own skin, she disbelievingly made her way down the corridor and past several other halls until she paused outside her bedchamber door.

She swallowed against the tightness of her throat knowing Ridley had almost died.

Though she had tried to battle her heart over the reality she had bound herself to since meeting him, she knew that every breath, every day, every week, every month, every year, every letter, and every word had only ever whirled into one man. *Ridley*.

CHAPTER THREE

Having less than forty minutes, Jemdanee banged open the door.

It was time to pull out all female ammunition right down to the jasmine.

Ridley had earned it.

Frantically unravelling the entire length of the sari from her body, she whipped it and kicked it aside. She tugged on the calling bell several times and skidded from one side of the room to the other fully naked, her mind unable to function.

Scrambling across her unmade bed piled with countless books she knocked over, she grabbed a honey stick from the glass jar and stuck it in her mouth to eliminate the lingering taste of apple brandy. Chewing the sweetness of the honeyed wax in an effort to stay calm, she rolled off the bed and jerked open all of the cluttered drawers of her dressing table, trying to locate hair pins.

There were none. She groaned.

Swatting aside the insect netting, she angled-open the shutter of the massive window to flood the shaded room with enough light to see.

The muggy heat of the morning outside and the distant shouts of the regiment gathering at the gate made her all the more anxious.

She finished chewing the last of her honey stick and spit out the wax into an ash pan. The time had come to wear the gown she had commissioned from Russia.

It had been sitting in the trunk for almost a year, waiting to be revealed.

The doors opened and Kalpita breezed into the room barefoot in her morning sari, a pained expression on her dark oval face. "You never call for me, *sahelii*. What sort of trouble are you asking me to partake in?"

The woman knew her too well. "I require assistance with the Russian gown."

Kalpita lowered her chin. "The heat."

"I would normally agree, but Ridley will be at the gate shortly." She couldn't believe he was actually here. "I only hope he is worth the angst I have suffered."

Kalpita's dark sultry eyes brightened. "Given the amount of letters he has written, I have no doubt." Clasping her brown hands, she shook them before touching her own bindi. "Bless yourself with *ittar* until you are glistening and offer him carnal suffering, for it is the only language men understand."

Ah, the glory of Kalpita.

Unlike the rest of the pucker-lipped Hindu women righteously serving the Government House in an attempt to erase who they were, Kalpita embraced her life with the shake of her hips and her head. Prior to her service in the kitchens, she had served as a veil dancer for a *chakla* and specialized in far more than silk.

There wasn't a man Kaplita couldn't bring to his knees.

It was going to be useful.

Jemdanee tried to remain calm. "I will forgo the stockings and slippers." There was no need to further swelter and no one was going to see anything beneath the mass anyway. "The gown is in that trunk. I only hope there is no mildew on that silk. I have very little time. Might you assist?"

"*Haan, haan.* Come!" With the flick of her mint-oiled black braid, Kaplita swept past, the veil of her palomino sari flowing against the warm wind blowing in through the netted window. With the extension of slim arms, she thudded open the trunk.

"I do not see any damage." Kalpita pulled forth the massive gown that continued to unfold from the trunk despite standing back several times, running her fingers over the fabric. "*Sahelii, sahelii,* you are dishonoring our culture with this circus tent. Are you certain you wish to wear it?"

Jemdanee rolled her eyes and assisted in dragging out the rest of the gown's weight. "Ridley is a sophisticated European that deserves acknowledgement. There are worse things a Hindu woman can do in the name of a white man."

"*Jee*. Debauchery."

They giggled.

The off-the shoulder gown was a very glorious magnolia color with elegant, pin-fine stripes. With her skin tone, she was going to look *magnificent*.

After yanking a chemise over her nude body, and arguing with Kalpita about which way the corset was supposed to go, they eventually pulled over the mass of crinoline over another mass of petticoats (the weight!) and yanked the silk fabric of the gown over it, shifting it to fit into place.

The gown was *tight*.

Her cleavage was heaving out almost to the brown of her nipples. It didn't look right. She adjusted her glasses. "I do not remember it being so tight."

"You have been eating more than usual. Even I noticed."

Nerves. "Is there a fichu for this gown?"

Kalpita squinted up at her while arranging the gown. "*Fichu*? What is this... *fichu*?"

"I believe you answered the question. There is no fichu." Jemdanee angled herself toward the mirror, her usually tame cleavage appearing massive and top-heavy. Shiva. "They almost reach my chin." She patted each one in an attempt to deflate them. "Is it too whorish?"

"*Nahin*." Leaning left and right while hooking her in, Kalpita chided in Hindi, "If he complains about the size of your breasts he is unworthy of them."

She bit back a smile. "You are quite right." Regally positioning herself after arranging the weight of the magnolia silk around herself, she set her chin. "How do I look?"

"Russian. You know what they say about Russians women: *crazy*. Which you are." Kalpita winked, snapping out a fan. "Use it against him and the heat."

Jemdanee swept forward and took the ivory handle, slipping the string onto her wrist. "Now the banana has a peel."

"May he be the nimble monkey." Kalpita wobbled her head.

DELILAH MARVELLE

"Shall I assist with the *ittar*?"

"*Nahin, nahin.* You have duties." Jemdanee kissed her fingertips in thanks and pressed them against the woman's cheek. "Go! I thank you."

"May your reunion be born of bliss. Are you in need of an amulet?"

Fourteen of them. "Gather whichever one you believe will be helpful."

"I will dig through what I have." Kalpita's dark eyes grew playful. "Your Dunning called on my kitchen this morning and ate more than three men in need of souls. Do they not feed him over at the barracks?"

A breath escaped Jemdanee. "They treat him like a sepoy. Be gracious."

"Since when do you know me to be unkind?" Kalpita leaned in and cooed, "How he stares at me and blushes. One would think I was the only brown woman in the land. He looks like a boy but towers like a giant! How old are his freckles and what are his finances?"

Jemdanee lowered her chin. "Leave him be, lest the Field Marshal see him shot. The boy suffers enough at the hands of everyone on the compound and to break his heart would be cruel."

The woman puckered her lips. "Better he learn that lesson now then later." Kalpita departed with the sway of hips she slapped.

Uff. Knowing time was against her, Jemdanee bustled to the other side of the room, the skirts on her rear wagging. Tossing out ribbons and garters and stockings from her dressing table (all useless), she dug through the bottom of each drawer, plucking out random wooden pins for her hair. "Not even a mantra swami with a magic towel could ever clean *this* up," she muttered.

Jemdanee unraveled her braid, loosening its long waves and seductively bundled all of the black curls before the carved wood mirror, pinning it up into a soft chignon with every wooden pin she could find. She teased out several long curls, letting it fringe against her bronzed throat and cheeks.

Peering at the mirror, she removed her railway spectacles, revealing her pale blue eyes. Picking up the lip rouge the Government House never permitted her to wear, she dabbed it generously onto her lips and carefully followed the outline of their shape, rubbing it to ensure they were glossier, fuller and red.

Red. Like her bindi.

Red. Like the color of the blood she intended to boil in Ridley's veins.

Without sex, there was no possibility of rebirth.

Without sex, life came to an end.

And Ridley would feel the glory of what her passion would bring.

After she made him crawl.

Tugging open a drawer, she plucked up a French pair of *lunettes*. Adjusting the dainty brass lenses onto her nose, which gave her a sultrier and sophisticated look, she uncorked a bottle of jasmine *ittar* and turning it over, paused, realizing it was… empty.

She frantically clanged through all five of the other small empty bottles.

Empty? All of them?

"*Dhatt.*" She had a habit of using too much except for when she needed it most.

Grudgingly, she knelt at the low side table set in the corner and struck a match against the flint. One by one, she lit all four of the resins of the *commiphora wightii* tree sticks set in the brass incense stand. Gathering fresh jasmine flowers from the water bowl beside the small banyan altar she had created, she set the flowers onto the statue of Krishna.

"*When our eyes meet, return him unto me, so I might embrace the glory of a passion that will bring me love.*" She touched more flowers to her lips and placed them at the blue feet of Krishna, rotating the incense stand three times. "*Guide us to happiness we deserve.*" She paused, knowing she ought to address the mess. "*May Bradley—*" she preferred not to play with karma by cursing him to die in the next hour. "*—find his Delilah and unearth love, passion, and peace.*"

She leaned down and blew at the brass stand, letting incense smoke. With cupping hands, she rolled the smoke toward herself, letting its heat and wood fragrance give her strength and guidance. Taking a freshly hewn lotus flower from the bowl, which had been blessed by the incense, she tucked it in her hair, ready.

The hall clock chimed followed by the one on her mantle.

Knowing she would have to pass through fourteen other rooms and the massive entrance to get to the Eastern Gate, she decided on a detour.

She unlatched the window and pushed it wide open.

Chunmun, who had been waiting outside in the tree, perked. His eyes darted toward her as he bobbed, reaching out fingers like he always did when asking for food.

She giggled. "Is that all I am to you?"

His frantic fingers kept waggling as he bobbed.

She rolled her eyes and held out her arms.

He jumped toward her and nuzzled his furry head into her shoulder, yanking on her hair hard.

"Ay, ay." She poked at his small hand, releasing her hair from it. "Leave some for my head as you have plenty." She smirked and gestured to the bowl on the floor beside the bed. "Go."

Chunmun jumped down and scrambled past her into the room.

"I am off to meet a gorilla," she called.

Gathering the weight of the gown up past her knees, she seated herself on the massive sill and swung her bare feet over the ledge of the window and slid downward in a mass of silk onto the thick grass.

Turning, she regally swept through the unending row of banana palms, passing the vined walls of tennis courts, the aviary, the Garden House and countless colonnaded verandahs where Hindu servants in turbans sat cross-legged, snipping and sewing uniforms.

She lifted her heavy skirts higher to permit a much needed breeze and eased out a calming breath knowing Ridley was coming.

Krishna, guide me into being a queen bent on ruling.

Jemdanee released her skirts to the gravel to cover her bare feet and bustled over to an already established greeting line of men, her heavy skirts rustling.

"Miss Kumar!" the Field Marshal called out from the distance, leaning forward to look at her from the other far end of the line. "Officers first, civilians last. This way, if you please."

Swiveling away against the biting hardness of the gravel that pinched her bare feet, Jemdanee snapped open her fan to cover her face knowing the dress was going to startle a few of the men.

She quickly walked *behind* the long row of men hoping to avoid attention.

No such luck.

Chokes, whistles and shouts echoed as officers turned and leaned out, extending gloved hands they wanted her to take.

"Damn the saints!"

"Jostle into a spin so I can see that rear."

"*Lapis*!" Officer Barker rolled his hand and kicked out a boot toward her gown. "Lift it to the knees. *To the knees*!"

At least she knew the gown was serving its purpose. Albeit these pigs were exaggerating. "I still have access to the laundry room and sumac," she warned, glaring. "Must you always act like boars who mate with swine?"

"*Bring it on, Lapis*," Officer Shaw hollered, jangling the trousers of his uniform.

She rolled her eyes, wishing she could start shooting.

The Field Marshal stalked out of the assembly line, his dark mustache twitching as he pointed at heads. "*Enough of this contemptable behavior*! Or every last one of you will be lifting sacks of sand for three hours without any water."

At least the Field Marshal was attempting to control them.

Officer Greenly held up a gloved hand and whispered from behind it, "*I'll give those native hips children. Fifteen. All white boys*."

Because that was an offer every Hindu woman would jump on.

She held up five fingers as she passed what was now nearing the end of the long row. "*This* is how many fathers each of you have and they all drowned in their own piss before your mothers could save them. I dare you to act like heathens around Ridley. I dare you. He will shake you out of your uniforms and leave you dead."

One of the Brigadiers leaned toward another. "Did you see him take a chair to Thornbur?"

Someone snorted. "It wasn't a chair. It was a table."

"It couldn't have been the table. The tables in those barracks are bolted to the floor."

"Which he *ripped* from the boards. *I was there*."

Uniformed backs greeted her one by one as they eventually fell silent.

She eyed them, dread seeping into her womanly hackles.

What was she about to get into?

She settled herself in a patch of shade behind the arched gates where hawkers and crowds and squadrons of red-coated sepoys tramped along the vast, dust-ridden road leading through Calcutta.

The slowing gallop of several military horses weaving through the massive din of crowds eventually revealed a group of uniformed officers who were permitted to pass through the now opening gates that clanged.

Several men from the regiment rode in on their horses toward them through the open gates, following the manicured path toward the greeting line she stood in before the Government House.

The massive amount of dust being kicked up was like watching demons roll in.

The group of riders stopped on the other far end of where she stood, making it impossible for her to make out very much.

One by one, uniformed men dismounted.

Despite protocol, she leaned further out to better see.

Glimpsing him beyond the assembled men and saddled horses, her throat tightened.

Dressed in a white linen shirt, a regiment-issued waistcoat and linen trousers that displayed a tall, muscled physique, Ridley landed on the gravel beside his stallion with the thud of large leather boots. Ridley winced against the impact, his rugged features instantly remolding into an unaffected calm as he adjusted his leather belt weighed with weapons.

Her lips parted in agony. Given what she'd seen of his gored leg in London three years earlier, he shouldn't have been walking on it at all, let alone hopping off horses.

It hinted he refused to give into letting anything control him. Even pain.

She edged back so he couldn't see her, but strategically positioned herself in a way to be able to watch him through the gaps set between the officers lined beside her.

Adjusting the satchel slung over his muscled shoulders, Ridley swept out a cane from the side belt of his horse. Impaling it into the ground, he leaned his broad frame against it, his hand gripping its black iron head. Scanning the vast grounds, the profile of his well-tanned, rugged face fully appeared.

Her pulse roared.

With a puff of smoke that finished a cheroot between his masculine lips, Ridley extinguished it against the leather of his saddle and tossed it. Dark cocoa-colored hair cascaded forward against the hot wind which he swiped back with a large, ungloved hand as he made his way toward the greeting line with an uneven but long-legged stride.

Time had changed nothing.

He was still a rugged-featured dominating man molding the world around him and forcing it to bend to his will. Right down to his leg that shouldn't have been moving at all.

It felt as if she were waiting for the lightening to strike the iron rod she held.

"*At attention!*" The Field Marshal finally boomed with a full turn.

The long line of officers to the right of her thudded their polished leather boots together and snapped their right gloved hands to their low slung caps, positioning themselves for the greeting every military guest received at the Government House.

Muskets were fired, booming. Crack. *Boom*! Crack. *Boom*! Crack.

She winced against each salute that echoed into the morning air, scattering birds out of surrounding trees until all ten shots faded.

Silence eventually returned, her ears now pulsing right along with the rest of her.

It was all too symbolic of her life.

The Field Marshal stalked out and with unprecedented gusto grabbed Ridley hand and shoulder, exchanging a few quiet words, their heads leaning in to each other.

It was obvious they had formed an alliance.

The Field Marshal turned. "Before the musket regiment that hails our king and country, we extend our unending gratitude," he announced in his typical I-am-your-God voice. "Your dedication honors our regiment that formally acknowledges your bravery and service."

Jemdanee peered down the long line of chin jutting officers which she stood at the end of, her forefinger pushing the down-sliding spectacles up on her nose.

The Field Marshal introduced Ridley to each and every man, leading him systematically down the farthest end of the

41

line. "Officer Greenly. Officer Jasper. Officer Fisher. Officer Barker. Officer Mercer. Officer Graham. Officer Shaw. Officer Harrison. Officer Lawson. Officer Andrews. Officer Barr. Officer Kirkpatrick. Officer Drake."

It was taking too loooooooong.

Why did everyone get to see him fist?

They weren't involved with him! They weren't—

Ridley's towering frame halted before her with a cane, his well-faded leather belt weighed with pistols and a satchel slung over broad shoulders. The achingly familiar peppery scent of his Parisian cologne drifted toward her through the heat.

She almost fainted.

Between half-breaths, her gaze veered disbelievingly up his military-issued waistcoat. The fabric indented and stretched against a broad torso and thick-bulked biceps, hinting at over-defined muscles pressing beneath every inch of a body she no longer recognized.

Their gazes locked.

Smoldering mercurial amber eyes that were far more soulful and far more *everything* rattled her into accepting that forever was now.

Her knees felt like *targola* jelly.

He wore no cravat.

The top ivory button of his linen shirt was seductively unfastened, revealing the curve of a strong throat and the alluring hint of a smooth muscled chest. His face and the skin visible beneath his unfastened shirt was well-bronzed by the sun, hinting months spent in Bombay.

She had promised herself not to be angry.

With a regal bow that was representative of her culture, Jemdanee removed the incense-blessed lotus flower from her hair and lifted her cupped hands toward him, presenting the unfolding pink petals of the lotus. "*Namaste*. Unto thee, Mr. Ridley, I gift the symbol of India's supreme beauty: *padma*. The lotus. Despite its seed growing within the thickness of mud, where its stalks are forced to reside, it *rises* from dark waters to find the light that produces the glory of this bloom. Despite its arduous journey, it remains remarkably unstained, its vibrant color unaffected by the darkness it had arisen from. It is my hope, that you respect the journey this lotus has taken in your honor and that you never reduce it to mud again." She stared him down to punctuate the delivery.

The clear-cut lines of Ridley's rugged features flickered. He searched her face, his shaven jaw working. "I am in need of your forbearance," his voice was low and broken. "I have dishonored you and myself, Kumar, and am here to return your faith in me. Might you forgive me?"

Tears overwhelmed her. He had almost died twice in her name.

He tapped his chest gently, still holding his cane, imploring silently for an embrace.

A tremor raked through her knowing he had only ever sought to love her.

Unashamed, she threw herself into his arms with the rustle of skirts and fell against his solid frame with a thud, reveling in his warmth, his peppery scent, his tensing muscles, his…

Ridley.

She sobbed, crushing the lotus in her hand.

It was too metaphorical, for she herself had long been crushed by him from the moment she had lain her head onto his lap one dark London night.

Tears traced her cheeks and dripped toward her trembling lips. In her honor, he had not only travelled to her homeland, but had even taken up squadron duty to return to her the freedom she had so foolishly tossed.

She fought against another sob and buried her face against the fabric of his military waistcoat, gripping the linen hard.

Ridley tugged her harder into the bulk of his arms, jerking her upward and off her bare feet. He buried his face into her hair, pressing her savagely against the solid warmth of his chest, tucking and molding her against himself.

It was gloriously too tight.

She quietly sobbed, the joy of holding him outweighing everything.

Slowly setting her feet back onto the ground, his large hands smoothed her hair as his fingers dug into her chignon. "I will never forget this," he rasped into her hair.

Jemdanee pressed her cheek harder into his cologne-scented waistcoat, drifting through blurring emotions of knowing that whatever they shared, it was too strong to ever break.

His taunt muscles shifted against her, his broad chest rising and falling with ragged breaths. "Your forgiveness means everything." He tightened his grip in her hair to stinging, his lips digging into her head. "*Everything*."

Her quaking fingers tucked the crushed lotus into the upper stitching of his right pocket. She smoothed it whilst sniffing. "I am... still... *very angry with you*." She poked at his chest, sniffing at each poke so he knew her tears weren't frivolous.

He smoothed her hair. "We can be angry with me together," he murmured.

A choked laugh escaped her.

Dipping his lowered head, he trailed his masculine lips downward from her forehead to her cheek and inward toward her lips.

Everything faded against the hot wind.

Although she didn't turn her trembling lips up toward his that hovered, she didn't move, either, chanting to herself that letting him kiss her wouldn't mean she was weak.

Only that her heart was still his.

Ridley grabbed her face with large hands, tilting her glasses. "Not here," he rasped against the side of her mouth, smoothing away her remaining tears with his thumbs.

She half-breathed, gripping his waistcoat hard.

He leaned back, the set of his jaw and the lines of his rugged face hinting at his angst as he searched her face and aligned the frame of her spectacles. Kissing her hands, he released her and inclined his head, never once breaking their gaze.

It was like meeting a completely different man.

It felt different. As if every heartbeat was going to matter.

Jemdanee swiped at her tears beneath the frames of her spectacles and eased back into the greeting line. Her limbs were quaking and she could barely stand.

One would think she had drank a quart of *bhang lassi*.

She was floating.

Adjusting his cane, he tugged out the pink lotus from the stitching of his pocket with his other hand. With a theatrical turn, he veered in close. "Permit me to return this to you in honor of what it represents."

Twirling the stem, Ridley tapped it against her nose and tucked it back into her hair, pushing it into place. "You will always be the lotus and I the mud," he offered in a low, husky tone. "This mud acknowledges that."

Their eyes met and her core quavered.

His hovering knuckles trailed across her gathered hair toward her forehead and touched the bindi she had never worn in his presence.

Her soul tingled.

Leaning back, he widened his stance, the intensity of his gaze remaining riveted to her face before raking over the rest of her. Shifting his jaw, he dropped his eyes from her glasses to her exposed shoulders to her corseted breasts.

A knot rose in her throat in an attempt to remain indifferent to his uncensored perusal.

His brows came together. Using the end of his cane, he dragged it against the silk folds of her Russian gown, rearranging the fullness around her thighs and knees. "What are you wearing?"

Her heart jolted and her insides jangled. It was as if he didn't like it. "Surely, you jest."

He held her gaze. "This concoction of a raiment announces you have no understanding of what we share. It's ninety-four degrees out. Burying yourself in more fabric than a field of cotton is lunacy. You should have worn a sari."

Only a man who dismantled everything with his investigative mind would turn her gown into a lecture. "Do forgive the disappointment."

His countenance softened. "You look extraordinary, but I came for something else. Pardon me for being a complete exhibitionist in a greeting line full of thirty men but I have to do it."

Tossing his cane to an officer beside them who fumbled with it, Ridley captured her hands with his large calloused fingers and brought them up and molded her fingers into the heat of his wide palms one by one, threading their fingers together as if stitching them together for life.

Skin to skin, palm to palm, finger to pressing finger, his mellow baritone remained edged with what he was most known for: control. "*This* is what we share, Kumar. *This* is what matters. Pulse to pulse. Do you understand?"

Between steadying breaths, she tightened her own fingers on his.

This was why she had been unable to embrace any other.

Never once breaking their gaze, he squeezed his dominating hold tighter and too tight, as if to ensure she felt his pulse and the bones beneath. "There is no need to impress me with silk. You *are* the silk."

Every inch of her, including both of her well-gripped hands, burned.

This is what Bradley and others didn't and couldn't bring: *sweaty appendages.*

Dipping his head downward, Ridley feathered his masculine lips against the inside of each wrist before dragging his teeth across her skin. "Kumar?"

Her bare feet, buried beneath the weight of her gown, seemed to drift off the gravel. "Yes?"

Lowering his gaze to her hands, he outlined them with large fingers and paused at seeing the gouge on her palm from the pin. He grazed it and kissed it. Twice.

Because she wasn't cursed enough to revere him.

He dragged his full lips across four out of her five fingers as his other hand drifted up from his pocket and slipped a black diamond ring onto her finger.

Her eyes widened. Unable to keep her quaking hand still, she swallowed.

"A token of my commitment." Ridley dragged his hands out of hers with rigid fingertips. Taking back his cane from the officer, he gripped it. Inclining his head, he offered, "In ten minutes, *mon dévot*, we will return to each other."

Averting his gaze, he stepped back, shifting his weight into the cane. Being further directed by the Field Marshal, he stiffly sidestepped to another officer beside her.

With a pang she felt all too deeply knowing he was still limping but attempting to hide it, she swallowed against the tightness of her throat.

He had once told her that the right man would know how to put her together when it was time, yet probably he did not expect that it would be the right woman putting *him* back together.

Everything after that was a droning blur.

Her trembling fingers grazed the glinting three-carat black diamond that weighed her scarred finger, hinting at the weight of everything to come.

She knew his mind well enough to say he was paying homage

to a past that seemed to whisper of a dream. Her raw wrists he had tended to and saved without having ever asked anything of her.

He'd even kissed her scarred fingers which had been gashed by his teeth during his seizure.

In between his conversation with several officers grouped together, Ridley locked a hand behind his broad back, widening his stance and cane. His brows drawn, he commented about something in a deep low tone she couldn't quite make out given the distance between them.

Unlike all the other officers, he wasn't wearing a coat, so she could see that hidden beneath his loose-fitting linen trousers was a muscled rear and equally well-muscled thighs set below overly broad shoulders.

She was in angst.

To be so close to him yet… so far.

Feeling unashamedly needful and lustful from looking at his rear, she fought against the equally searing heat of the gravel that continued to annoyingly pinch into her toes.

A patch of grass to stand upon would have been nice.

Turning, she made her way toward—

Her pulse roared.

In the distance, Bradley was propped against one of the columns, the collar of his uniform unbuttoned to the chest and his blond hair scattered against the wind as he smoked a *bidi* and sketched. He blew out smoke through lips and nostrils, whispering of things she didn't know.

Was that her *bidi*?!

The one she had left half-burning in the vase?

Noticing that she was watching him, he wagged it, as if announcing he was turning a new leaf, and returned to sketching.

It unnerved her. What if he did something stupid and complicated everything?

She would kill him!

Hearing heavy boots slowly thudding into the gravel, she knew Ridley was coming.

Chanting to herself to remain regal and calm, she turned with a sweeping effect and froze, realizing a chest was already blocking her entire view.

It was Ridley.

47

CHAPTER FOUR

Everything grew quiet, save her own breaths and the chirping of birds.

At over six feet, compared to her five, Ridley towered above her like a stone temple awaiting neck-craning worship.

He said nothing despite his eyes saying everything.

The muscles quivered in her thighs.

Adjusting the heaviness of the black diamond ring on her finger—upon her soul was it unusual and gorgeous!—she forced her body *and* her mind to remain calm.

She sensed he was determined to make them both crawl.

"Apparently, you have arranged for us to stay at Spence's." Although it was the swankiest of luxury hotels in all of India built barely three years earlier, located across the street from the Government House itself, she feigned ignorance and offered him her sultriest of voices. "How are the accommodations?"

His amber eyes prolonged the moment. "As resplendent as you," he offered in low, husky tone. "How have you been, Kumar?"

Sweat tricked down her neck and into the silk of her gown as the sun blazed over their heads through the shade of the gulmohar trees. Why was she nervous?!

This was *not* the conversation she had expected to have with him after the sort of letters he'd been writing. "Why not altogether discuss the weather, Mr. Ridley?"

He lifted a brow. "'Tis *Ridley*, if you please. Or Evan. Or

Oswald. No mister. I belong to you now. Much like you belong to me, *Jemdanee*." Rounding her slowly, he held her gaze. "What were you hoping to discuss?" The low pitch of his voice was like hearing the roll of his hips.

She couldn't *breathe*. He clearly sought to be the stone and make her the vine.

Little did he know a vine knew how to find cracks and invade the mortar.

She set her chin. "I find your attempt to control your passion for me amusing."

His mouth quirked. "We have plenty of time to pursue passion and what it will bring and do to us. Why annihilate the inevitable?"

She wanted to grab him and rip every piece of clothing from his body so all of India might know of it. "In other words, three years was merely an introduction to a lifetime of suffering."

"You introduced it." He loomed before her and angled his cane. "Explain to me, *mon dévot*, why you didn't write for three years. I want to hear it before we move on to the esoteric subject of our passion."

Uff. Why did she feel as if she were talking with a professor moving into his own classroom?

She *had* written.

Enough to make her fingers sore and her heart sick. She simply never sent any through courier for they were either too loving or too harsh and she hadn't really wanted to corner herself into being either. "Perhaps I required your commitment to be far greater than mine after what I went through. For although I am permitting us to embrace whatever our association will bring, it *does* come with a baleful warning."

She stared him down, letting the sting of her seriousness gash him with a stern tone. "You will *not* be given permission to turn my life into a mess like you did back in London. Tears I do not need. Pain I do not want. Freedom from both was why I left. I may have forgiven you, Ridley, but I still remember the savagery of the pain you made me feel. It will *always* be there and if you *ever* tug on that pain again, *ever*, I will lay with another man that same night merely to make you *perish*. Do you understand?"

There was an arrested expression on his face.

Edging in close, he reached out and dragged the entire bridge of his rigid thumb across the fullness of her mouth, before smearing her still-wet lip rouge slowly *down* to her chin with calloused fingertips. "Perfectly."

To her exasperation, the fluttering of her heart betrayed the nail-scraping, lip-biting, knees-digging attraction that had never left her.

She jerked her chin away from those large fingers and stared up at him with enough sauce to ensure he knew where to dip it. "Was it necessary to assault the rouge?"

He lowered his gaze to her. "*Mon coeur*," he rumbled out. "Nothing I ever do is *unnecessary*. The smearing of your lip rouge is allegorical. For now you look *exactly* how I feel. Smeared to the chin by what we share. Unrecognizable." He leaned down and breathed hotly into her ear, "Imagine what will become of us once we kneel to this. We'll be fucked."

Jemdanee swallowed.

Leaning back, he snapped out a handkerchief from his waistcoat. He unfolded it and dragged it across her lips, rubbing the softness of the linen against her chin and mouth. "Hold still."

More than her lips trembled.

With the tilt of his head that sent thick chestnut hair falling onto his brow, he watched his fingers curve the linen beneath her lower lip. "Red lip rouge signifies audacity, confidence, and a need to be noticed." He shifted his jaw. "You should make it your signature. One that only I get to smear."

His gaze bore into her in silent expectation, tingling her stomach.

There had *never* been a man who had *ever* captivated her with such alluring and equally dark but gentlemanly mystery.

He was the enigma she sought to lick with her soul.

Folding the handkerchief with one hand, he leaned in, the scent of his Parisian cologne drifting toward her. He held up the folded handkerchief. "You cried into this same handkerchief when I first met you. I freed you from prison only to then chain myself. In honor of what we share, I promise you will never cry into this linen again."

She melted.

Ridley tucked it into his pocket, thudding it into place. "Now I have a memento. Your rouge on the same linen that introduced us."

Unable to hold in her adoration, she gushed, "I had hoped you were still the same."

"The same? No. Worthier? By a touch." He held her gaze. "Did you read all of my letters?"

Her mouth went dry. Those. "*Haan.* I did. Some of them more than once. Some of them as many as fourteen times to ensure I was reading what I thought I was reading and it was exactly what I thought I was reading. They were all very..."

"Necessary." Ridley tipped her chin upward. "Conveying my passion is the one thing I swore I would do for you. Unlike too many shackled by convention, I am the sort of paramour who finds the word 'cunt' to be as beautifully effective on the tongue as it is on the mind. Especially when spoken in the presence of a beautiful woman who intoxicates my inclinations. What are your thoughts on it?"

That hotel was going to get razed.

She moistened her lips, noting he was looking at them. "If it amuses your gentlemanly disposition, who am I to keep an intellectual from exploring the broad usage of the English language?"

One corner of his mouth lifted. "Every breath you take defines me. You are my *angustia.*"

She bit back a smile. "That is Latin for trouble. T-R-O-U-B-L-E."

His eyes brightened in amusement. "May you never stray from it. Unlike our time in London, I hold *nothing* back. If it's in my head, you will be cursed to hear it. If it's in my body, you will be cursed to feel it. Are you at ease with that?"

Holy—Jemdanee lifted her still burning feet beneath her rustling skirts, annoyed that the gravel had not lost its heat yet. "I will manage."

He paused, glancing past her for a tense moment. He shifted his jaw.

Stepping toward her, he curved a large hand to the small of her back and prodded her toward a hidden path beyond. "Come."

The possessive pressure of his weighing hand spread as his large fingers dug into the fabric of her gown and veered downward toward her rear. He smacked it. "Move."

She dragged in an astounded breath, swatting at his hand. "Ridley!"

He leaned into her ear and bit out, "Move into that grove now. *Move.*"

She choked, sensing something had changed, and frantically gathered her skirts, ensuring she didn't lift them too high lest her bare feet show. Darting further and deeper into the hidden grove, she winced as her skirts dragged and kicked up dust. When her burning feet finally touched the soothing coolness of the shaded grass, a soft breath escaped her.

The tamarind trees now hovered above and over the winding path that buried them completely from sight, nestling them in silence.

Smoothing her skirts away from her rear, she glared. "Whatever was that about?"

"You tell me." Ridley's muscled stride rounded her in the silence of the secluded garden, his cane following. Taking her arm in his and molding it against his forearm, he tugged her close and forced her to walk with him, bringing them deeper into the shaded silence.

He was miffed.

He wasn't yelling but he didn't have to.

She glanced up at his commanding veneer that demanded obedience. "Should I be concerned?"

"What sort of man do you take me for?" His gaze remained trained on the grass path before them. "Where are your shoes, *mon chou*? Why are you not wearing them?"

Her gaze snapped toward him, knowing full well he couldn't have seen her feet. She'd kept them well buried beneath her gravel-dragging gown. "Once an inspector, always an inspector."

He forced them to walk farther into the overhanging, dense grove. "Shoes make a distinctive sound against gravel and it was fairly obvious by the amount of fidgeting you were doing that your feet were burning."

Tightening his hold on her arm until it pulsed, he gave her a pointed look. "Aside from offering us privacy, given there appears to be a particular officer overly keen to watch our interaction, I moved you into the shade to spare your feet." He searched her face. ""Are you always in bare feet? Or are you running from trouble?"

She almost waved her fan violently against the heat of her face, but knew it would only come across as a sign of nervousness.

How was she going to tell him about Bradley without introducing a war?

"I need you to talk to me." He bent his head toward her. "What happened to your hand?"

It was as if he already knew something was amiss. "Ridley?"

"Yes, Jemdanee?"

"What sort of man are you?"

He eyed her. "What sort of a question is that?"

She eyed him, in turn. "It is a question posed for the safety of everyone involved."

Ridley squinted, then released her and stepped back. Dragging his cane across her skirts, he used its end to lift the hem to her knee. "Whose safety are you worried for?"

She swatted at his cane. "Might you not do that?"

He searched her face. "Explain."

She didn't want this ending in a Bradley/Ridley brawl/duel. The Field Marshal was known to hang his own for less.

She picked at her fan, twisting it. "Ridley?"

He released a breath through nostrils and adjusted his leather belt that hosted his weapons, still holding her gaze. "Turning my name into a question isn't easing the tension, dearest."

That belt and low tone unnerved her.

He eyed her. "If we say everything right now, there won't be enough for later."

She cringed. "Given what every military man on the compound has been saying about you since you arrived into Bombay, I fear telling you anything. One would think the cultivated gentleman I met back in London was a contrived form of camouflage. *Was it?*"

A muscled flicked in his jaw. "Nothing you say or do will make me raise a hand to you. Do you understand? My voice… maybe. My hand? Never. Even if you did the things I hope you didn't do, I will be what you need me to be. Calm. *Barely*, but I will be. Fair warning: I may pummel everyone else."

"I do not want you pummeling anyone. I have seen enough of it being surrounded by military men who think violence is a solution to the world's problems."

Except the rustling of trees that shaded them from sight, everything grew quiet.

He sighed. "Give me your hand."

Ridley positioned the head of the black iron cane shaped

into a raven between them. Gripping her fingers, he set them around the heat of the iron his hand had warmed. "Animals know the true nature of any man and Chaucer never once feared me despite being less than twenty-five inches in height. Take his lead and trust that I would never hurt you. Not even if you hurt me."

Jemdanee lowered her gaze to the head of the raven, her throat tightening.

Ridley used her fingers to unfasten the beak, dragging back the iron to nudge it open.

Tucked in its narrow hidden cavern was the lone black feather of a raven. *Chaucer*. Her fingers grazed it delicately, tears blurring her eyes. She had somehow become his raven given Chaucer was no more. She had sobbed when he had written about the loss he had felt responsible for.

And now, Ridley was silently asking her to be on his shoulder at all times.

Blinking back the burn of too many tears she had cried well before his arrival, Jemdanee fastened the downturned beak back into place with a click and gripped the weight of the handle.

Holding his gaze, so he might know she felt his pain, she drew up the black iron raven toward her lips and kissed it. "He will come back to you in another form. He will make himself known when he is ready to be yours again. Believe it. Until he does, I am at your side and on your shoulder."

His brows flickered but he conveyed no other emotion. "Are you?"

She grazed his full masculine lips with her fingers, entranced that she was touching him and that he was letting her. It was surreal. "Never doubt what we shared in London."

Ridley lowered the cane, and broke the contact of her fingers against his mouth, no longer meeting her gaze. "Who was the officer watching? The one sketching? Who is he to you?"

She swallowed. *He knew*. Scotland Yard pounded on his door for a reason. "Knock any thought of infidelity out of your head. Would I be standing here subjecting myself to your level of intensity if I had given myself to another?"

Lingering, he nodded but still didn't meet her gaze.

Turning, he intently scanned the path and beyond it into its gardens. "I've read quite a bit about your culture in my attempt to better understand you before coming to India. In that enquiry, I found myself drawn to the *Aghori Sadhu*. I had an incredible opportunity to meet a few of that sect whilst traveling into Bombay. They belong to no one family, live on cremation grounds, meditate whilst coating themselves with the ashes of the dead, and consider nothing to be malevolent. I found their mindset fearless and wish to explore that mindset as it relates to us."

She tried not to twitch at the sentiment, especially given he had veered so very, very far off the topic. She sensed he was gauging her. "They are also known to drink from human skulls and eat human flesh," she said out of the corner of her mouth. "Are you wanting that for us, as well, o Morbid King? Or are you insinuating you intend to drink from *my* skull?"

He gave her a withering look. "I merely consider it refreshing that they live without taboo. I want that for us. That you can be who you are and I can be who I am without either of us harboring a distaste. To the *Aghori Sadhu* sect, nothing is unholy. They believe God lives within each of us and therefore *everything* we do is sacred and *nothing* ever defiles us."

Oyo. "Why do I feel as if you are trying to rationalize whatever bad behavior you intend to display?"

Ridley lowered his chin. "Jemdanee. I am attempting to have an intelligent and productive conversation with you about your culture despite wanting to rip another man's throat out. Would you rather we discuss something else? Like why you're wearing non-prescriptive spectacles?"

She awkwardly adjusted her glasses. "I hardly wish to bore you with my newfound tastes."

Given his height, he glanced down toward her. "If I had wanted to be bored, I would have remained with the officers. Did you know Officer Barker, despite his name, owns four cats?"

A startled laugh escaped her at the unexpected jab at Barker.

"*Ah.* There she is." Reaching out, he skimmed her exposed shoulder, dragging the material downward. "The girl I first met." He dragged her gown down hard and harder. "The girl who once told me I was worth the pain when she pleasured herself in my name."

Those words and the rigid skimming of his weighing large fingers against her exposed skin made her body tingle in too many places. Her chest tightened as she dragged up the lacing on her shoulder knowing the mess that lay ahead. "Ridley—"

"I have heard my name said enough times to think I was thrusting." He squinted. "Tell me about your officer." His voice grew strained. "I have *two* questions. When you first met him, when your pale blue eyes captured his in that half-breath of an introduction, did you find him attractive? And did I, the one who wrote you over seven hundred letters dripping with devotion, disappear from your thoughts?"

Her face burned.

Krishna save her from leaving Calcutta and disappearing into the jungle. For yes, her first few interactions with Bradley three years earlier were not as chaste as they should have been. She had overly smiled and even flirted.

Until she got to know him.

She had been so livid and detached from Ridley after what he had done she hadn't read any of the first dozen letters he'd sent. Instead, she had forcibly flirted with Bradley to spite Ridley *and* herself, and perhaps *that* was what had ultimately led Bradley to think he ever had a chance.

She had unhinged a grimy padlocked door.

Her throat burned. "For a small while your raven flew to another window, but she never once wedged her beak past the ledge. Once I set aside my anger, which took time, I finally started reading your letters and that was when…" Her voice cracked with the emotion she had felt even then. "I became yours again."

He said nothing.

Adjusting the weight of the black diamond ring on her finger, she set her hand out, wanting to change the subject for the sake of peace between them. "I thank you. 'Tis truly beautiful."

Ridley gripped her hand, until their fingers entwined and directed them toward a bench. "The black diamond represents eternal commitment, even in dark times."

How fitting.

Her fingers wove into his large fingers, needing assurance. She peered up at him. "You broke my heart and a vile part of me wanted to break yours, but I did stay true to what we once shared."

"What did we share?"

"More than most."

Ridley turned toward her without breaking his limping stride or their grip on each other's hands. He started walking backwards, so he could get a better view of her face.

Tugging her to a halt, he jerked her into his muscled arms, tilting her forcefully back. "Look at me."

She stilled, every inch of her skin turning to his and fire, as the bulking hardness of his shifting biceps tightened around her.

He surveyed her, pressing the cane against the fullness of her skirts. "You got what you wanted from me: *everything*. You, who once crawled into my bed one night as if it were you right, insisting on a man who then poured himself into being yours for three years. Only there is something you aren't telling me…" He dipped his head downward and slid a rigid, hot tongue across the pressed rounds of her breasts, tingling them to the nipples.

Her chest quaked in disbelief as she attempted to draw in breaths she couldn't.

His fingers dug into her arms to burning as he lifted his head, staring her down. "Apple brandy." His amber eyes grew lethal. "An officer's drink. I can smell it on your skin. Why is it all over your breasts?"

Blood pounded into her brain, leapt from her heart and made her very knees tremble knowing there was no burying *anything* from him. Not even if she wanted to.

Her pulse roared. "Before you think the worst, understand that he and I—"

Releasing her with the flick of hands, he tossed the cane away from himself with a thud as if he didn't trust himself not to use it. His rugged features wavered, then stilled. "Keep it to one word. Willingly or unwillingly?"

Yet again, he returned to being that jaguar after a meal, casually cleaning his teeth with his tongue whilst every gazelle in the field watched. She knew the intelligence of his mind was going to turn every argument into a chess game she never wanted to play.

That intensity unnerved her.

Knowing she and she alone had been responsible for sending him to what had almost been another death, she choked out, "I did not invite what he did."

His eyes widened. Tugging her savagely into the bulk of his

arms, he thudded her into his muscled chest. "Breathe," he rasped against her hair, his hands jumping frantically to her face. "I am here with you. *Always*." He cradled her harder. "What was the extent of the assault?"

She cringed against his waistcoat, realizing he thought she'd been assaulted.

And… yes… but… no.

She quickly leaned back, her hands quaking against the shifting, tensing mass of muscle beneath her fingers. "I was not—I am fine. All that matters is that you survived."

"*That I survived?*" His brows came together as he intently searched her eyes. "Did he hurt you? Did he fucking hurt you?"

She shook her head violently. "No. No, no, he—"

"Jemdanee." Ridley grabbed her hand and held it up, turning it toward her face. "Did he hurt you?" His tone indicated he already knew but didn't want another lie. "Did he do this?"

Why did she have to fall in love with an inspector? She could never tell a lie. "No! It was the pin on his sash when I…" This was horrific. "He kissed me and then he… told me about you and your assignment and I…"

"My assignment?" He gently rattled her, setting his nose to hers. "You aren't making sense. I cannot understand or help unless you tell me everything. *What happened?*"

This was going to be her life.

No thoughts left untouched.

His nose to her nose and everything open to speculation as the inspector ticked through every scenario like an emporium list that required all shelves be stocked. They weren't even on the subject of her heart or her body.

She tried to remain calm and lay out each moment like a row of seeds she was planting for harvest. "He offered me brandy, only I shoved it away and it spilled everywhere." She gestured toward her own chest. "He then… kissed me. Only I shoved *him* away, which *gouged* my hand against the pin of his sash after which he felt guilt-ridden enough to confess that he had signed off on your assignment." She tugged him close, knowing how it could have ended: tragically.

He leaned back out of her embrace. "Where did this happen?"

"In the Council Room of the Government House."

Easing out a long audible breath between straight white teeth, his expression became a mask of stone. "I want a name. Who is it?"

If she didn't take precautions, this would end in blood. Eight pints of blood judging by Ridley's intensity. And whilst, yes, Bradley deserved it to lose every drop of blood in his biblical body, the last thing she wanted was for Ridley to get arrested and/or hanged.

She smoothed his hair adoringly, attempting to steady her own breaths. "I suggest you put that stone face away. There is no need for you to get involved in this."

He gave her a dark long look, edging away from her touch. "*Name. Now.*"

It was Armageddon.

It was as if everything would *always* be Armageddon.

She sensed retribution and the Field Marshal would be what he always was: unforgiving. "I do not want you getting hurt or arrested, Ridley. Leave it be. Let it go."

"*Kumar.*" Dipping his head toward her so that they were eyes to eye, he spaced out each syllable between teeth. "Protecting a man who didn't protect you from himself is wrong. *Name.*"

She pointed at his head as if she were about to poke a hole through it. "I am not at all protecting him. I am protecting you!"

He tapped his chiseled cheek. "Might you set your hands against my face, please?"

She blinked. "My...? What?"

"Your hands. My face." He snapped toward them and pointed to his jaw. "*Up here.*"

Bewildered, her hands jumped to his smoothly shaven but taunt face. The flicking muscle of his strained jaw beneath her fingertips made her feel the pulse of the ticking tension of his cheek.

"Good." He held her gaze. "Do you feel that, *mon dévot*? What do you feel?"

Why did she want to kiss him? "You are... ticking like a clock."

"Exactly. *This* is what you have done to me for three fucking years. This. I have no peace. None. Never. Not since you left London without sending me a single missive *until* I got into Bombay." He leaned back, breaking her hold. "Are you in love with him?"

Ew. "Of course not," she said with the twist of lips showing her disgust. "No and no and no."

He said nothing. Still searching her face, he smoothed her shoulders with tense hands before releasing her.

A shaky breath escaped her, wondering if she had lost her mind thinking she could handle this man. For everything in his mind was a crime scene.

Stiffly walking past her and over to the cane he threw, he rolled it with his boot and kicked it upward to keep himself from kneeling. Catching it, he thudded it into the ground. "Is it Lieutenant Bradley?"

This one might as well be Krishna. Unnerved, she breathed out, "How did you know?"

He closed the distance between them, stalk-limping. "He was supposed to be in the greeting line but wasn't. He was also in charge of your employment and the Field Marshal informed me he had asked for your hand several times. It's called deduction, my dear *Watkins*."

That mind never stopped digging. "Trust this Watkins when I say it is over and it is done. Bradley knows his place."

He stared. "Why are you referring to him as Bradley?"

She panicked, sensing he thought… "We were *never* that! Ever." She leaned over and demonstrated with a spit. "If anything, go pummel Peter over in Turkey for that. He encouraged Bradley at every turn."

Ridley swiped his face with a trembling hand. "Fuck. I thought he had raped you."

She paused, seeing past the curtain of what he had tried to hide: his emotions. "Ridley." She grabbed his hand, squeezing it tightly. "*Ridley*." She softened her voice adoringly and leaned in. "Not everything is as horrible and dark as you imagine."

He squeezed her hand. "If you had written, I might have been in a better state of mind."

She kept her voice soft. "If I had written, the words would not have been what you deserved. I was hurting too much for too long and I would have hurt you more. It was yet another reason I did not write. You had attempted suicide despite my devotion to you. How was I to embrace that? What sort of words could I have written?"

He touched her cheek. "I'm so sorry. It may be difficult for you to ever understand, but I was mentally bleeding. When you came into my life, Jemdanee, I was barely functioning. I was disconnected from everyone, including myself, and I'm still not…"

He averted his gaze, his jaw working. "If I were to listen to my jugular right now, and my jealousy and everything I am hiding deep within me knowing I missed out on three years of your life whilst another gloried in it, I'd be in that building, spraying that officer's blood for even looking at you," he rasped. "For that is who I really am. Do you understand? *Reason* is saving him. *Reason* is ensuring I don't scare you. That is why I'm usually this. Reserved. Rational. Gentlemanly. Because anything else and I am unrecognizable even to myself and I don't want you to be scared of me."

She eyed him, her throat tightening. "Listening to you say that *is* scaring me."

He said nothing.

She hesitated, wondering if the rumors were true. "Who is this Earl of Hell? How am I not to fear you or panic over what you will do next when everyone has stories about you shooting and beating men with pistols and canes. Are you truly that?"

There was a pulsing moment of silence.

Ridley slowly adjusted his leather belt, hooking his thumb through it as if to announce the two pistols and the massive sheathed blade was normal. "I have a work persona," he admitted in a low tone. "Not including the assignment that went wrong outside of Bombay, I've been responsible for the deaths of nineteen people."

Her eyes widened. "Nineteen? You… *killed nineteen people*?"

An exasperated breath escaped him through straight white teeth. "No. I take responsibility for any life slain during an assignment that goes wrong, and unfortunately, in my field, there are quite a few. In truth, I have never learned to abide by an eye for an eye sort of retribution, Jemdanee. I have always embraced more of a tooth for a tooth retaliation given men have a hell of lot more teeth to knock out than they do eyes. Do you understand?"

Using the fan, she attempted to cool down her skin that had overheated from the weight of the gown and the weight of being in Ridley's presence. "No. Not really. What you survived as a child does not mean you now have to put the fear of death and murder into others."

He said nothing.

She swallowed. "Helping others given what you endured is honorable, but it is clearly affecting you too much and making the world think the worst of you. I do not want that for you." Her voice cracked with emotion. "Everything you do reintroduces you to the pain of what happened to your father. Why live like that? I saw it written into every one of your letters. You return to the grime of these criminals as if they were your family and never give yourself peace. Do you never tire of it?"

He nodded gloomily. "Sometimes, I do. Yes."

It meant that maybe one day he would retire.

It gave her hope for his safety.

She reached out and gripped his hands. "Ridley. You drank an entire bottle of laudanum as if it were champagne. And that is what I fear most. That you have already crossed over beyond my reach, pursuing a justice you will *never* reach for you have seen too much and fear *nothing*. Even death does not scare you, and *that* scares me. What if during the course of our involvement, we end up with children?"

His gaze snapped to hers. He squinted. "Are you saying you want children? *With me*?"

The very thought of *this one* becoming a father sent her into a heaving panic. Instead of ducklings, they would be called... deathlings. "No," she confided awkwardly, tugging her hands free of his. "Between my being an Indian and you being an inspector who puts himself in constant danger, such a thing would be *baleful. What on earth would we do with them*? Take them on jail tours and teach them how to decipher poisons in a greenhouse whilst loading lead balls into pistols by the age of four? All they would know of is death."

She shook her head. "No. Not my child. Not my children. The world will put them through enough given who I am: an Indian. But you? You, o *Earl of Hell*, are leading a life unworthy of any child. Do you doubt it?"

Ridley shifted from boot to boot, the silence pulsing between them. "No."

She sighed. "You once told me you hid the devil. Is this the devil you were referring to? Is he your... work persona?"

His jaw worked. "Amongst other things."

She lowered her chin. "What *other* things are there?"

Ridley dragged a heavy hand through his hair. "I was hoping to actually discuss this with you in private on Friday." He held her gaze. "At the hotel."

Her mouth throbbed. "I had a chance to read the bible."

Rolling his tongue against the inside of his cheek, he held her gaze. "Did you?"

She nodded. "I am not about to preach to you in the way I was preached to by these women and men, but I did learn a few things about the one who calls himself the devil."

Nodding, she tried to distract herself from his gaze by adjusting his waistcoat. "Despite everyone always offering 'scary' descriptions of what 'the devil' is and what he is capable of, nowhere is it written as to what actually makes him so frightening. It is all heresay. Except, of course, for when he verbally taunts Jesus in a desert without ever once striking or when he slithers up to Eve as a snake without ever biting her. In truth, verbal taunts, harsh lands and hissing snakes never really frightened me. I was born and raised in India."

He squinted. "Your point being?"

"Despite the devil being notorious for tempting so many people to sin, he never once grants himself or any human in that bible any miraculous powers that enables him to control anything and so I am incredibly confused as to why he is given any credence at all." She squeezed his arm in assurance. "I suggest you not give this devil in your head any credence, either. The only power he holds over you is the one you give to him. For you are what I know you to be: *a gentleman*. Give credence to that. For you *are* that. You have always been that to me."

He held her gaze. "I'm no gentleman, Kumar. Did my letters not convey that?"

She rolled her eyes. "All men are lustful in nature."

"Some more than others." Shifting his jaw, he snapped out his hand. "Take a turn with me."

This one was still what he was back in London: a riddle. "Do I need a chaperone?"

"No." He grabbed her hand hard and wove his fingers forcefully through hers, walking them out of the grove. He skimmed her low décolletage. "You need a fichu."

Rolling her eyes, she squared a hand around her top heavy breasts. "I did not realize a low décolletage could offend your delicate sensibilities."

He leaned in. "I don't mind risqué, Jemdanee, but I came for a relationship. A bit of maturity. *Not this*. You accuse me of being unable to control the devil, but I am accusing you of something far worse. Playing with my cock. A bit of advice: don't." He flicked her lip *hard*. "We have to be strategic."

She eyed him, her face burning.

"Are you trunks packed?"

She hesitated, leaning away. His casual approach toward everything, including death and sex was... ruffling. "*Nahin*. I have had too many apothecary orders and most likely will not find any time to gather my effects until Friday evening."

Releasing her hand, he quickly removed his watch and flipped open its gold casing, noting the time. "Unfortunately, I have to leave in twenty minutes."

She jerked toward him. "You are leaving again?"

He puffed out a breath. "Yes. Aside from meeting with all of the officers from the greeting line, I have to ride back to the Eastern barracks on the outskirts of Calcutta. I'm still training men in criminal profiling until Thursday night." He weighed the watch, blankly looking at it. "How about I gather your effects when I return on Friday? That way, you don't have to do it and you can go directly to the hotel. I'll meet you there."

Jemdanee bit back a smile. "You would do that for me?"

He tapped her chin. "What wouldn't I do for you?"

She slowly rolled her fan shut, remembering that gold watch all too well. He might as well have frozen himself in time. It was as if nothing about him had changed. Not even the watch he carried or the cologne he wore. "Still ticking fast, I see."

He shut the casing with a flick. "I merely respect what controls us all: time. Which brings me to a most endearing point." Tucking the watch away with the push of his thumb, he jerked them to a halt and removed a folded parchment from the other side of his waistcoat pocket. With the turn of his wrist, he held it out between two fingers. "For you, my raven."

Jemdanee eyed him. "What is it?"

"We adhere to it." Edging in, he held it out, grazing the smooth flat surface against her lower lip, which he further dragged to her cheek and down her throat. "It's only temporary."

It made her curious.

She tugged the parchment free, unfolded it and paused, momentarily unable to comprehend what she was looking at.

TEMPORARY SCHEME

6 a.m. to 8 a.m.—Rise, bathe, dress, contrive the day's business and breakfast with Ridley.

8 a.m. to noon—Squadron duty for Ridley/recreational time for Jemdanee.

Noon to 1 p.m.—Alfresco dining with Ridley.

1 p.m. to 6 p.m.—Squadron duty for Ridley/recreational time for Jemdanee.

6 p.m. to 10 p.m.—*Mis en place*, supper, examination of the day with Ridley.

10 p.m. to 6 a.m.—Retire into separate quarters until logistics of sexual congress is agreed upon.

She snort-laughed and sent it fluttering against the hot wind where it belonged, tumbling into a nearby shrub. "The hours after ten in the evening are poorly allotted." She lifted a brow. "Whatever are you about? Is this a clever way to get me to cooperate?"

"No. It ensures you never submit to anything unwillingly." He leaned back, adjusting the cane. "I have to reconvene with the Field Marshal in the next fifteen minutes. That will give you time to catch up on your own work given you're behind on forty-two prescriptions. Forty. Two. You'll be here well past Friday if you don't rattle the windows of that greenhouse."

She jerked toward him.

He knew the amount of prescriptions she was behind on.

Only her logs were aware of it. Logs she kept locked in her greenhouse with the keys always in her satchel. "How do you know how many prescriptions I am behind on?"

He cracked his knuckles. "Sleight of hand. I had a few hours last night. Your logs are a mess."

This one had been digging! "Judge not. A few messes are to be expected. I have been servicing almost a hundred people on the compound with *no one* assisting me."

"Hence the schedule. You could use it." An inexplicable look of withdrawal came over his face. "I've seen how you utilize the

65

clock, Kumar. Not very wisely. Yesterday, you took a two hour walk into the city and wove through countless markets despite never buying anything. How is that useful to anyone?"

Her lips parted. "Were you spying on me?"

"I was getting to know you again given you only started writing when I arrived in Bombay."

This man was exhausting her.

He set his shoulders. "How long have you your *semnopithecus priam thersites*?"

Twisting her lips in an attempt to further understand him, she blurted, "My *what*?"

"Chunmun. How long have you had him?"

She lowered her chin. He knew everything. Everything, everything! He even knew the Latin name of the species Chunmun belonged to. "Almost eight weeks."

"Is he your version of my Chaucer?"

She blinked. "Why would you think that?"

"*Chunmun* has the same amount of letters as *Chaucer*."

This one's mind needed more rest. "It never crossed my mind."

He hesitated. "You didn't plan that?"

"No. A monkey is not exactly a raven."

He gave her a withering look. "A monkey is also more work and requires an insupportable amount of resources, guidance and space. What were you thinking?"

She groaned. "He peered out at me through the cage and I became a mother."

"I see. You once accused me of keeping a raven in an unnatural habitat but somehow think a monkey is… any better?"

She cringed. "Are you accusing me of animal cruelty?"

"Yes. Monkeys need other monkeys and more than a bedpost to swing from."

Her throat tightened knowing he was right.

"Was he captured in the wild?" he pressed.

She felt like a *goodna*. "*Haan*."

He searched her face, his deep voice softening. "You do realize, *mon chou*, I purchased Chaucer as a hatchling from the Zoological Society. He never knew life outside of people."

A miserable breath escaped her. She hardly needed a lecture. She'd been meaning to do it, but… she grew attached. "I always intended on returning him to the wild."

"I'm glad to hear it. Where was he taken from? Do you know?"

"Near Bishnupur."

He sighed. "Bring him to the hotel on Friday and we'll release him together after a few days. It's a three hour ride to Bishnupur but you owe him a better life. Agreed?"

It was inevitable. No amount of fruit in a bowl would change that Chunmun's life needed more than four walls.

She half-nodded. "You certainly seem to be well informed about my life. It hints you have been here longer than a day. How long *have* you been in Calcutta?"

"Long enough." His amber eyes grew playful. "I had to catch up on everything I missed."

"So you investigated the animals I keep and pummeled a man."

He widened his stance, gripping his cane. "I was ensuring your wellbeing."

"Is that what you call it?" She stared him down, willing him to remember the day he almost died. "Despite what you think, Ridley, I have *always* been able to take care of myself *and* others. You, however, appear to be in dire need of guidance. You should *not* be assaulting men who are well known for being idiots but otherwise harmless. It does not suit your gentlemanly and academic nature."

He thudded the cane into the ground, leaning in. "Is the keeper of wild animals lecturing me?"

She set her hands on her hips. "*Haan.* I am also asking the jaguar out of London not use his career as an excuse to advance his personal life or intimidate others."

He released an exasperated breath through teeth. "If I had wanted to advance my personal life, I would have already damn well thrown you over my shoulder and taken you *to* London screaming. My life is *there*. Not here. Not in this depraved gallimaufry Britain created. They are all out of their fucking minds. The criminal rate is doubling in England with each passing year, yet these merchants, lords and pasty-white politicians think pouring all of their resources into another country is ingenious?"

Tipping forward, he added, "My contract with the intelligence squadron terminates in five days. After that…" He adjusted the sleeves on her gown as if laying out the grand plan. "London needs us. Between your expertise and mine, it will be the greatest partnership to have ever touched a crime-infested city since Vidocq put a blade to Paris. Imagine what we could do for London. *Imagine.*"

Jemdanee tugged her sleeves away from his hands. She was *not* going back to London. It held no fond memories.

Prison. Poisoned oranges. Dead people at theatres as if *that* were the real show.

And that didn't even include the memories of his sweat-dampened skin. The trembling of her own hands wrapping his gored leg each and every day with fresh gauze.

She could still hear the scraping sound of the razor she had used to shave him as he lay unconscious and sometimes still heard it in her head at night. Right along with the clicking of the metal spoon against his teeth which she had tucked past his parched lips, willing him to live when he had only wanted to die.

All while he had gazed past her without even knowing it was her.

His so-called career did that to him.

And then there were... *the crowds.* One would have thought the king had been shot.

The sea of spectators and journalists pressing their faces against his iron gates on Basil Street, whilst shouting and yelling about his attempted suicide, had made it impossible for her to leave through any door. The few times she *had* attempted, men and women shoved in disturbingly close, touching her hair and brown skin as if she were an animal in a cage and they had come to an exhibit.

Never again. "Setting aside everything I endured at your hands and whatever you call a career, I am *never* going back to an all-white city and its definition of what an Indian should live through. I have more respect for myself than that and will stay here until my braid goes silver. You can say it in French and I will say it in Hindi."

His voice softened. "I remember you once wanted to stay in London. I remember you insisted you would never leave my side. Do you remember that?"

She pointed. "Do not use that overly soft tone with me and think it will charm my bindi into cooperation. I am *still* recovering from seeing you half-dead. The demands of your career is what ultimately led to your attempt at suicide."

"It was more complicated than that." He adjusted his leather belt. "It won't happen again."

She squinted, trying to understand what she never seemed to be able to: him. "Is that what you think I fear? That it will happen again? Ridley, you fool of a mercenary who knows nothing about women. *It already happened*. I already lived it!"

He tugged up the sleeve of his linen shirt, rolling the cuff and shoving it up. "You survived me and I survived you."

She paused, her gaze settling on his strong bared forearm that had been heavily scarred by what appeared to be letters that spelled out... *JEMDANEE*.

Startled, her heart flopped, sinking down to her bare feet and toes buried in the grass. She frantically grabbed his arm, disbelievingly touching her fingers against the raised ridges of long-healed lettering that had whitened against the olive tone of his skin.

What did he do? "*Ridley*... this is *not* something you can ever erase."

He gave her a withering look. "Why would I want to erase a woman who did this to my soul? At least this way, you can see the damage you've inflicted. Blame yourself."

She glared. "*I did not inflict this on you*! Ridley, this is—First coca/limestone, then eight fluid ounces of laudanum and now a razor?! *Are you mad*?"

"Cease yelling." Reaching out, he gripped her hand, kissed it hard, and then guided it to the linen shirt over his sizable bicep. He pressed all five of her fingers into it, molding it hard. "When you're ready to face who I am, ask me about it."

The pulsing of her fingers against ridges of what felt like rope bundled against corded muscle hinted of too many feral things unsaid.

She jerked her hand back.

If he could razor her name into his skin and bind rope around his bicep as if it were a bouquet of roses waiting to be given, the intensity of what his mind, his lips and his body would bring to her made her realize her knee caps needed iron reinforcement. "Marring yourself is wrong."

His hair ruffled against the breeze, as a shaft of sun struck his hair through the branches of the swaying trees, making his chestnut hair gleam. "Do you think overcoming a broken body that was addicted to coca/limestone was easy? Most men don't even overcome that much for themselves yet alone the woman they seek to claim. It's a mindset I took on in your name and carving this into my skin saw me through the worst of my addiction. So don't insult me by saying it's wrong or you're insulting what I feel for you."

It was *torture* knowing she had afflicted him to the point of him needing a razor.

She shook her head, riled. "Carving yourself violates the respect I want for you."

He stared her down. "You are misusing the word 'respect'. The true definition of respect is and I quote, 'a feeling of deep admiration for someone or something elicited by their qualities'. *This* is me showing *you* respect, Jemdanee. For I admire your qualities. I am embracing you for who you are and am asking you to embrace me for who I am. That is the foundation of a good relationship. Unlike other men, I am excessively passionate about my devotion, but I would never hurt you. *Ever*."

Her throat burned. "You once did."

Turning, she quickly crossed out of the shade and whipped past low-hanging branches that pushed her into the adjoining garden. She hurried across the extensive lawn toward the side entrance stairs leading into her three acre greenhouse, her bare feet burning against the hot pathway stone. The burning against her feet and the burning against her soul and the weight of the gown made her hyperventilate.

Seeing her name razored into his skin was too much.

It brought back her own pain. Her angst. Him almost dying. Him with the bottle of laudanum in his hand and his blank stare that almost killed everything and who she was.

Her breaths became choked and unmanageable.

"Ey." His booted steps and thudding of his cane quickly followed. "You aren't leaving angry after you mauled me with silence for three years. *Trois*. Show a bit of maturity."

She glared back at him, walking faster. "Do not lecture me on maturity as you razor yourself with my name!"

His large frame drew closer. "Whilst I admire your tenacity to make an effectual point, *mon chou*, we are cultivated enough to address all points in conversation without yelling. I'll be gone for four days and won't be able to function if you toss me off like this.

So bring that fourteen-pound dress back here. Turn around."

Breathing raggedly through flaring nostrils, she shook her head, refusing to speak to him whilst angry. For she would only hurt him. She would only make this worse. "We will talk on Friday," she bit out. "When I am calm and not as resentful."

"*Jemdanee Kumar*," he rumbled out. "Turn around. I won't ask again."

Her tongue was one of the smallest parts of her body, but one she brandished like a sword. It was her greatest weapon and her greatest flaw since childhood. Too many times she had made her own *maa* cry with hateful, hateful words she'd never be able to take back, especially now that her *maa* was gone.

It was something she lived with and something she always regretted.

Much like plants, which varied in their use and level of toxicity, words had the power to destroy and Ridley didn't need her to punish him.

He needed her to do what no woman had ever done in his honor: guide him.

Which was why… she was biting her tongue to bleeding.

She gathered her skirts and marched up the long set of stairs leading to her greenhouse. "I am *far* too angry to have a rational discussion with you and will say things I will regret. *So leave off. Leave off!*"

She darted up the remaining stairs.

Ridley tossed the cane with a loud clang and jumped three stairs at a time beside her with a long-legged run, wincing in an effort to pass her on the terrace of the greenhouse.

She gasped *knowing* he was coming after her full force. She sprinted, frantically lifting the weight of her skirts against her scrambling bare feet, while trying to move against tangling petticoats.

Ridley skidded and grabbed her waist hard.

She choked, shoving. "I am attempting to respect you by not… *saying anything*!"

He jerked her into place against himself, tightening his hold as his chin dug into her hair from behind. "Unlike most men, Jemdanee, I can swallow whatever blade you throw." He adjusted his tensing hold, molding her backside to feel every rigid muscle in his body. "So throw it."

She shoved him. "Cease—"

He adjusted her harder, his muscles rigidly shifting and leaned in from behind, grazing his lips against her neck. "Shhhh."

Given he was holding her shoulders hard and she couldn't move forward or back against the rigidness of that embrace, she used her elbows and her legs which were buried beneath useless skirts to try to connect with anything she could. "*Ridley*, I am... *warning you!*"

"I embrace that warning willingly." With his teeth, he dragged out pins, spitting them out. "What do you want?" he intoned, dragging his lips back toward her throat. "What do you need?" He set his hot mouth on her throat and sucked at her skin, moving up and up.

She gasped against the moist heat of his mouth, unable to breathe, and staggered back against him, the lotus fluttering out of her hair as locks fell in curtains.

"Isn't this better than arguing?" he breathed hotly into her ear.

She staggered.

Spinning her around, he shoved her against the entrance of the door she had been looking to escape through and held her hard in place. "*Bonjour*, gorgeous."

The rest of her pins tinkered out and she couldn't see past her own hair.

She peered through her black waves of hair realizing he was only a breath away.

Ridley squared in with the bulk of his large muscled frame.

He searched her face. "You're ignorantly poking for a fight and I'm telling you right now, I'll end it before you start one." He waggled his large fingers at her eyes as if casting a spell. "So I razored my forearm. Oh dear me and *gasp*. It wasn't your arm, dearest. It was mine."

Jemdanee almost slid down the length of the door, venting out three horrid years of too many words unsaid to a man who had tortured her heart, her body and her mind. Unable to believe she was already losing control of her mind, she choked out, "Nothing about this association is normal, Ridley. *Nothing!* You are—I cannot *think* when I am away from you anymore than I can *think* when I am with you and you—"

"I feel the same." He smoothed her hair, leaning in. "No more of this. I'm imploring that you not muck up what we share with irrational displays of emotion neither of us can handle. Talk to me knowing words are my rooks. Play the game with me."

In that moment, she realized… he was far more forgiving of her than she was of him.

A tear she couldn't hold onto escaped her eyes, revealing all too well what she had felt for him all along.

He tilted her face upward. "Ey."

Their eyes locked and her heart rushed to her toes, her fingers, her breasts and her elbows. The single tear traced its way down her cheek.

He dragged it away with his thumb, searching her face. Lowering his head, he set his forehead against hers, the pulse of their pressing foreheads emphasizing what they shared. "Persephone and Hades," he rasped. "That is who we are. Persephone never wanted Hades but he was unable to live without her. He dragged her into his realm and there she was forced to stay. She gave him no children, yet remained faithful to him and he to her. Always. Why? Because they came to an understanding of who they were to each other and the power it brought."

Ridley leaned back to look at her face. "Everything about me will unsettle you. Get used to it. Well before my father was taken, I was still this, Kumar," he admitted. "*This*. A riddle unto myself. I once spent an entire afternoon on the stairs of my home as a child counting how many nails went into building that staircase, pulling up the carpet until my fingers were raw. My mother had me nail every piece of carpet back into place, yelling in French, but how could I not be fascinated by the very thing that allowed me to move from one floor to the next? It was how my mind worked. By the time I was eleven, I could read eight books at once and still be bored, needing more. Is that normal? I cannot say. I had intelligence on my shoulder with an angel trying to choke the devil out. The only difference was that as a child, I feared that devil. Until I met the devil one night and realized it was human."

She eyed him.

His expression stilled. "The devil lives in all of us, but unlike most, I understand that same devil can yield great power and protect not only me, but those that matter most. And damn you, you matter most."

A knot formed in her stomach.

"I will *always* choose to protect you over myself and I don't think it's wrong," he rasped. "I have never felt this way toward anyone. Not even my former wife. So if you want to know what scares me… this does. *You do*. Because drinking a bottle of laudanum is only the beginning of what I would do in your name, and yes, that should scare us both."

A shiver of awareness skimmed through her knowing he meant it.

Holding her gaze, he said in a grudging tone, "This goes beyond love, *mon dévot*. I call it hell and you do nothing but keep me in it. You aren't the prisoner here. I am. Yes, I have an incredibly macabre persona, and yes, I have always been a villain to these criminals, but they never show the world mercy, so why should I show them mercy? How have they earned it? *By breathing*? Taking breaths doesn't make you human. Animals take breaths, too. There will be times you will see a dark side of me that will make you think I am one of them, but with you holding me, I promise to stay loyal to what I want most: *you*."

She sniffed in exasperation, trying to return her mind to a breathing calm she had yet to feel knowing he was hovering close. Too close. His heat and his cologne was penetrating her senses and her mind.

Pressing each hand outside of her shoulders, he shifted his large frame toward her. "Are you still attracted to me despite the limp?"

She swallowed. "Yes."

He grabbed her face, startling her. His large hands tightened against her face, tilting her glasses upwards. "*I needed to hear that*."

She couldn't breathe.

Holding her gaze, he used his calloused thumbs to touch her face beneath the lenses, dragging away another lone tear that escaped. "I regret not showing you what I felt back in London." He re-looped the wire rims behind her ears, to ensure they were back into place and rasped, "I regret not getting into that water with you and flooding the floor and our lives, but you weren't ready for me any more than I was ready for you. I needed you to be what you are now: bolder, stronger. Strong enough to ensure you don't break when I hold you." He rigidly traced his thumbs over the curve of her cheekbones, his features wavering.

She lingered, her breaths difficult to take as those large, heated hands possessed her.

Ridley gently rattled her face, the pads of his fingers dragging upward toward her lips. "Many women have passed through my life, but I have *never* had a Jemdanee. You're going to feel what I feel and it will scare you enough to run, but don't think for a moment you'll ever be able to. *We're bound.* Pain is incredibly subjective and experienced differently by every person. To me, a razor against my skin is no different than the pain you continue to dole. You enjoy hurting me. You revel in it. It's who you are."

She glared. "That is not true."

He tapped a finger against her lips. "You don't know yourself very well. For three years you let me suffer offering nothing but your silence as I fought against my own body and my own mind to be able to stand here. You let me suffer because you couldn't handle the pain I made you feel. *That* is the difference between you and I, Kumar. I can take the pain. I can take it until I'm dead. You, on the other hand… *can't.* You seem to think life is all about sunshine and good weather, when in reality, every human story comes with quite a bit of thunder and rain. *Especially* when it comes to those you love. You've been an orphan too long not to know otherwise, but if you don't ever feel pain for those you love, you're not in love with them at all."

She swallowed.

He traced her throat with his knuckles. "I'm going to ensure you can't breathe without me. I'm going to crawl into your skull and leave scars and you'll not only *let me*, but will love me for it."

She could see by the set of his jaw and the riled heat in his eyes that *this* was about to go well beyond the usual bond men and women shared.

This would become everything that defined Ridley… bone deep.

She tried to breathe knowing every minute in his presence was a second hand of a clock tapping and tapping at who she was. Digging. Digging deeper to the bone and skull he wanted.

"You appear to have caged yourself." Reaching out, he removed her spectacles, his fingers grazing her skin. He folded them and tucked them into his own waistcoat pocket. "Hiding behind a pair of non-prescriptive spectacles tells me you have permitted the world to negatively influence you since I last saw you. Why are you wearing them?"

The tightness of her throat made it almost impossible to speak. "I find them fashionable."

He tapped her nose. "Don't lie. Not to me. Why are you wearing them?"

Damn him for knowing everything.

She veered her gaze to his. "My eyes are not meant to be blue."

Ridley weighed her, his expression taut and derisive and final. "You and I are far more alike than you think. You accuse me of mutilating myself, yet you openly mutilate yourself, in turn. If you disrespect the half of you that is white, how do you expect anyone to respect the half of you that is Hindu? *Hm*? The world will seek to destroy whatever side you take, which is why it is up to you to show the world you are capable of embracing what they never will: *both sides*. My duality is hero and demon. Your duality is Indian and white. Your struggle will *always* be greater than mine, but the moment you choose one side over another, you limit your potential and your mind and become a villain to yourself. Don't wear these spectacles again. Don't. Fucking don't."

She swallowed knowing he was already crawling back into her brain as if she were in London again. Even worse, he was trying to crawl into the veins of her soul and seep into the one place she swore she'd never let him rip apart again: her heart.

"*You're done hiding.*" A muscle quivered at his jaw. "I addressed a long list of contemptable vices back in London in your honor so that I might offer you a better man. Whilst you? You're a mess on the rise. Even your corset is on *backwards*."

Her hand jumped to her hidden corset buried beneath material she knew he couldn't see through. Her fingers gripped the clinging material hard, her pulse roaring.

Smoldering constraint lit his eyes. "Unlike other men, I have the mental capacity to see past your antics." He tapped at her stomacher, dragging his finger across it. "You wore this contraption to make me crawl, but how about I make *you* crawl instead? I'm going to make you wait for the fuck we both want."

Explosive currents raced through her. She smacked away his hand.

His hand rigidly skimmed her waist and dragged up to her

breasts. His fingertips grazed her exposed skin, spreading them down toward her nipple buried beneath the fabric.

She choked.

With the quirk of a brow, he snapped up the hand to demonstrate it was no longer inappropriately touching her.

She staggered, unable to control the need she always felt in his presence.

His eyes darkened. "I have to leave. I will see you in five thousand, seven hundred and sixty minutes." Leaning in, his hot tongue grazed the corner of her mouth, dipping and dragging past her lips and across her teeth.

Moisture flooded her cunt and she gasped, wanting to be tongued and filled and impaled. Her skin was ablaze, her core demanding his thickness. She grabbed his shoulders hard and veered her hands down between them, grabbing for the flap of his trousers. "Pleasure me," she choked out trying to reclaim his mouth that annoyingly stayed out of reach. "Before you go. Four days is far too—"

"Ey. Ey. Ease off," his voice came low against her cheek. "Your officer is watching."

She froze against uneven and harried breaths. Her gaze snapped beyond Ridley's broad shoulders to the lingering figure of Bradley in the distance. Watching.

A knot formed in her stomach.

"He can't seem to let you go," Ridley intoned, his chin digging into her cheek. "Why?"

She almost buried her face against him in mortification. "Why not go and ask him?"

Leaning back, he gave her a pointed look, his amber eyes sparking. "I have squadron duty and have no time for this. I'll see you on Friday. Maybe by then you'll tell me more."

The last thing she needed was for him to think there *was* more. She swallowed. "He signed off on your assignment that you took into Bombay. Were you aware of that?"

He nodded. "Yes. His signature was there for me to read. Why?"

"Did you also know it was a *felo-de-se* assignment?"

He squinted. "Yes. I knew."

She stared in disbelief. "*Yet you took it?* Knowing you could die?"

"You needed me."

She glared and thudded his chest. "Not at the expense of yourself!"

His tone hardened. "What the hell is this? What aren't you telling me?"

Jemdanee pressed her hands to his smoothly shaven face, thankful he hadn't been hurt. "Bradley gave you that assignment thinking you would never return from it."

His expression cooled. He leaned back, breaking her hold on his face. "Why? What happened between you and him?"

She tsked. "With such a lofty attempt to slander, I am astounded you did not have my hymen investigated."

Something flared in his eyes. "Now is not the time to toss jokes."

She gripped his arms in assurance. "*I am not a case.* This is not an investigation. Cease treating me as if I were a criminal looking to turn against you. Nothing happened outside of what I already told you."

He glanced toward the Government House. "I'm going to assign someone to stand outside your door within the hour. Do you know Brigadier Jasper?"

"I... yes."

"He will follow you everywhere until I get back. Don't go anywhere alone."

"Ridley, I have been here for three years without an incident."

"Except for the one that happened today." He pointed. "I'll be gone for four days and hardly need the distraction of worrying about you. I'll assign him to your door."

"I appreciate the concern, but there is no need to—"

"Don't argue." Edging toward her, he jerked her toward himself. "Give me what you owe me." Seizing her lips, his tongue rigidly slid into her mouth, pushing deep toward her throat as if thrusting his cock into her womb.

She gasped, her pulse roaring in disbelief. He was... *kissing her*!

His fingers dug into her, stinging her over-sensitized skin as his masculine mouth worked with ferocity, opening her mouth wider to him. His hot tongue tasted, penetrated and dragged against her teeth.

She almost fainted.

Pressing into him with the intention of climbing onto him, she tongued him frenziedly, glorying in a moment she had dream of for too long. The prickling heat of her skin beneath the fabric separating them was unbearable.

Their ragged breaths mingled against each other's frantic mouths.

Dragging his large hands downward from her throat to her shoulders to her breasts, his calloused palms almost burned her from the friction.

Jemdanee staggered against his muscled frame, her hands jumping up in anguished need to touch his smoothly shaven face, his strong throat and his broad chest as the bulk of his arms crushed her closer. She moaned in ecstasy knowing this was real!

Gripping and tugging at his waistcoat, she submitted to his driving tongue as he sucked her own tongue deep into his mouth, stinging it to the root.

Her lips burned in an effort to keep up with the mounting intensity.

The solid muscle beneath his clothing tensed and shifted, warning of building tension.

He thudded her back *hard* against the greenhouse door, jarring her into gasping against his mouth from the impact vibrating every limb.

Growling, he nipped her lower lip, and slid her hand down between them, forcing her to rub the thickness of his rampant cock which pressed against the linen flap straining past the buttons that were shifting. He curled her fingers around the swollen length and imposing size of that cock, inflaming her to forget whatever pain it would bring.

Her mind reeled, her thighs wet.

She couldn't breathe.

Ridley broke away and released her, removing her gripping hands from his flap and his waistcoat, by unfurling every last one of her fingers on both hands.

Her face felt as if it had been burnt to the muscle by an iron left atop of sizzling coals.

Ridley lingered, silence pulsing between them.

His eyes darkened with emotion. Wetting his lips, he eventually half-nodded.

A muscle flicked in his jaw. "I'll see you Friday."

Stiffly walking past her and over to the cane he'd thrown earlier, he swept up the cane. Without another word, he thudded it into the ground and headed toward the direction of the gathering squadron with a long legged limping stride that shifted the clothing against his imposing, broad frame.

She lingered, grazing quaking fingers to her scorched lips.

There would be no separating their breaths again.

He had marked her to the bone and she was now his raven.

CHAPTER FIVE

Friday afternoon
The Government House

Evan Oswald Ridley wasn't a man known to step outside of his own head very often. When he wasn't miffed with himself, he rather liked it in there. His mind, after all, held an extensive amount of serviceable information he had ceaselessly gathered throughout his thirty-five years of life, and it was far more organized than the rest of the benighted world around him.

For he knew what to expect from his thoughts.

He knew what to do with them.

He knew how to apply logic and get results.

More importantly, he rarely disappointed himself when he followed his own set of axioms. While there were too many axioms for him to list, he still abided by each and every one.

For instance, he knew that getting emotionally and physically involved with a woman made a man do stupid things. And in his world and in his life and given who and what he was, there was no room for stupidity.

It led to iniquitous mistakes that could never be undone.

For every half-second that his watch couldn't show him, it revealed a thread leading to countless lives that had yet to be saved.

One wrong tug and they ceased to exist.

One wrong tug and no evidence remained.

One wrong tug and a killer was left to do what they did best.

Whilst too many people seemed to think he was a genius, his mind was only really extraordinary because of one thing: he knew how to retrieve and utilize the information to see past the jargon.

Unlike these fucking military men surrounding him, who only looked at women and saw a pair of tits, his mind saw into the muscle holding that woman together which allowed her to not only move, but exist.

He hadn't always been so enlightened.

Once upon a time in that often fog-ridden land of London, after he'd solved his first double-homicide back in 1820, there hadn't been a woman who didn't notice that, *oui*, he was good-looking, and *oui*, he had a subtle French accent, and *oui*, his overly educated mind wanted the attention, and *oui*, he was ready to fuck whoever he wanted and however he wanted.

Back when he was two and twenty, he'd been cocky enough to even fuck the fetching wife of Flanders, a highly ranked lead inspector of the Bow Street Runners. She had been flirtatiously sending him perfumed missives, attempting to engage his newfound popularity.

Given Flanders had refused to let him in on *any* cases and had even repeatedly denied his application to the Bow Street Runner's, Ridley had called on Mrs. Flanders one afternoon and twenty minutes later banged her on the back stairs of the man's own home like she wanted.

He even left the used condom on the man's desk with his rejected application.

Three days later, Flanders hired two burly Irish men and they rightfully pummeled the British blood out of him in a back alley.

That incident veered him toward what he called French enlightenment.

For he had lost sight of what mattered most: absolute justice.

Setting aside the moral issue that came with penetrating another man's wife, he had brought justice shame by forgetting his purpose and thinking revenge and any fuck was more important than his duty toward the rest of the world that was always dripping in blood.

To compensate for his aberration, he focused on what he did best: deconstructing atrocities and connecting them to the criminals whose heads he slammed into prison walls.

Over too many years of occasionally visiting birch clubs when loneliness got the best of him, he met Elizabeth who dragged his teeth across the pavement until he said 'I don't'. After their divorce, he'd learned to take greater pleasure in more subtle things.

Like pushing aside the skull and looking at the brain. How much could it endure? How much would it embrace? Did it panic? Did it like to experiment? Could it match his intensity?

That was what mattered.

But Jemdanee, Jemdanee made him realize... none of those questions mattered.

The taste of a raw honey stick she had sucked on still clung to the memory of his mind since Monday. The sounds of her uneven breaths and the feel of her small fingers gripping his prick made it impossible for him to focus on anything but what he wanted: her.

She was the only reason why he was making his way through the vast, silent corridors of the Government House. For three years she had lived in a world he had never wanted her to be part of. For three years, he'd been left to imagine what did and didn't happen given she never wrote.

He knew he had earned her vengeful silence, but his need to piece together the years he'd missed was messing with the commonsensical part of his mind.

It all veered into that dangerous, shadowy and unpredictable bailiwick known as his heart.

Before deciding on what to do with *Bradley*, he decided to keep it simple.

He was going to crawl into her mind first.

Past her unsaid words.

Past her pain.

Past his own.

Ridley set his cane against the wall outside her bedchamber.

By packing her effects, he would be unpacking misunderstandings and erasing the three years spaced between them in the only way he knew how.

He dug out the key the Field Marshal had given him and

unlocked the door leading into her room with the jerk of his wrist and pushed it wide open.

Stepping into the silence of her bedchamber, he closed the door behind himself, locking it to ensure no interruptions. He then did what he always did before sectioning off a crime scene.

He did nothing but stand in the room and breathe.

Scent. Jasmine *ittar*.

It lingered in the air and yet… it had not lingered on the heat of her bronzed skin when he'd last seen her. The scent was as mouth softening as it was overpowering. Like the color of her gorgeous eyes that were not a mere blue but the color of lightning that lit up the sky during the rage of a storm.

A storm he couldn't wait to fuck so he could smell the burn of electricity.

Ridley shifted his jaw and rounded the massive room, his booted feet echoing as he opened the shutter enough to let in more sunlight. He paused at seeing a maze of hemp. Looped through bolted hooks, the unending rope had been shaped into intricate macramé patterns that upheld countless jars filled with plants which decorated the entire ceiling.

His lips parted in disbelief. Few things ever astounded him.

"*L'Appel du vide*." It was… his overlord rope.

The one he thought was still in the attic of his house on 221 Basil Street.

Why in knucklebones had she…?

"You *minx*." If a sky could be strewn with possibilities he was looking at it.

Veering to one of the woven nets she had created for her plants out of his rope, he disbelievingly grazed his fingers against the roughness of small seashells wedged into the hemp for adornment.

She put fucking seashells into his overlord rope.

Seashells. As if the twisting of hemp into bare skin wasn't enough to produce a burn.

It was scatological.

He imagined positioning them over each of her budding nipples heavily moistened with his tongue, whilst guiding the rest around her bronzed thighs, rubbing her slit.

Too much of him knew she would never be that given his razored arm alone unnerved her.

Ridley dragged the rope grudgingly, swaying the entire maze of plants and set the macramé adorned rope against his face. It hurt his heart knowing he was folding her into a life she would never understand or come to embrace.

It was the price a man paid for thinking he could erase all obstacles in the name of love.

Easing out a breath in an effort to refocus on what he had come to do, he paused.

Despite it being two in the afternoon, the linens on her bed were bundled and hanging off the low-lying mattress. Several saris were tossed onto the other side of the bed with equal disregard.

Two of the three pillows were on the floor.

Stacks of books and parchments and quills, along with several inkwells that had spattered the linen of her bed with ink, were all stacked from the head board to the footboard on the right side of her bed as if it were its own person.

A low whistle escaped him at seeing piles and piles of tangling saris that had clearly never been folded or placed into her wardrobe.

It was rather obvious she yanked out a dozen, before settling for one.

Her countless slippers and sandals, which anyone would be hard pressed to find its matching pair, were falling out of a trunk that was propped against the wall.

That didn't even include the mess on her dressing table, where ribbons and pins and glass bottles of tonics were piled together like stew spilling out of a pot.

Ridley scrubbed his head in a riled effort to erase the mess he was seeing. "My study never even looked like this," he muttered.

He'd long since organized that study right down to the ink.

Because of her. Because one couldn't think straight when buried in a mess.

And yet… *she* lived like this?

His boot tapped at a porcelain bowl full of unevenly half-chewed browning apples. He tilted the bowl with the tip of his boot.

He leaned down, keeping his injured leg from bending as best he could and picked up the bowl. He glanced around, curious to meet this pet of hers.

Going over to the window, he edged it open and let out a low whistle. "Chunmun."

A grey-haired monkey with a charcoal face scrambled up the tree and peered at him.

Ridley lowered himself against the sill and set the bowl onto the ledge, tilting the apples as he held that eager gaze. "Was that the face you used to win her over?"

Chunmun jumped down and using hairy hands yanked himself up onto the ledge, which he now sat on. Glancing up, Chunmun dragged the bowl over, uncertain.

Holding out a hand, Ridley let it graze that narrow little chest. "Don't you miss your old life?"

Chunmun shoved away his hand and knocking over the bowl back into the room, jumped down and darted across the garden, disappearing into bushes.

"If life in the jungle was that bad, we can talk," he called teasingly.

Narrowing the window back to what it had been, he gathered the bowl and the apples.

Going over to her washing basin, he soaped his hands and cleaned them. He flicked off the water to ensure the stickiness of the apples didn't remain and glanced around.

He was looking to see if she'd associated with this Bradley beyond what she admitted to. He trusted her, but... he'd also trusted Elizabeth once and that didn't end so well.

Relationships had too many veneers and one of them was a need to possess a bit of sanity.

He had already decided back in London that when it came to Jemdanee, he wasn't leaving a single drawer unopen. For that lead to misunderstandings and he was far too passionate in nature to trust himself not to muck this up.

Veering his gaze to the copper hip bath set on the marble floor, he approached, the strain of his stiff leg reminding him he was not without sin. He leaned down toward the tub. With a finger, he dashed it across the oily residue of the tub, creating a line and rubbed it against his fingers, the scent of jasmine *ittar* drifting toward him.

She even used it in the bath water.

Ridley stalked over to her dressing table, pushing himself past the pace of his leg. He repositioned her hairbrush and angled each glass bottle and a few small jars.

Peach oil tonic for her hair. Very Hindu. Very nice.

He dabbed some onto his fingers and slicked it, drifting it toward his nostrils. Dragging in a breath, he reveled in the scent he'd buried his face into when he'd been picking out hair pins from her black silk hair. Angling in, Ridley ticked through the rest of the jars and bottles.

Lip rouge.

Kajal for the eyes.

Red ochre paste for her bindi.

Empty bottles of… Jasmine *ittar*, jasmine *ittar* and… jasmine *ittar*.

Women.

He scanned the piles and piles of stockings and garters and picked up a silk stocking, dangling it before himself. "France and India unite."

Skimming his fingers across the smooth silk, he shoved it into his pocket. "Let us see how long it takes for you to notice it's missing. I estimate… *never*."

He would pack everything up in a way to teach her how to better organize, because this was fucking ridiculous. Even at his worst, he'd never been this.

Opening the drawer on the nightstand next to her bed, he paused, his pulse roaring.

Countless pieces of crushed, then smoothed and folded parchments were stacked within.

It hinted she had attempted to destroy them but decided against doing so.

Glancing toward the main entrance door of her room, he fished out one of the heavily crinkled parchments and unfolded it.

An unfinished letter was written in her hand in English. It was no longer the perfect and neat cursive he knew her by three years earlier.

It was quick and harried.

It was… to him.

He lifted a triumphant brow knowing she *had* attempted to write.

Ridley,

I am ever so sorry about Chaucer. I know what he meant to you. Even as I write this tears blind my ability to see, but it does not blind my ability to feel. I apologize for leaving you and London without waiting for you to be fully conscious of what I had decided. Aside from the chaos of people coming to the door on the hour, and them treating me like an exhibit at the museum, understand that when I had stumbled upon you and thought death had taken you from me, I realized you had stolen what I cherish most. My ability to smile. My ability to laugh. You had told me that you needed someone more broken and in pieces. I am that now because of you. I would have never

It was left unfinished.

Ridley's chest tightened as he lingered with those words burning into his soul.

It would always be there.

The scar of his teeth on her fingers and the bottle of laudanum in his hand. As if his own guilt and his own hatred for himself wasn't enough.

Folding the letter, he kissed it and tucked it back into the drawer, leaving the other letters untouched, and closed the drawer. He hardly needed to see any of the other unfinished letters to know he had destroyed the most beautiful soul he had ever met.

He had turned it into a tangled mess of knots and left the frayed ropes to hang by her ceiling.

He had *tried* to pretend she hadn't marked his mind.

Unfortunately, the overlord in him had spoken and that motherfucker owned ninety percent of his brain. Sometimes more.

He shoved the phytology book off her bed, letting it thud to the floor and leaned over the bed and touched a hand to the coolness of the pillow she had slept on, smoothing his palm and fingers downward and beneath it.

Turning toward the massive row of trunks which needed to be packed with the contents of the room, he crossed the space. Fighting against his limp to feel more like a man, he paused, something on the far wall catching his eye.

It was at shoulder height.

Walking backward, he veered right and toward the wall.

Though barely visible, it was hairline seam in the bamboo paneling that dented inward.

His finger slid along the seam.

Squinting, he thudded the wall with his fist hard. It swayed.

His pulse roared as he unsheathed his dagger from his leather belt and stabbed it into the seam. Wedging it loose with the grit of his teeth by pushing against the handle, a creak and a reverberation unhinged the narrow two-foot-wide door.

Shoving it open, he paused.

It was a corridor.

"Son of a bitch." He braced the frame of the narrow opening and leaned in, peering into the darkness beyond. Only a single sliver of light on the farthest end, several feet in, outlined what appeared to be the other end of the door. Sheathing his dagger, he quickly wedged himself in, realizing it was going to be tight. His arse and the flap of his trousers were almost hitting the front and back of the corridor wall.

Pressing his back hard against the uneven mud walls studded with nails, he guided himself down the darkness of the corridor toward the sliver of light, shifting his shoulders to unhinge his waistcoat that occasional got caught on nails.

His jaw hurt from gnashing his teeth not to rip anything.

His leather-booted foot and bare hand pushed the outline of another doorway, creaking it wide open. He peered out, realizing it was an empty servant's room.

The shutters were left open, pouring in light and a hammock creaked in the corner.

Ridley wedged himself out and scanned the small room, seeing only a trunk.

Stalk-limping toward it, he leaned down, wincing against his leg that shot up pain to his hip and weighed a lock that held it shut. Eyeing the rest of the room that was eerily empty, he noted that everything else in the room was heavily caked in dust. Unused.

Even the hammock had cobwebs.

He slid his finger across the top of the trunk. Pristine.

It was being used. "Fuck."

Dragging the trunk away from the wall with the grit of teeth, he paused when it slid easily toward him.

He didn't like it.

Quickly rounding the trunk, he used his leather ankle boot, thudding it on each side, looking for any weakness in the wood paneling and leather. None.

No need to be polite.

Removing his pistol, he stepped back two feet and angled it downward toward the lock knowing it would take at least eight direct shots at its center.

He paused, checking his brace of bullets.

He only had three.

Of all days. He usually carried nine.

It was best. Pistol shots would only bring attention to him and the trunk. He needed to pack up Jemdanee's life and get her out of this mess first. For while she damn well thought he overanalyzed the world, his analyzing exposed the grime she clearly refused to see.

Not everything is as horrible as you imagine, she had said.

Gritting his teeth, he kicked the trunk, jarring it. "Sometimes, it's worse, *mon chou*."

It was something she would have to learn, because reality couldn't be miraculously altered with a positive attitude and a smile.

Shoving his pistol back into his holster, he stalk-limped over to the door of the room and unlatched it, swinging it open. He edged out into the corridor and seeing a male servant, called out in Hindi, "*Sahib*. Might I ask a favor of you?" He wagged his fingers toward the man in the red-linen turban.

The young, dark-skinned man hurried over.

With a quick bow, he met Ridley's gaze with uncertainty. "How might I serve?"

Inclining his own head in greeting, Ridley glanced down the otherwise empty corridor and dug into his waistcoat pocket, removing a handful of gold *mohurs*. He grabbed the man's heavily calloused hand and set all ten into his palm. "What is your name, *sahib*?"

The young man's lips parted in astonishment at the amount of coins weighing his hands and brightened. "Amit."

"A pleasure, Amit. Do you speak English?" His Hindi wasn't as good as it needed to be.

Amit nodded and quickly offered in a heavy accent, "Yes, sir. I have been with the Government House since I was a child."

"Excellent. It will be less painful for both of us." Ridley leaned in, lowering his voice. "This stays between us. It's incredibly important you tell no one. Can I trust you to protect a fellow Indian? Her name is Miss Kumar. Do you know her?"

Amit's brows rose, flickering. "*Haan*. She tended to my mother several times and gave her medicine when no one else would. She…" Amit sheepishly hesitated. "Does she need me?"

His woman was stealing too many hearts.

Ridley thudded that lanky shoulder. "Yes, she does, but not in that way, my boy, I do that," he chided. "Do you like her?"

Amit beamed and offered from behind a calloused hand, "My mother insists I offer on her, but there is a man by the name of *Sahib* Ridley and she does not entertain anyone but him."

Well, well. Ridley almost did something he never did: smile. "It's a pleasure to meet you, Amit. I needed to hear that."

Stepping back, Ridley gestured toward the lone trunk in the room. "I'll give you double what you have in your hand if you take this trunk and have it delivered to Spence's Hotel to the valet under the name of Mr. Ridley." He tapped at his chest. "That would be me. *Sahib* Ridley."

Amit blanched. "*You are…*?"

"*Haan*." He held the young man's gaze, needing to lay out the importance of what he was asking. "Given what Miss Kumar has done for your mother, keep her in mind and do this without delay. Take that trunk and deliver it to Spence's Hotel to the valet under my name. It's important and has to be done now. I need it out of this house lest it disappear and I can't have anyone seeing you do it. Can I trust you to this?"

Amit nodded, shoving the coins into the pocket of his stitched kurta. "I have time to do it."

"Good. The hotel is just across the street. I'll ensure you get additional compensation by tonight." Ridley hesitated. "Where is the Lieutenant Bradley at this hour?"

Amit extended a hand beyond the corridor. "He just returned from the barracks and is in the Council Room in the east wing."

"Thank you." Ridley gestured toward the trunk.

"It will be delivered at once, *sahib*." Amit hurried toward the trunk.

Once Amit was well down the length of the corridor with the trunk and out of sight, Ridley was about to walk out to the corridor door that lead into Jemdanee's room, when he realized… he had locked the door. "Fuck."

Ridley quickly stepped back into the empty servant's room and latched the door to ensure he left everything else like it was. He grudgingly headed back to the hidden door in the wall and wedged his way back through, shutting the paneling behind himself.

Pressing himself through the uneven mud walls studded with nails, he guided himself back down the darkness toward the light and back into Jemdanee's room, thudding the door closed and smoothing the seam.

Who else would know about the secrets of the Government House but the appointed right hand to the Governor General? This Lieutenant Bradley was going to get a visit and it sure as fuck wasn't going to be friendly.

With the grit of teeth, Ridley set both hands against the now hidden door, easing out breaths that were permeated by Jemdanee's *ittar*. Who knows how many times or how many nights her peace had been violated without her knowing it?

Ridley's eyes burned as he dragged his hands down the paneled wood.

This was his fault.

She would have *never* came here if not for him.

She would have *never* been forcibly touched by another if not for him.

She would have *never* spent three years outside of his embrace if not for that fucking laudanum.

He slammed his head into the door, jarring his skull.

He needed tobacco.

Or he'd keep hitting his skull and that… wasn't helpful.

Grudgingly setting his shoulder against the wall, he flipped open the leather casing of his own stash from within his slung satchel slung around him and stuck a cheroot into his mouth. Striking the flint of the match, he lit the end of the cheroot and dragging in several breaths, ignited the hissing tobacco. He eased out smoke between teeth, tossing the flint and matches back into his satchel.

A knock on the main door made him pause.

He checked his watch, flicking open the casing. It wasn't even noon. Who…?

He left his cane outside the door, signaling he was in her room. Damn it.

Ridley tucked away the fob back into his waistcoat and stiffly walked over to the main door leading into the room. Hitting the bolt, he unlatched it and pulled the banyan paneling open, sticking his cheroot back into his mouth.

White magnolias momentarily blocked his view before they were playfully lowered.

Jemdanee peered over them, her pale blue eyes meeting his. Her oval bronzed face brightened. She no longer looked like the European doll she had attempted to be days earlier, but had transformed into what he wanted: her.

He almost staggered.

The straight severity of the center part of her black hair had been perfectly smoothed with peach oil that drifted from her braids. A frayed burgundy linen sari had been sensually wrapped and pleated around her curves, making her doubly alluring.

"You were missed," she offered softly, that regal Indian accent humming into his veins. "Welcome back." Her full lips curved into a smile. "I was hoping you would be here packing my effects like you had promised and I wanted to thank you for that."

It was as if his heart and his soul had summoned her.

Dragging in a mouthful of smoke he needed to remain calm, he draped the doorway, the heaviness of his body overtaking each breath. He'd been up since three this morning, stressed, but finally being in her presence… relaxed him.

He blew out smoke toward his shoulder, chanting to himself not to grab for her and bring an end to the raging need sitting in a very tight, heavy sac. A need his deprived body had harbored well before she choked out, 'Pleasure me'.

His shoulder dug into the wood of the frame. He flicked fingers against one of the orchids with the hand that held his cheroot, ensuring he didn't singe any of the petals. "An ostentatious bow to what few men get: equality. You would be the first woman to deliver me flowers."

She tucked them into his arm. "May I be the last."

Holding her gaze, he edged back into the room and set the flowers onto the side table beside the door. "I'm sorry I had to leave after what our mouths did to each other."

She bit her lip as if reliving it.

He shifted his jaw knowing full well where this was going.

She, who panted and lost control, merely by him introducing a tongue to her mouth.

It was inevitable that he'd have to dilute the ink that made him who he was. For despite her blazing ways, she was still as conventional as a cup of tea with no sugar steeped only in overly bright smiles. "It's your last day on the compound. How are prescriptions progressing? Are you almost done? How long do you think you'll be?"

She eyed him. "It may take as long as eight this evening."

He shrugged. "I expected as much. I know the hotel is across the street, but I'll send a rickshaw to fetch you. Give the valet your name when you arrive at Spence's. He'll be waiting. In the meantime…" He gestured toward her room. "I have to assemble."

She edged in closer, lingering. "Ridley?"

He lowered his chin, the heat of her body taunting him. "Yes?"

Those overly large blue eyes peered up at him. She reached up and dragged her hand up to his bicep, gripping the bound rope beneath his linen shirt. Holding his gaze, her slim fingers curved around it.

His pulse roared.

She fingered the rope. "Why did you bind it to your arm? What is its meaning?"

His throat tightened in angst.

Life without the rope or any sex had done *insufferable* things.

To compensate for what his anatomy wasn't procuring, his mind ceaselessly frigged the obscene by ticking through unnerving possibilities of where his veined, swollen prick could onanistically pump out a full sac of semen without hurting her.

Many claimed that through abstinence it got easier over time.

That wasn't fucking true.

What used to be a soft breast he once sought to suckle turned into a knocker he wanted to bite off. What used to be a velvet opening to the womb turned into a cunt and a slit to *bang, bang, bang*. The overlord in him born of France was *disgusted* by the lack of refinement. His British counterpart, however, who had been raised in England and known for kicking the devil, demanded her cunt lips drip with semen.

He was losing the last of his well-cultivated mind.

It was exactly why he needed to ease into this or more than

her hymen was going to rip.

Ridley removed her hand rigidly from his rope-strapped bicep, informing the rational side of his brain that his prick needed to stay out of the conversation. "Whilst I'm honored by your sense of adventure, its meaning is involved."

He kept smoking, taking longer drags in a restrained attempt to ease the tension coiling within too many needful muscles. "I leased the entire first floor over at Spence's. It will allow you to have separate living quarters until we settle in with each other."

Her eyes grew playful. "Not that I am by any means a complete whore, but why are you insisting on separate living quarters?"

It was like being back in London and having to manually remove her hands from the belt of his robe. He thudded the frame of the door. "Jemdanee," he warned in a low tone. "This is me giving us time to adjust to each other. Do you understand?"

He stared her down to ensure she did understand. "The moment you permit me to penetrate more than your mind, your body becomes a door I will be walking through on the hour and it won't be confined to a bed. Are you saying you're ready for that?"

She lowered her chin. "I did not realize I was about to become a piece of furniture."

He held her gaze for a lingering moment, memorizing far more than her eyes as he dug his fingers into the wood harder. The future he had seen for them back in London was at hand. She wasn't a child anymore. Even the way she spoke and carried herself was different.

She and that mind and those hips could whiplash him in the way he needed her to.

His gaze lingered. "Given you are notably more conventional than I ever will be, let me lead in this. Your first few times should be in a bed and we wait."

She set herself against the doorframe opposite him. "I may have never lain with a man, but who says my taste in lovemaking is conventional?"

"I do." He dashed some of the ash from his cheroot and gestured toward her sari with it, flicking his gaze to the outlines of her curvaceous body. "When it comes to my tastes, me inside of you is the easy part."

She lifted a dark brow.

Taking in a long drag of his cheroot, he turned his head and breathed it out between teeth. Leaning in close, he offered in a husky tone, "Try not to start anything because I don't have three hours to give you right now." He flicked her cheek. "Maybe this is where you crawl."

"If I arrive naked, I will not be the one crawling."

"You seem to forget who you're talking to." He dashed out his cheroot against the frame behind himself and tossed it out in the corridor.

Let the government deal with it.

He raked back his hair from his eyes. "You embezzled my rope. Was there a reason?"

She hesitated. "I meant to tell you."

"Is that so?" Tilting his head, he offered, "After my divorce, it was buried beneath a set of books inside a trunk I wedged up against the attic. It took *a lot* of effort to find. Why were you in the attic?"

Lowering her somber gaze to her fingers, she picked at her nails and shook her braided head.

He propped himself against the doorframe, intrigued. "Why are you so quiet?"

Her gaze remained fixed on her fingers. "Mr. Fulton and I scoured your entire house after your attempted suicide. We... discarded everything that could have been used to hurt yourself. There was not a trunk or a drawer that we did not overturn in honor of your safety. Razors, rat poison, we discarded everything. When I found your rope, I was going to discard it, as well, given you could easily hanged yourself with it, only I remembered the woman you pointed to beneath the glass of the table. So instead of discarding it, I... kept it. I brought you with me."

His throat ached knowing it.

It made him realize all of his letters and breaths had amounted to what he already knew: she was his. For that rope, which he had commissioned when he was in Paris, had seen him through his own understanding of not only himself but women.

It was a way to control and sexually explore without limits while eliminating the inward panic he had first known when stripping to his most vulnerable state.

It turned into an art form he sought to perfect.

96

It had taken him years to overcome the image of a faceless, nude woman creeping into his sphere at night. One of a breeze rustling bed curtains around his mattress that displayed overly pale skin moving through the shadows with an ax.

It hadn't exactly inspired him to think gloriously of women.

Ridley half-nodded, sensing this conversation of his attempted suicide would never go away. Jemdanee would look at an object, then at him and think the worst. "I buried that part of me when I divorced. That rope holds great meaning. It was commissioned by Jean Maximilien Lacour and enabled me to embrace a level of comfort with women I didn't feel for years."

She eyed him. "I respected your rope," she quickly offered. "The plants were simply easier to tend to whilst hanging. It gave them more light."

The overlord in him was amused. "I'm pleased you enjoyed exploring its array of possibilities. Maybe one day…" He lifted a brow.

She lingered then pushed away from the doorway and walked back out into the arched corridor. "I have a long list of herbs I have to mortar and pestle. I am attempting to finish as early as possible."

His rope had been slapped. He leaned out against the frame of the door and watched those curvy hips sway as her rear shifted against the silk. He *knew* she was putting extra sway into those hips due to him watching.

Damn flirt. "Jemdanee."

With bare feet that peered out from beneath her flowing sari, she sashayed to a pause and glanced back at him, her blue eyes appearing over her propped shoulder. "*Haan*?"

He held her gaze. "I'm going to talk to Lieutenant Bradley about something I found in your room. Are you at ease with that?"

She squinted. "What did you find?"

"A hidden door."

Startled, she swung toward him. "Are you saying he was coming into my room?"

He shrugged. "I'm not certain, but as the right hand to the Governor General he would know of such passageways. Did you want to see it?"

She set a hand to her throat. "No. My life here is done." She hesitated. "What do you intend to do?"

"I'll dig out whatever son of a bitch was making use of it and have the Field Marshal deal with it."

Her eyes widened. "Be careful, Ridley. I cannot have you—"

"You needn't worry. Go. I'll see you later tonight."

She hurried back toward him, reached up and grabbed his face hard. "Promise me you will not get hurt or arrested." She kissed his lips and teased, "We have yet to make love."

Tightening his jaw, he permitted her touch and her words with agonizing revere, but refused to engage it out of respect for how quickly he had unraveled when he had osculated her on Monday. "No distractions," he said down at her. "I need to focus on whatever the hell this is."

His mind had already seen more than enough disorder these past three years because of her.

She hesitated, sensing his reserve and half-nodded. Smoothing his hair away from his forehead, she smiled, despite her eyes being troubled. "Be careful."

"Always." He thudded his chest and pretended to toss his heart at her. "Go finish those orders."

She swatted at the air, catching the heart he'd thrown and popped it against her mouth, chewing. "In answer to question, it tastes sweet."

Har.

She nodded and bustled down the corridor, disappearing.

Dragging his tongue across the lips she had grazed with her own, he eased out a breath. *Knuckle down.* Shoving past the door and into her room, he winced against the muscle strain in his always aching leg. "Christ. You had to go for a younger woman."

Setting his shoulders before the mirror in her room, he repositioned his waistcoat and ticked through his appearance. The government expected him to be in a cravat at all times.

Not today.

"Hail the Queen." He unbuttoned another button on his linen shirt beneath his waistcoat and set his shoulders again. Much better.

He billowed his linen shirt against his waistcoat, trying to bring his mind to a calm.

Don't get arrested.

CHAPTER SIX

Once everything had been packed, fastened, stacked and delivered to the hotel, Ridley made his way back toward the domed east wing of the Government House. The Council Room was less than twenty feet from Dr. Harper's office where, according to the Field Marshal, Jemdanee had spent most of her time.

Three years of this.

Three. Years.

Few blessings ever touched his life but knowing she hadn't seen any harm was one of them.

Cracking his neck and his knuckles, he set his shoulders to relieve a sliver of the tension coiling in his muscles. Observe. Assess. Decide.

He softened and eased his limping step.

Ridley paused outside the Council Room whose banyan door was slightly open, showing a brightly lit room. Quietly setting the cane against the wall in the corridor, Ridley slowly fisted the end of the heavily faded leather on his belt and eased the holster loose from his trousers and set it as gently as he could onto the marble floor with a soft *clack*.

The last thing he wanted was to let emotion curve around the trigger of a pistol. He wasn't in London and Finkle wouldn't be able to get him out of prison if he overstepped his bounds.

Ridley edged past the open door.

An oak-leaf embroidered military coat had been slung over the side of a teak chaise.

The lingering scent of oak moss cologne tinged the muggy air.

Across from the open plantation shutters of a massive window, in a cane chair, sat a well-muscled man of about thirty, his pensive gaze lowered to a bible he held.

A bible? Those sins apparently were great.

Linen trousers were rolled crookedly to the knee as extended bare feet soaked in a porcelain basin full of water. Blond hair brushed back with tonic showed the lines of a comb. His features were good-looking, disrupted only by a crooked nose and a fresh, sizable gash that streaked his forehead.

This one defined what every female would want laying in their bed.

Younger. Fitter. Highly placed.

It made him, Evan Oswald Ridley, feel like a mangy mutt rolling in mud.

With a limp.

The unexpected swell of jealousy suffocated Ridley with an inner torment he hadn't been prepared for. An image of Jemdanee struggling as she attempted to thud away the broad, muscled shoulders of Lieutenant Bradley who smeared his mouth on her throat made Ridley's mind *snap*.

His chest burned to the sternum with a need to *rip* flesh, but thoughts of Jemdanee holding *him*, accepting *him*, loving *him*, kept *him* human.

To release the explosive coil of energy roiling through tensing muscles, Ridley whammed open the door, slamming it against the wall with an earsplitting *bang* that reverberated beneath his own booted feet to announce his presence.

Lieutenant Bradley startled, sending the porcelain bowl clattering across the tile floor as water sprayed. Snapping his gaze to Ridley, his hand jumped for the sword set against the chair, seizing the handle and slowly rose to his sizable six feet.

Startled green eyes held his moment.

Feeling more in control given he had set the stage of unease, Ridley inclined his head in gentlemanly greeting and scanned the expanse of the room, looking for anything that might have been physically jarred, altered or out of place. Ticking through the obvious furnishings, including side tables, he paused, noting that the campaign desk against the wall had one end tilted forward.

It had never been adjusted.

He casually limp-strode over to that campaign desk where… no surprise… a decanter of apple brandy sat atop a ledger. He held up the crystal decanter and swirled the amber liquid, squaring himself against the desk.

Lifting a conversational brow, Ridley offered, "I hear you forcibly osculated the vitality of my existence."

Lieutenant Bradley squinted. "Pardon?"

Ridley spaced out his words through teeth. "You kissed my woman without her permission well before I had a chance to kiss her myself. I take offense to that."

Lieutenant Bradley set aside the sword against the cane chair, next to his bible. "We finally meet, Mr. Ridley. I would say it was an honor but I'd be lying."

Spreading his arms out wide, with the decanter still in his hand, he offered, "Are you disappointed I survived your *felo-de-se*?"

Bradley's square jaw tightened. "I genuinely regret that."

"Do you?"

"Why do you think I told her?" Bradley hesitated. "I wish we had met under different circumstances but it is what it is. You will not see the best in me and I will not see the best in you. As the closest hand to the viceroy, I will still attempt to be at your disposition. All I ask is that you do right by her given her heart has decided on you. Perhaps it is best we become more acquainted given our mutual interest in the same woman." He gestured toward a sideboard. "Would you like a glass for the brandy?"

This was all a bit too artful for his liking. "No. I didn't come to drink."

Bradley lowered his hand. "I understand your reservation." Emotion overtook his face. "I never meant her any harm. I swear it."

To hell with your lies. "I didn't come here to treat her like property. This is about ensuring you don't continue down whatever dark path you've chosen. So let us be gentlemen about your inability to be one and answer me this. Regardless of whether she was spoken for or not, why did you forcibly kiss her?"

Bradley stared off at nothing at particular. "Maybe I was hoping she would see past your antics and give me a chance. For three years, I have only ever sought to protect her. For three years, I have touched whatever wall she touched and prayed she would notice. Yet she never did." Bradley stared him down. "I will not deny it. I want what you want. I still want what you want. She is an amazing woman. But do you know what I want most for her? A life outside of the one you lead. She deserves more. She is more. Let her go."

This one wasn't in lust.

This one was in love with his Jemdanee.

He could see it. He could hear it. He could feel it. He could smell it.

It burned his chest knowing this man had spent more time with Jemdanee than he had.

It hurt. It dug. It stung.

Ridley half-nodded, swirling the brandy. "Who wouldn't love her? Jemdanee Kumar, who was first appeared to me as Jemdanee Lillian Watkins draped in too many shackles and a turned-in bolt, defies logic. She and her eyes of blue and her gorgeous skin of brown laughs when the world spits. She sees light in every darkness and makes a cheerless man like me, who has sinned well beyond what your bible could hold, feel worthy. *Unfortunately*, my barefooted friend, loving someone doesn't constitute the right to physically violate them against their will. If it did… *I'm about to love you to the marrow of your bones*. And I'm not even that sort of man."

Bradley said nothing.

Still swirling the brandy, Ridley gestured toward the expanse of the brightly lit room around them. "Show me where you kissed her. I want the exact location." He already knew but he was going for effect.

Bradley said nothing.

Waiting.

Waiting.

Ten seconds.

Waiting.

Waiting.

Twenty seconds.

Not a very intelligent soul.

Squinting, Ridley offered, "You aren't in any position to be acting like a thimble-wit. The only reason your auriferous head hasn't already smashed through all eight windows gracing this room is because I'm not looking to get arrested. That is why I'm attempting to reach into the darkest part of my soul and find something called: *don't kill him*. Show yourself mercy, my boy, because I'm usually far less tolerant toward those who engage in criminal praxis and none of those pricks had ever even touched my woman. Do I need to say more?"

Bradley held his gaze, then crossed the space between them and pausing beside him, tapped on the desk. "Here."

Jemdanee had scrambled and pushed here.

Don't backhand him. Don't touch him.

Or you'll be in prison and won't be able to protect her.

Breathe.

The swaying of a key on a silver necklace around Bradley's throat made Ridley pause.

It was... similar in size to the opening of the lock on the trunk Amit had taken.

The. Same. Size.

This one *had* been going into her room. He'd been—

Don't fucking kill him! Don't—

Ridley cracked his neck. "Did you enjoy taking her against her will?" he asked in a low, low tone, chanting to himself not to smash the decanter into those teeth. He set aside the decanter lest he get any ideas. "Did you enjoy taking her against *this* desk?" He tapped it. "Did you?"

The man no longer met his gaze.

"I should hope not." Ridley rolled his wrists and gestured toward those bare feet. "Soaking after a long day? How nice. Do tell me. How devoted are you to the bible, Lieutenant?"

Bradley said nothing.

"This is where you and I trade places. *Usually*, I'm the one to play the devil, but in this case... I think you beat me to it." Ridley wagged his fingers toward that throat. "I want the key."

Bradley's gaze snapped to his. "I suggest you leave. You already have what you want: her." He buried the key beneath his billowing linen shirt. "This belongs to me. It's all I will ever have of her given she decided. Let me keep it."

It had depravity slathered all over it.

Ridley jumped and grabbed that throat hard, gritting his teeth as all five of his fingers dug into the esophagus which he chanted to himself he wouldn't break. "Bradley, I need you to listen to me. I already have the trunk. The question is… what were you doing with it and why *the fuck* were you using that passageway to get into her room? Were you observing her in the nude? Or were you squirting all over her linen?"

"*No*. What are you—" Bradley shoved him with the grit of teeth. "I've done nothing but look after her. I never once—"

"Never once?" Ridley tightened his hold. "*Lex talionis.* Have you heard of it?"

Bradley shoved. "The law of… retribution."

"*Exactly.*" Leaning in to that perfect face, Ridley breathed out, "If I find anything in that trunk that displeases me, all of India will hear your screams for seven minutes before it goes silent." Ridley violently shoved him away with the full force of his meaning, sending Bradley crashing into a side table that flipped as both crashed to the floor.

Sitting up, Bradley's chest heaved, his green eyes blazing. "I would bury that sense of righteousness if I were you. My intentions were never as base as yours."

Narrowing his gaze, Ridley bit out, "Is that why you osculated her before I did?" Grabbing the decanter of brandy, Ridley jumped toward him and smashed his boot down against that bare foot, purposefully grinding and casually poured the entire contents of amber liquid onto the flap of his trousers. "A bit of holy water to exercise those demons."

Bradley glared, his other foot swinging up and—

With the grit of teeth, Ridley blocked it with his arm, but it still connected to his injured leg, sweeping into the scarred muscle and bone. Searing pain blinded him into staggering back and off to the side. He seethed past breaths, hating that he wasn't what he used to be: stronger.

Bradley jumped onto his bare feet and snapped up both fists. "Whoever falls first. *Gauntlet!*"

Gauntlet? Was this prick for real?

Who used that word anymore?

Dragging in calming breaths through nostrils, Ridley widened his stance, mentally adjusting to his own physical pain. "No. You'll have no satisfaction in turning me into a villain." He held up both hands. "These hands and these knuckles walk out of here clean. I'm not going to prison."

Fists still up, Bradley rounded him. "I thought you wanted the key."

Ridley gave him a withering look. "I'll just shoot off the lock." Tossing the empty decanter onto the chaise, Ridley strode past. "Excuse me while I return to a woman who will *never* be yours."

There was a pulsing moment of silence.

Bradley sprinted at him full force from behind.

Abecedarian. Skidding aside, everything slowed barely enough for Ridley to tick through what to grab.

The marble bust on the pedestal. It would kill him. Glorious idea, but…

A sizable ledger on the—Good enough.

Ridley swiped up the ledger and swung it out full force just as Bradley rushed again. The thudding impact against that head with the leather bound ledger snapped Bradley's body sideways. Sweeping out his good leg, Ridley accosted Bradley's stumbling frame to ensure a hard topple and shoved Bradley head first onto the chaise.

Both flipped.

Bradley jarred the chaise out toward Ridley, causing Ridley to stumble back against his limp with a muscle straining hiss that sent him against a sideboard. He winced in disbelief.

Jumping back up, Bradley sprinted and thudded into Ridley full force with a muscled thud.

Everything after that was a bit of a blur.

Furniture was overturned. Vases were shattered. Curtains were ripped from the rods. Shirts were used as choking devices and buttons were being popped off every waistcoat as noses, jaws and heads and fists were thudded to bleeding.

Ridley was morbidly impressed by the challenge.

The son of a bitch could fight.

His mind blanked as he let the devil do the rest.

Knuckles. Head. Jaw. Head. Mouth. Face. Face. Face. Face. Blood.

It spattered their clothing. Some of it was his.

Delivering one last downward solid blow, that sent Bradley to the floor, Ridley whipped off the key from that throat, snapping the silver chain that left a blood mark.

Ridley shoved the chaise between them. Between evening ragged breaths, Ridley stepped back, folding himself back into his mind.

A warm liquid line traced its way from his own nostril toward his lip. Ridley staggered against his aching leg that felt as if he'd ripped a muscle. Fuck. He was getting too old for this. "You ran at me," he growled, pointing rigidly down at Bradley who was wheezing. "Remember that when the Field Marshal asks. Remember that *or you're fucking dead*."

Bradley glanced up from the floor he was now on, his hair hanging in his eyes and blood smearing his entire face, mouth and nose. "You'll be the one dead if you don't look after her," he bit out.

Ridley refrained from delivering another blow to that golden head. "I would lock yourself in a prison cell right now to ensure I don't get to you after I open that fucking trunk." Still pointing, Ridley stalked out before he backhanded the son of a bitch with the decanter that was still on the chaise.

Spence's Hotel—an hour later in that afternoon

It annoyed him that he had to now call on the Field Marshal and explain why he had roughed up the viceroy's favorite Lieutenant. News of it was going to be all over the compound and Jemdanee didn't deserve to have her name dragged into any more than it had been.

With a blood-stained towel on his shoulder, Ridley grudgingly squatted before the trunk and seated himself on the marble floor, wincing against the stab of pain from the blow Bradley had delivered to his injured leg. "Prick."

Dragging in a mind-steadying breath, he gritted his teeth and quickly pushed in the key to the lock, turning it. The bolt unhinged and he removed the lock, setting it aside with a clatter.

Unstrapping the lid, he pushed it open, letting the lid thud against the wall behind it.

His brows flickered.

Gathering a handful of parchment, his gaze settled on *hundreds* of...

Charcoal sketchings. One of Jemdanee sleeping, with her hands curled peacefully beneath her cheek and the linen spilling over her chemise clad shoulder. Another of her ink stained hand unfurled against a prescription ledger, where she dozed at a paper strewn pedestal desk. Another of the ropes and plants hanging in her room. Chunmun digging into a bowl of papaya. Slippers overturned and kicked beneath the bed.

Swallowing against the tightness of his throat, Ridley slowly gathered more and more and more and more, angling his head to see each and every one. He sifted through countless images, glimpsing stolen moments he himself had lost and had been unable to witness, yet ones that had been captured for him to see.

His eyes burned as he frantically gathered more and spread them out, breathing past every moment he had missed. Her head buried beneath a pillow with her knees curled, her braid frayed. Another was with her mouth unattractively open as if she were snoring.

None of them were provocative or inappropriate in nature.

It didn't make it any less disturbing.

He hadn't been there to protect her from a man coming into her room.

It could have ended badly.

Ridley eased out a shaky breath. "Fuck."

And that is what I fear most. That you have already crossed over beyond my reach, pursuing a justice you will never reach...

The bloodied towel from his shoulder slipped and rustled to the floor.

Staring at the trunk, he slowly gathered all of the sketches and numbly returned them one by one into the trunk, realizing he had failed her.

He, who always looked for the devil on the head of a pin to be able to nail it, had missed the most important pin.

Why save the world when he couldn't save the one who mattered most to him?

If he was distracted by cases, while bringing more and more loons into their lives, her in peril was only the beginning. He wasn't about to fool himself or the impediment of his limp that he'd be able to protect her when it mattered most.

He couldn't even remember the last time he'd ever been physically bested by another man but it happened. It. Happened.

Gritting his teeth, he latched the trunk and locked it.

He was doing what he should have done when he married Elizabeth.

It might have saved their marriage.

He was retiring. Tonight.

Spence's Hotel—Early evening

The double mahogany doors leading into the massive lavish private quarters were swept open by a dark-skinned Persian dressed in a flowing emerald-green garb bound by a thick, red sash.

With a slight bow, the Persian gestured toward the long marble corridor beyond. "*Sahib* Ridley insists upon your warm welcome. The calling bell in the corridor will bring me to this door."

With Chunmun on her hip, she felt like a zookeeper in need of shelter.

She brightened in disbelief. "I thank you." She slowly entered the mosaic corridor lit by torches and lanterns, the unending gleaming white marble strewn with jasmine and marigold.

The gods were in awe.

As was she.

The banyan doors closed behind her, introducing a silence of grandeur that made her feel like a harem girl arriving to entertain the prince.

Chunmun grunted and tilted over heavily against her arms, signaling he was done being held.

She quickly set him onto the floor.

He glanced up at her, confused.

"I am as overwhelmed as you are," she breathed out. "Whoever thought he was this posh."

Chunmun turned and picked at the marigold on the floor and tossed it.

She smirked and seated herself beside him, gathering the flowers into a pile.

He eyed her and shoved the pile.

She grinned and gathered the pile again.

He darted down the corridor, tail up.

Thrilled by the entrance to her own private floor, Jemdanee scrambled up onto her feet, whirled twice, and then sprinted down the gleaming white marble in bare feet after Chunmun, past countless rooms and doors, throwing open door after door to reveal massive receiving rooms and bedchambers with domed ceilings. "Choose a room!" she called to Chunmun. "Any room! Which one? *Seize it before I do!*"

He disappeared into one and moments later, emerged, dragging linen.

She laughed. "Well chosen."

Quickly veering toward a banyan door that had been marked with chalk patterns, she peered in, noting all of her trunks were stacked within the room.

She wandered in, grinning and trailed a hand across the mosaic walls leading her into the room before a four poster bed covered in netting.

She paused, seeing another adjusting door to another bedchamber.

It was closed.

Something whispered to her that it was *his* room.

She bit her lip.

Pausing before that door, Jemdanee quickly glanced at the clock on the mantel, noting it was almost eight o'clock at night. "Ridley?"

She tapped at the handle of the door and pushed down. It opened.

Pushing open the door, she edged in. "*Ridley?*"

There was no answer, but a lone lantern had been lit.

Her skin prickled in awareness as the scent of his cologne lingered in the massive bedchamber.

She could *feel* his karma in the room as if he were still in it.

It whispered of the sophisticated man who spent too many

hours in his own head.

Slowly, she circled the massive mosaic bedchamber, realizing the room had already long been settled into with personal effects. He was far more organized than she remembered him to be.

From the keen, alphabetized organization of scientific books to perfectly folded Parisian clothing in his wardrobe to his desk where even the parchment was aligned by a ruler and the quills set equally straight, it was obvious every detail mattered to him. Even all three inkwells had been filled at the same level in each crystal, whispering that he had carefully measured and controlled the amount of ink he poured in.

It bespoke of a man who had been touched by a need to showcase every detail.

It was who she used to be prior to the Government House.

She went over to the books he was reading.

Careful not to disrupt the entire row of spine-aligned books, she gently nudged out one and started paging through it. Letting it fall open to one page, she read:

These properties therefore (always the concomitants of fluid bodies) produce these following visible effects: First, they unite the part of a fluid to its familiar solid, or keep them separate from its dissimilar state. Hence quick-silver will stick to gold, silver, tin, lead—

She pulled in her chin and slapped it shut, examining its worn leather binding.

Seeing there was no title on the leather binding, she quickly paged it back open to its front. Her brows shot up as she read aloud, "*Micrographia: or some physiological descriptions of minute bodies made by magnifying glasses with observations and inquiries thereupon.*"

Mmm*huh*. "Only I would love you."

Awkwardly closing the book, she tucked it back into the space she'd taken it from. "I am at a loss as to what your mind finds attractive. What does that say about me? Not very much."

On the side board was an expensive looking bottle of French cologne and shaving blade whose ivory handle she breathlessly touched knowing it had scraped the contours of his jaw every day.

She paused, noting a copper bowl.

Angling in close, she peered into it.

A ripped piece of parchment revealed the words…

Lay on the bed and wait for me.

It was as if he knew she would come into his room and read it.

She edged back, unnerved.

How did he know she would peer into the bowl?

The soft rustling and billowing of the net hanging over his bed made her turn and walk up to it. Fascinated by what continued to be the mystery of him, she sat on his bed.

A thud made me smile. "Chunmun?"

With the dragging sound of linen that came in through the open door, Chunmun wobbled and arranged himself on the floor beside her, burying himself.

She grinned down at him over the edge of the bed and patted the mattress. "Come."

He peered up at her through linen and laid his furry head onto the floor, picking at the linen sleepily from where he was.

"Oye, oye, life is exhausting," she teased, watching him. "Imagine if you were human. It becomes very complicated."

He picked at the linen until his lids grew heavy and his overly long fingers stilled, eyes closing.

"Dream of fruit trees and jungles," she whispered. A soft breath escaped her knowing Ridley was right. She couldn't keep him like this.

She stared up at the ceiling.

Bored, she let her bangles jangle against each other.

She decided to stay in Ridley's bed as he had asked.

Maybe he'd get inspired.

She unraveled her emerald green sari to better showcase her midriff and waited.

And waited.

And waited.

And waited.

And waited.

And…

Somehow, she fell asleep, drooling onto the pillow.

It was the *sonti* she'd had at supper with Kalpita celebrating her departure.

Silence. Darkness. Dreams.

Hands curving. Fingers grazing. Warm lips.

Silence.

When Jemdanee startled awake, sunlight poured in through open shutters.

She staggered up in a frizzy curtain of her own hair and wrinkled sari to find she was no longer in Ridley's bed, but… her own.

The man was being too much of a gentleman.

Grudgingly scooting off the bed, she paused.

Her entire room appeared to have had a wand touched to it. All of the trunks had been unpacked.

Her piles and piles of tangling saris which she always kicked off to the side and into corners, had all been methodically folded and placed into the open wardrobe. Her countless slippers, which were always falling out of the wicker basket and missing pairs due to her inability to dig to its bottom, had been removed from the basket and aligned onto a shelf beneath her wardrobe.

Her cosmetics and brushes, which she usually shoved into a drawer, had been all set out onto a dressing table which had undergone its own transformation of aligning all of her hair brushes by size, ribbons by color, and combs by assortment.

It was *magic*.

And on the marble floor—

Marigolds had been arranged beside her bed to spell NAMASTE.

She slowly grinned. "Someone is going to get kissed."

A dreamy breath escaped her as she turned toward the side table where a marigold was laid beside a stack of gold *mohurs* and a missive.

My little raven,

I apologize for abandoning you and not returning on time. Indulge in a meal and enjoy the emporium knowing I am cursed to finish the last of my squadron duty. Not many more days remain until all of my hours are yours. Chunmun is enjoying the company of the valet who will be taking him for the day. Dress for comfort knowing sandals are a necessity and meet me at the Eastern gate outside of the barracks at 4 p.m. I look forward to seeing you.

Ever your servant and overlord,
-R

She kissed the missive twice.

CHAPTER SEVEN

Squinting against the blazing heat beyond the gates of the barracks, Jemdanee lifted her newly purchased veil and tugged its coolness further down over her eyes to keep the sun out.

She paused at seeing Ridley.

He adjusted the straps of the saddle weighted down with weapons and a leather satchel on the lone horse. His cane was already tucked into the belt of that saddle, as well.

She eased the fluttering in her stomach at seeing him.

Her sandaled feet kicked up dust as she made her way over to him. "Only one horse?"

"You are late," he rumbled out, tightening the thick belt with the strain of bulking muscles.

"By a minute."

"By seven." Ridley quickly turned from adjusting the saddle and captured her gaze, the overly concentrated lines of his bruised face softening. "One horse will allow us to better maneuver through the crowds."

Her lips parted into an O. "Whatever happened to your face?"

"Bradley."

She gasped. "He did that to you?!"

Ridley gave her a withered look. "I faired a bit better than he

114

did. I straightened his nose."

Jemdanee glanced toward the barracks, trying not to panic. "The Field Marshal is going to—"

He snapped up a hand. "I already spoke to him." Ridley hesitated, adjusting his leather belt. "I wasn't looking to hurt him. It happened. The Field Marshal assured me Bradley will be transferred in the next seven days to another compound. Unfortunately, that will be the extent of his punishment given there are no laws for being a prick."

He swiped his face and winced against the bruising. "I wish I could have done more. In my opinion, he should have been arrested for violating your rights on every imaginable level."

She eyed him. "Why was he using... the door?"

"He fancied himself an artist. I will leave it at that." Angling toward her, his throat worked. "Yesterday unfolded quite a few things for me." He searched her eyes. "I can't keep you safe if I'm distracted with a career that will only bring you harm. Unlike three years ago, I am physically compromised and I'm not bold enough to say I can guarantee anything anymore." He was quiet for a long moment. "I'm retiring. The moment my contract expires with the government, I'm thinking of becoming a professor of criminology, instead. I could continue to offer my expertise in an educational setting, but without the mess. What do you think?"

May Shiva keep her from kneeling.

Through the roaring din, she breathed out, "I think it brilliant. Your career only ever made me worry about you."

He searched her face but said nothing.

She lifted a brow. "With such news, why do you not smile, *Professor*?"

A congested expression settled on his face. "Smiling has always been on the lowest of my priorities." He pointed to his set mouth. "This has been etched into my nerves to the point of instinct. Changing it requires a lot of effort."

She laughed. "It is not as complicated as you think." Using her fan, she gently tapped at the straight line of his lips. "I promise nothing will rip."

His amber eyes remained hooded like a hawk. "We have places to be, *mon chou*." Grabbing her waist, he spun her around and hoisted her up into the air and sideways onto the saddle of the horse beside them.

Startled, her hands jumped onto his muscled shoulders to keep herself from falling. "Do warn a woman."

"I was hoping you would be wearing lip rouge again," he said in a low tone, positioning her hips and rear on the saddle. "Maybe even some kajal for those eyes."

Tracing smoky black powder around her eyes was indeed something only Ridley would request. He truly was a lover of all dark things. "Lip rouge I will honor, but I would never wear kajal. I consider it overly ostentatious even for me."

He lifted a brow. "Then why do you have it on your dressing table?"

She sighed. "Kalpita gifted it to me."

"She has good taste." Ridley set his foot into the stirrup and attempted to hoist himself up behind her, but was unable to. He winced, adjusting his one leg and tried again.

She held out her hand, her voice softening. "Do you require assistance?"

"Ey." He pointed at her in warning.

She rolled her eyes.

Hoisting his large frame up behind her, he wedged her firmly against himself, his arms coming around her to grab the leather reins and hold her in place.

He leaned in toward her ear, his chin nudging aside her veil. "How is that?"

Too much.

The heated scent of his Parisian cologne overtook her half-breaths as the flexing bulk of his arms tightened around her. "Where are we going?"

He smoothed his hands around her as if mapping her out. "On through town. Dr. Wallich is expecting us."

She paused. "*Professor* Wallich? From the university?"

"Yes. I put in an application for myself this morning given you stubbornly wish to stay in India. Whilst I do that, you'll be going through his entire inventory of flora. He insisted."

Dr. Wallich had been responsible for rejecting her application to the university. All fifteen times. She jerked toward Ridley, trying to look back at his face. "He never invites anyone to look at his private collections. Not even other professors."

"He made an exception for us."

Men like Wallich didn't make exceptions. She squinted. "Did you threaten him?"

Ridley stared. "A little."

She quirked a brow.

He still stared. "A lot."

Jemdanee snorted. "You cannot—Ridley, most people accept that one does not always get what they want."

His eyes and tone grew warmer than molten. "I always get what I want." He nuzzled her cheek with his lips, lingering.

This man—*this man!*—might as well have been a leopard pup with dangling paws and big eyes. Oyo, it was cute now, yes. Until it got older and mauled everyone, leaving blood on the floor.

She leaned back, nestling into him. "Dr. Wallich is as staunch as professors come."

He tightened his hold around her. "He has his moments. Did you know he spent several years in West Hindustan and Burma gathering over three thousand seeds from forests that have long since been devastated? And *you* will get a chance to wade through all of it and keep whatever indigenous seeds you want."

Her eyes widened. "Ridley, that is marvelous!" She craned toward him, half-grazing her lips against his cheek she couldn't reach. "I would turn in this saddle and *osculate* you, but I would probably fall off."

"I'll collect later." He hesitated, leaning into her ear. "The Field Marshal is hosting a garden party tomorrow night. Are you going?"

She paused. "Are you inviting me?"

"Are you accepting the invitation?"

She made it this far without dying. "Maybe."

"That had better be a *haan*."

"Ridley?"

"Yes?"

"How did you know I would go into your room and look into the bowl last night?"

He tightened his hold on her. "I was merely curious to see what your mind gravitated to. I was surprised you paged through one of my favorite books, *Micrographia*. What did you think? Did you read a few pages?"

She made a face. "It was unreadable." She paused. "How did you know I even looked at it? I put it back in the exact location I took it from."

"It was pushed in."

"Oh."

His voice warmed. "Fasten that veil against your braid, *mon chou*. We have a city to get through before three." Pressing his boots into the sides of the horse, they galloped down the nearest dirt pathway through carts and people and horses.

A group of young Hindu women in flowing veils paused with their baskets to stare.

All five stared up at Ridley, turning toward them.

It made Jemdanee pertly set herself against him to ensure they knew their place.

"Jealous, are you?" he rumbled out.

Of course he noticed. "They only stare because I am a Hindu riding with a white man."

"Liar. They never even looked at you."

She snorted as they picked up speed, the hot wind pulsating against her face.

Gripping the reins and his large hands, she breathed in this glorious, glorious moment of something she sorely missed. Adventure. Wind. Heat. Ridley. This.

They angled in through tight spaces at a dirt kicking speed that made her grab his arm in an effort to warn him.

He pressed in his heels into the horse.

She grinned, more than ready for the speed.

He sped them onward faster.

Her flapping veil tugged and whipped off floating somewhere into the hot wind behind them.

She gasped, reaching out behind them.

He dug his chin into her shoulder hard in reprimand. "I told you to hold onto it."

"I just bought it!" She gripped the reins and tried to glance back behind his shoulder that was blocking her ability to see. "We have to go back!"

"Have to? My dear, it is always forward and never back. Let someone else enjoy it." Riding faster, he veered the horse, riding them down a long pathway between stone walls.

The looming walls grew… narrower.

Glancing back toward him, she squeezed in her sandaled feet lest the tips of the embroidered leather scrape the walls. "I *would* like to be able to walk after this."

"No need for insults."

"I was not thinking of you, but myself! Why are we even going this way?" Clinging to the reins, she leaned back against him in dread. "There are other paths!"

"Trust me." He sped the horse faster as the looming walls around them sharply narrowed.

It looked too small for them to fit and they were speeding at it to the point of the hot wind whistling as it further narrowed.

"*Ridley*!" Dearest no and dearest— She slapped one quick hand over her eyes and the used the other to hold on, holding back a scream. "*Ridleyyyyyyyyy*!"

"Oh, come now," he hollered. "Don't tell me you've turned into what other women are: *boring*," he continued to holler over the whipping wind and thundering gallop. "*Feel the heat*! Feel the sting of the wind coming at you!"

"The walls are *narrowing*. Have you no eyes?!"

"Trust me." He sped faster and faster, leaning into her and the saddle.

"Ridley! Slow down! Please!"

He tightened his hold. "Trust me, *mon chou*."

Hearing him use *mon chou* made it worse. "No! No, no, no, no—"

They galloped through, the wall almost scraping their elbows.

He rattled her. "We made it. Elbows, knees and arms."

Her pulse still racing, she elbowed him hard. "There is an elbow for you. We barely made it!"

"Four inches on each side is more than barely. Learn to measure." He slowed their horse and veered them down another dirt street. "Cease thinking the worst of everything I do. I may appear reckless, but I would *never* put you in harm's way. Why do you think I'm retiring?"

She eased out a breath.

He nipped her throat with teeth hard, starling her. "Learn to trust me."

The sting on her throat said otherwise. "That hurt."

"Good," he said into her ear. "Today's lesson was: *trust your overlord*. I have nothing but your wellbeing and safety in mind. Even if you don't think I do."

"Are you saying you did that on purpose?"

"Nothing I ever do is without purpose." He dug his chin into her hair. "You failed me. Lamentably. Grievously. It's obvious you don't trust me."

She cringed. "I did not trust the walls."

"Why not blame the horse next?" He sighed. "I know in the corridors of your mind I'm still a suicidal, despondent addict, but I'm here to prove to you, I'm none of those things. Not anymore. Not ever again. I *can* be trusted." He squeezed her. "Let me live up to that honor. I want to. Can I? Might I?"

Gripping his arms, she melted. "The honor is all yours."

After spending the afternoon and early evening perusing the most extensive collection of flora she had ever seen, Jemdanee felt as if she had finally touched a finger to the future of her career.

She tapped at the glass casings of the observatory they were in, wishing she could travel into Nepal and document plants that were fading into extinction.

One day.

"'Tis my unending hope you will visit again," Dr. Wallich insisted. "I found myself endlessly and pleasantly surprised you know anything about phytology at all."

She tried not to be offended. He'd been saying it all day.

Turning, she extended her hand to him and shook his hand, attempting not to break it off. "I thank you for being so generous with your time. It was inspiring to meet someone as devoted to phytology as I."

"Of course. Was there any particular breed you were interested in seeding?"

She perked at the offer, gesturing toward a potted plant nearest them. "Yes. What is this one here? I find it to be so incredibly unusual, like a creature with five fingers. Is it an orchid?"

He nodded, reaching out and grazing the palm with protruding tubers. "Yes. It isn't in bloom quite yet. It's known as the *dactylorhiza hatagirea*. The tribes in the Himalayas extract juice from these tubers for the treatment of pyorrhea. Its roots are also externally applied as a poultice on wounds and the treating of bone fractures."

Oyo. She excitedly waggled fingers at it. "If you would be so kind, I most certainly would be interested. I specialize in medicinal plants."

"Of course." He patted her cheek. "I will have it potted and delivered to you at the hotel."

"I thank you," she gushed. "This has been an incredible day. Truly."

"I was happy to oblige." The older gentleman's brown eyes glanced warily down the corridor leading into the rest of his house. He cleared his throat. "The university, as you well know, has a strict policy on keeping its classes dedicated to developing male minds, *however*... I would consider hosting you in a classroom on occasion. I sent a syllabus over to Mr. Ridley earlier in the day and hope it meets your satisfaction."

Jemdanee blinked. What did Ridley do?

"I insist," he added.

This had Ridley all over it. "Are you insinuating the university has miraculously changed all of its policies in the name of admitting its first Hindu woman into an all-male school?"

He eyed her. "No. You would be placed in a one-chair setting."

A one-chair setting.

Which meant... not really a classroom, but a dark corner in a backroom.

The glory of knowing she could step into an actual university like she'd always wanted to *should* have been glorious, but seeing Professor Wallich clutch his coat with white knuckles as if he expected to die for not allowing it had *never* been her dream.

It wasn't real.

A soft breath escaped her knowing Ridley had arranged it.

She wanted to adore him for it, but she also wanted to smack him for making the entire university now think she had enlisted the military to get what she wanted. "You will be pleased to know I will not be taking up the invitation, but I do appreciate the offer."

The man flushed. "I think it wise. There might have been riots."

She refrained from rolling her eyes and gestured toward the adjoining rooms. "Have you seen Mr. Ridley at all?"

He cleared his throat. "I believe he is still in the library."

Of course he was. Where else would Ridley be?

"Assure him I have done my part."

Pathetic. "You need not worry in that, I will."

The man inclined his grey head. "Feel free to leave the entrance doors agape as my servants always permit the night breeze to flow past a certain hour. I bid you both a good night." He edged back. "Do inform Mr. Ridley that I—"

"Yes, yes. I will. Thank you."

He stuck his pipe between his lips, turned and hurried down the arched corridor, glancing back.

Ridley, Ridley, Ridley.

He seemed to think he could open doors with the bang of his leather boot a bit too wide.

Jemdanee heaved out a breath and marched her way through the corridors and toward the library where he was. She quickly veered into the room and dashed right into the wall known as Ridley, knocking over a pile of books from his hands.

She cringed as pages and bindings rustled and cracked.

He steadied her. "Ey. Weren't you accusing me of rounding corners with the horse a bit fast? *Slow down*." He gave her a pointed look and lowered himself to the floor, adjusting his stance to fold his leg enough to permit himself to kneel. He winced, hissing out a breath and gathered the scattered books.

She quickly knelt beside him. "You should not be straining your leg like that."

"There are plenty of things I should not be straining." He methodically gathered the books, stacking them. "Did you finish with Dr. Wallich?"

"*Haan*. Oh, yes. He was most gracious and will be delivering a list of indigenous plants I have requested from his collection."

"You see? People like you."

The cad. "He invited me to be part of the university for a one-chair setting," she continued trying not to let on that she was on to him. "This from the same man who denied my application fifteen times."

He shrugged. "Policies change."

The jaguar. "Do they? Is that why he kept glancing toward the door as if someone was going to stab him with his own pipe?"

He eyed her. "I never threatened him with a pipe."

She tsked. "This reminds me all too much of when you decided to remove me from Millbank without the permission of the British government."

He pointed. "Sometimes a man has to go above the law to deliver it."

She leaned in close, lowering her voice to sultry. "Why am I cursed to adore you?"

He dabbed her nose. "The curse is mutual and digs deep."

She bit back a smile, feeling as if they had been married for too many years. Pertly gathering the books with him while still on her knees, she adjusted the fabric of her sari to give herself better movement and helped him stack the sizable pile.

Ridley paused, his eyes falling to her exposed leg.

Her pulse beat erratically realizing she had… unknowingly invited him to play.

Lowering his head, he dragged his lips across her knee and trailed his hot mouth upward toward her thighs.

She fumbled against him, grabbing his shoulders. Her tongue grew too heavy to speak.

Ridley leaned past her and swiped up the remaining books. "Admittance into a university should be based off merit, not right. You're brilliant and in my humble opinion, they're fortunate I didn't stab them all with pencils and bury them beneath their desks." He rose.

Her heart flopped to the floor and back up again realizing he had no intention on pursuing what his lips had earlier initiated. Her face burned knowing it.

Why was it *she* was the one crawling?

I'm going to make you wait for the fuck we both want.

Exasperated, she rose with wobbly knees, balancing the stack of books and held them out.

He took the stack from her arms, then turned and finished going around the room without a cane, returning books to where they had originally been taken from on the shelves.

She trailed toward him and angled in before him near the

shelf. "You can," she offered.

He propped his shoulder against the shelf to better look at her. He shifted his jaw. "I appreciate the level of trust, but you aren't ready."

Her pride concealed her inner turmoil. "When is a virgin ever ready?"

"You screamed the moment I brought that horse to a trot."

She snorted and teasingly shoved him. "Only you would think high speeds were a mere trot. I *screamed* because you were being irresponsible."

He rattled her cheek. "As I said... you aren't ready. It's important we establish a measure of trust between us. I hardly want you screaming through our first time together."

She laughed. "Is it going to be *that* involved?"

He lifted a brow.

She eyed him. "What do you usually do with these women? Beat them with your cock?"

There was a smoldering invitation in the depth of his eyes. "If we are to be honest, I had one woman lose consciousness."

Her grin faded as her fingers nervously tried to straighten his stack of books, but tipped them instead. They thudded back to the floor. She cringed, the sound almost amplifying their situation.

He searched her face. "We're not even doing anything and you're jittering."

"Perhaps it is because you are tapping fear into my head, you grave-digging rake." She gestured in exasperation toward the corridor. "I will go crawl away and wait by the horse." She hurried past him.

Ridley jumped toward her, knocking over his cane to the floor, and bumped her into stopping with his chest, looming close. He held her gaze from above. "I don't want you standing alone in the darkness. Wait until I'm finished putting away these books. I'll let you watch."

She gave him a withering look. "You, Ridley, are an onion in need of chopping. Only I refuse to be the one to do it. For my eyes have no need for the burn and there are plenty of other vegetables in the garden."

Silence pulse between them.

He edged his chin down against his cravat. "Are you saying you want other vegetables?" he asked in a low, low tone. "As in celery? You haven't seen the width of this onion to judge."

Her mouth throbbed.

He leaned in. "You seem to think you can rattle this cage without letting anything out." There was a lethal calmness in his eyes. "The trouble with what we share is that we are uniquely passionate people unable to relinquish the control we have over each other. That alone is going to complicate our sexual relationship and I haven't even introduced you to this." He thudded at his bicep.

She lingered, his cologne and his words making her hazy. "What is your fascination with rope?"

Ridley guided her hand to the bundled rope around his bicep. "Are you curious, *mon dévot*?"

She jerked her hand back. "Keep *mon dévot* out of it. There is nothing romantic about choking a woman with hemp."

"You are villainizing what you do not understand."

She glanced around, gesturing toward the library. "I cannot believe we are discussing this in Dr. Wallich's library."

"You brought it up, not I." He turned away, putting away the remaining books.

She squinted, a part of her needing to know if… "Are you even capable of engaging a woman without the rope?"

He heaved out a breath. "Yes, Kumar. I am a perfectly capable functioning male and most certainly can and do enjoy sexual congress *without* rope. The rope, however, enables me to do more, be more, see more, feel more. I enjoy it more. Without the rope, it isn't really me."

This didn't sound very promising. "Maybe your need for the rope will fade over time once we… become more involved." She shrugged. "Maybe you will be cured of it."

Silence stretched between them.

He swung back to her, a riled warning settling into his chiseled features. "I was not aware that I suffered from a mental illness."

She cringed. "What I meant—"

"I know what you meant." His tone darkened. "I would never attempt to change you, Jemdanee. I respect who you are and yet it is fairly obvious you do not respect who I am. Unfortunately, the rope *is* who I am. It's who I have always been. And whilst I would never force you to embrace it, I will *not* have you speak to me as if I were mentally unsound. The rest of the world already thinks that and I hardly need it from you."

He stared her down. "I'm making drastic changes that include giving up my career and settling into another country whose cultural logistics will take me years to master. How are you making changes? Or am I too worthless in your eyes for you to consider making any?"

She lingered, her heart squeezing. "No. I…"

It was awful.

In that moment she realized, he was right. He was kneeling to change in her name, whilst she? She was not even offering to understand his need for the rope.

He searched her face. "What is your real opinion of me?"

Her mouth throbbed. "I adore you."

His jaw worked. "I don't think you do. I think you still see what everyone else does: a cacodemon."

She eyed him. "I do not even know what that word means."

"A malevolent man."

Oh. She cringed. "You most certainly can be intimidating. You are."

He squinted. "How so?"

"That squint, for instance. Is it necessary? That combined with your inability to ever smile or laugh or…"

He half-nodded and released a breath through his nostrils.

She gestured. "You see? What man does that? Dragons do that."

He gave her a withering look. "I take it you associate closely with dragons."

"China is not *too* far," she teased.

"Are you saying I frighten you?" he drawled.

She rolled her eyes. "No. You do make me question my own safety on occasion, but I am anything but frightened."

"Is that so?" He stared her down playfully. "I think it time we test your level of fear. You have two ragged breaths to adjust. Are you mentally prepared for what is about to happen next?"

She eyed him.

He lunged.

Half-shriek-laughing, she sprinted through the corridors of Dr. Wallich's house and out through the already open doors of the house. Still laughing, she darted straight past Ridley's horse and toward the banyan tree out in the dirt path road illuminated by moonlight. She giggled, shoving her way past hanging branches.

She glanced back at the door in exasperation as he appeared. "*I was startled*!" she argued. "It had nothing to do with you!"

Ridley appeared in the shadows of the dim lanterns that illuminated his frame. "Nothing to do with me?" he drawled. "Are you certain?" With the toss of a handle, Ridley snatched up a machete by the door on his way out. Quickening his long-legged limping step, he stared her down teasingly, and hacked and hacked his way through the hanging branches.

She snorted.

The roaring pulse of her out of control heart barreled her forward as she whipped her way through hanging branches that tagged her arms and face. "Any other woman would have fainted by now."

He moved faster. "Fortunately, you aren't any other woman, are you?" The downward thudding of the blade as it slashed through the branches against the rapid movements of his muscled arm, brought him steadily closer. "I thought you trusted me," he called. "Don't you trust me? It's only a machete!"

She laughed so hysterically, she could barely make her way through the swaying of the branches at higher speeds as he thwacked after her, growing nearer.

Lunging, he shoved her hard against the trunk of the banyan.

She scream-laughed, stumbling against the tree.

Pressing into her with the weight of his body, he leaned down and set his nose to hers. "Hello."

Her chest heaved against his, the heat of his large, muscled body pressing into her as they stood nose to nose, the machete still in his large hand.

She nudged the blade away. "Even for you, this is a bit much."

His voice grew low. "Our hearts racing should always define us."

She dug her back harder into the tree behind her. "If you overwork the heart, it will cease functioning."

"There are ways to strengthen it." He twirled the machete, then held out its handle. "I bought this for you. I may be retiring, but it's important we start teaching you how to better protect yourself."

It wasn't exactly a bouquet of flowers. She took the handle from him and dangled it between them. "Protect myself from who? *You*?"

"From everyone but me." He flicked the blade between them and then took the handle and tossed it away from her hand into the grass beyond with a thud. "If we don't trust each other, Jemdanee, we'll fail each other." Holding her gaze, he set his hands on both side of her. "Why do you never ask me questions about my life?"

"I…" She was a horrible, self-centered person. "I have been too preoccupied with surviving my own thoughts."

He nodded. "Try not to leave me out of those thoughts. Unlike most men, I enjoy discourse as much as I do intercourse. Now what would you like to know about me?"

She eased out a breath knowing the doors to the underground crypt were opening. "I…"

He lowered his chin. "How about we start with the simple questions. Ones that will benefit you as a woman. Like… how long was your longest relationship, Ridley? Prior to that unhinged wife you should have never married? Followed by questions of: How do you usually treat women? Do you offer them respect and equality despite the rope?"

She eyed him. "Do you?"

He gripped the bark of the tree behind her. "Unequivocally. Have I not delivered on both? Given you ask, however, here is a little something you need to know about me and my history. I've always treated women the way they treat me. Which is why it *never* lasted."

He squinted. "Women have a tendency to insult my level of intelligence by only seeing my face and finances. When I was younger, I reveled in taking what they so freely gave, but they never saw the real me and because of it, I got bored. It never lasted and the rope never came out because I knew it would scare their lily white tits off. Then I met Elizabeth.

"We were two extremists looking to be accepted for who we were, not what the world wanted us to be. Only she wanted more than the rope. She wanted to hang by it and I foolishly thought I could edge her away from the extreme pain she was drawn to. Prior to learning that she was brutally raped when she was younger, and how it affected her, I entertained a good number of her requests, which included backhanding and cropping her one night until she lost consciousness."

His features grew troubled. "I actually thought I killed her." He rolled his eyes, easing out a breath. "That was when I ceased engaging her requests, which only put a further wedge between us. Her excessive need for pain went beyond what I could swallow. I reserve that side of me for those I hate. Not those I love."

Stunned, Jemdanee said, "You backhanded her and cropped her until she… *lost consciousness*?"

He nodded. "Not my finest hour."

"Did you not love her?"

"Of course I did."

She blinked rapidly. "Then why would you…?"

"Why does any man try to prove himself to a woman? To make her realize he would do anything to please her. Even if it means going against everything he is."

A shaky breath escaped her.

His gaze fell to her lips.

Silence lengthened between them as a jackal cackled in the night beyond.

His large hand slipped down her arm with the rigid drag of fingers as he veered them further down to her thighs, shifting the silk of her sari.

She gave into that touch, her limbs quaking with a need to be touched.

The night breeze grazed the moistness that dewed what his finger circled.

He surveyed her for a long moment, the muscle in his jaw quivering. "It's why I fought you back in London," he rasped. "I knew no matter how much I would pour into you and this, I would never be the man you need me to be. I acknowledge what few men do: I am broken. What man glories in finding grime and beating it with a ledger? I do. What man chases his woman with a machete and thinks it amusing? I do. But you…" His throat worked. "You make me believe I can forcefully glue in a few of those missing pieces."

She knew he was offering her more than he had ever offered to any woman.

She could see it in his eyes and it was humbling.

How had she earned it?

She could pretend that raw and passionate darkness in him didn't exist and try to erase it by insisting he be like other men, but that wasn't what she wanted. She wanted him *because* he wasn't like other men. And unlike other women, she refused to have this extraordinary and unusual man walk away from her merely because he defied convention. She defied convention, too, and therefore needed to embrace him in the way he was embracing her: completely.

Even if it meant... swallowing some of that darkness.

She had more than enough light to oblige. "I am in awe of the flaws you never hide."

He lowered his chin. "I wasn't poking for lofty compliments."

"I am in awe that you embrace what others fear and yet remain what others hope to be."

He said nothing.

It's why she loved him.

She searched his rugged, bruised face. A face he had bruised in her name. He did almost too much in her name and she not enough. "Explain to me what other women never took the time to listen to. Tell me about your rope. What does it mean to you?"

Astonishment touched his face. "Your mind would never understand."

Her lips thinned. "Then you have already decided and I never will."

His expression grew tight with strain. He sighed. Averting his gaze, he removed an eight-inch piece of hemp rope from his trouser pocket, folding it. "This, as you already know, is my think rope. The rope that I... usually use on a woman is the one you swiped."

She wavered. "That rope is over a hundred feet long."

His mouth quirked. "It's an art form." He searched her face and gestured to the stone bench beside the tree. "Sit or stand, Kumar. You choose."

She eyed him, the pulsing intensity from his presence making her realize the air between them had changed. She glanced toward the lanterns and the night. "You intend to do this now?"

"You needn't worry. Your first time will be in a bed without any rope and me barely moving. I promise. It will not be here or now or like this. No one masters anything overnight. I merely want you to understand it."

Lowering his gaze to hers, he used his entire muscled body to bump her in the direction of the bench, taking her hand and sliding it down toward the direction of his flap. "Sit or stand before your hand reaches the flap."

She almost stumbled against the bench, her knees buckling. She sat, the weight of her gown almost making her sag.

"Stay seated." His voice now simmered to a rough velvet. "Meet Evan Oswald." He set his broad shoulders hard and widened his muscled stance to rigid before her, his rugged features taking on an implacable expression that was tight with stern strain. "I look the same, I talk the same but one thing is different."

He pointed to his masculine full mouth as it softened and quirked. "Welcome to overlord academy. Please reserve questions for the very end of this session as interruptions will not be tolerated."

Jemdanee blinked up at him her mouth widening against still close lips at realizing… he was… serious.

Ridley tapped at his chest. "I am an overlord," he intoned. "By definition I enjoy retaining control over myself and my environment at all times. It means I have reached a level of maturity through consciousness and self-knowledge that allows me to embrace not only myself but what others fears most: inner fantasies. Fantasies are incredibly dangerous because it erases reality. Too many never cross that line out of fear of what they will see and do and feel when reality is erased. That fear does not exist in my world."

He captured her gaze, his amber eyes pinning her into place with unspoken magnetism. "A real overlord's true domination does not start or end in the bedchamber. It's applied to *all* aspects of his life."

He surveyed her for a moment. "Much like any man who seeks a wife, an overlord seeks a bondswoman to share his penchant. His methods of subtly testing her level of conscious cooperation for his lifestyle varies. If asked, would she set aside all doubt and sit on his knee and share his cigar merely because he asks her to? Would she set aside prudery and frig her clit in a copper tub for a man she just met because it unraveled a need in her and in him all of society would otherwise dismiss as loose-moraled and filthy as opposed to a visceral connection felt instantly between two souls?"

Jemdanee's lips parted, her face heating at the memory of what she had allowed.

His jaw worked. "I will always give my bondswoman choices, but sometimes, she will have to choose between the wall and the wall. I call it real life. For we all have to make choices we don't want to and *c'est la vie*. Though you are not a bondswoman, and most likely never will be to me given you are what the whipping society refers to as a milk-and-water female, unable to swallow milk by itself… let us embrace a thread. Might I demonstrate?" He lifted a brow, waiting for permission.

It was like peering into a circus master's mind. "I…" She had always wanted an explanation of the woman she'd seen carved into the table. "*Haan.*"

"I thank you." He towered over her, blocking the entire view of the garden. Setting each trouser-clad muscled thigh around her bent knees, he locked them *hard* against each other with the compression of her sari that was now bundled between his thighs.

He tapped at his flap. "Look at it."

She stilled. Her face now hovered near the flap of his trousers. The linen fabric was form-fitted against a dormant but still very sizable indication that he was all male.

Her throat worked as her knees instinctively locked together, unable to look at much else.

Ridley smoothed the flap with the roll of the rope, outlining his dormant cock more. "Being able to control the urge is what makes me an overlord. The amount of restraint I have practiced over many years is what men lack when engaging women. As a result, you get more out of it."

She swallowed.

He stared down at her from above. "Grab the back of the bench with both hands to balance yourself and look up at me."

Jemdanee's chest constricted. The manner in which he had locked her knees made her breaths quake. "Ridley?"

He dug his knees tighter into her. "Yes, bondwoman?"

She almost fidgeted. "This is only a demonstration, *haan*?"

His features softened. "*Haan.*" He smoothed her cheek and then dangled the rope between them. "The moment you seek to regain control, say *Evan Oswald*." He held her gaze. "Now lean back and grip the bench."

She swallowed, half-nodding. Gripping the edge of the bench behind her, which forced her to lean far enough to better see him, she slowly rolled her head back.

Locking his gaze to hers from where he still towered above, he knotted the hemp once, methodically ensuring it was pulled tight. He held the hemp rope on each end and pulled it *tight*, causing the large knot to compact. He snapped it until the knot held itself at no return. "Do you trust me?"

"*Oh, haan*. I trust every white man with a rope who holds my legs together."

Amber eyes pinned her. "Humor hurts when it's offered in the wrong moment. Do you trust me, *mon chou*?"

She softened her voice. "Yes. Of course."

Holding her gaze, he dragged the section of rope across his tongue, wetting the hemp.

She felt her core tighten against her will with every rise and fall of soft breaths, watching.

He edged in closer, the solid muscle buried beneath his waistcoat shifting. Rolling the hemp slowly across his unfurled tongue, he lowered the knot down to her own lips, dragging its duality of rough smoothness against her own parted mouth. "Moisten it."

Jemdanee felt her jaw slacken and her breaths go faint as the delicate grazing of rope that had been christened by his tongue now christened her own.

The rope tasted of salt and had the scent of charred wood.

He continued to drag it gently back and forth against her tongue. "This is the flavor of the kingdom I bring. I am the tale and you are the fairy. Your sweat is the salt and I char your skin with my rope whilst I knot your body and your mind into submission."

Her thighs quivered.

The rope paused between her lips. "Bite the knot until your jaw aches," he rumbled out.

Unable to think under the power of his voice and his presence, she sank her teeth against the knot until it squeaked between her teeth.

His mouth softened. "Hold it and look up at me, *mon dévot*. Breathe knowing I would never hurt you without your consent."

Meeting his heated gaze, her jaw ached as she slowly breathed through teeth and nostrils, feeling an eerie sense of power for she could see she was giving him what he wanted.

"Even in this moment, though you feel powerless, we are equals," he whispered down at her. "You can take away my power whenever it pleases you. That is *your* power. Release your teeth."

Her jaw slackened.

He dragged the rope from her mouth to her chin and down her throat to the mounds of her breasts, grazing her exposed skin until a staggering shiver escaped her, turning her flesh to a prickling heat.

The quake of her arms made it almost impossible for her to hold herself up.

In that moment, between the uneven breaths and the roaring of her pulse which she felt within the rope itself, she would have begged him to wedge that hemp between her already moist-flooding thighs and slide the knot against her nub until she tremored to blindness.

"This I do not fear at all," she managed up at him.

His voice warmed. "Fear only exists when you have no understanding or control. You will always have both." His mouth lifted in a predatory acknowledgement. "The moment you become mine in this way, modesty is dead to us and unconstrained voluptuousness begins. *That* is when you learn to trust me to do things to your body you wouldn't even do to yourself."

She couldn't breathe.

"Pleasure is a gift. One I wholeheartedly respect, which is why *pain* has to be respected even more. It reminds me to honor every nuance of pleasure lest it be reduced to insignificance. The world is too blind to ever see past its own need for pleasure and that is why they see harm in it. People only seek out self-gratification thinking it's the path to fulfillment, and as a result, pain hurts them twice as much and they fall twice as hard. So imagine if you divide yourself between the two. You become so fucking powerful no one can touch you or your mind. It's what I practice. It's who I am."

He snapped the rope beneath her nose, startling her.

Her over-ignited nerves made her half-breathe.

Widening his muscled stance as the defined bulk of his arms

tensed against the coat and linen of his shifting muscles, his large hands stretched each end of the rope as far as it would go. "This is a demonstration. Nothing involved, nothing complicated. *Simple*. Say *Evan Oswald* and I will liberate you from whatever authority I impose."

His voice turned to velvet. "Lift your sari to your navel."

Why was she as intrigued as she was scared out of her mind. "Now?"

He tapped the rope gently against her lips in answer, seeking compliance.

Slowly releasing the bench as the hot wind blew between the swaying branches of the low hanging trees of the night, she swallowed and gave into the wet need he'd created, dragging up her sari. The fabric was too pleated to move up, resisting. She tugged and tugged again, but with him standing against her sari, she couldn't—

"Jemdanee?" he rumbled down at her. "Lean back, hips up and *lift*."

She almost shoved him, her face burning at how inexperienced she was coming across for not being able to even lift her own sari when it counted most. "This is not—"

"Shhhh." Hooking the rope into his teeth, he quickly yanked up the sari past her thighs and setting his nose to her nose, guided each of her hands to her thighs. "I won't look," he said through the rope tucked between his teeth. "I honor thee."

This. Him.

How she revered and adored him for always being more than what she expected.

His large warm fingers grazing her fingers, he slid her forefinger against the heat of her nub as he forced her other fingers to spread the lips of her quim open. Her body jolted then relaxed.

With the rope between his teeth, and still bent nose to nose with her, he slowly jostled her finger against the nub, making her gasp.

Releasing her hands, he removed the rope from his mouth and held each stretched end at her eye level. "Let me hear your breaths and see your lips tremble along with the rest of you."

Her fingers brushed her wetness and the hardness of her nub. She shuddered knowing he was watching. Blinded by the rippling of pleasure penetrating her core in waves, she stared up at that rugged face as she increased the friction, determined to release.

It was glorious. He was glorious. She'd always known that.

Faster. Her breaths hitched. Almost. Almost.

"Three years I have imagined you kneeling to me like this," he whispered.

Ridley wedged the rope beneath her chin, making the knot curve slowly into her skin as his amber eyes penetrated her gaze from above. He dragged it delicately back and forth, grazing the knot until her over-sensitized skin knew the gasping breaths of anguish and beauty of pleasure.

"Claim your need," he whispered down at her, rolling his hips toward her face.

She gasped as wetness flooded her fingers and her body quaked in an attempt to control it through breaths. She sped toward it, the knot pressing her chin as she lowered her gaze to his flap to see the outline of his thick cock. Her fingers slowed and altogether stopped realizing… his cock was dormant.

With the grit of teeth, he snapped up the rope and dug the knot hard and up to a searing pinch.

She flinched as her skin and jaw burned against the entire curve of the rope, all pleasure snapping toward pain as she stilled.

The muscles in his linen shirt visibly tensed as his breathing became slow and intense. "Do you feel that?" His deep voice simmered. "*This* is a reminder that you do not control your pleasure. I do," he intoned. "You lost focus on what you were tasked to do and as such, you will remove your hands. This demonstration is over."

She swallowed. "But…"

"Distractions during sessions are not tolerated by me. Ever. I take this very seriously given the amount of power you are entrusting me with and I try to keep emotions separate from this or you'll get hurt. Hands out."

She swallowed again, her chin still hinged against the knot of the rope knowing if she moved forward it would choke her throat and if she moved back she would fall off the bench. "I will focus."

"Hands out," he warned.

She was too riled to let him do this to her! "Are we not going to…?"

He jerked the knot harder and tighter into her skin, her teeth clacking.

Her hands jumped away from her thighs as her skirts slid back down with a rustle against the weight of the gown. The knot dug harder into her chin and throat, searing her senses with pain and making her choke out, "*Evan Oswald.*"

Lessening the pressure completely, he leaned down toward her and slid his entire tongue across her lower lip, tingling her mouth into forgetting the burn and pinch. His heated breaths fanned over her wet lips. "Next time, stay focused."

Blood pounded into her brain, leapt from her heart and made her very knees tremble.

He unhooked the hemp from her chin and edged back, searching her face. "Your pain tolerance is nonexistent. I was gentle." He quickly wrapped the rope around his hand. "Are you all right?"

Torn between being fascinated and disturbed, she nodded.

"Good." Holding her gaze, he leaned down and nudged up her chin. Inspecting it, he then kissed the skin, pressing the warmth of his lips against the fading sting. "Seeing you submit to the rope is beyond salacious."

He grazed his lips against her cheek then her forehead, curving his hand down her breast, flicking her nipple that was hidden beneath the fabric. "What did you think?"

Silence lengthened between them as a jackal cackled in the night beyond.

Jemdanee swallowed hard, the burn beneath her chin hinting she had lost her mind thinking she could handle this man. "While it had its moment, I find your interest in its nuances baffling. I do not understand it."

"Spoken with Jemdanee flare." He stepped back and tucked the rope back into his pocket. "If you were to ask a dog why it has a tail, do you think it would be able to answer? And do you think because of its inability to answer, that tail holds no meaning or value to that dog and therefore the tail ought to be removed?"

She eyed him. "As always, your mind overthinks everything."

"I know. It is what it is." Turning, he seated himself beside her. "Come." Guiding her head to his shoulder, he wrapped his muscled arms around her tight.

His tenderness toward her was unbearable and went against what his rope represented.

In that moment, his duality of hero and demon was all too real.

She could feel his steadying breaths against her forehead as he held her closer. She adoringly circled her arms around his waist and relaxed, sinking into his muscled embrace. "When will you make love to me?"

Tilting her chin upward, he caressed his masculine lips against hers. "Tomorrow night."

It sweetly drained what little was left of her. "Evan Oswald, I fear over time, we will erase each other with a need to prove ourselves to each other."

"There are worse things," he murmured against her mouth, his tongue sliding around her lips.

She faintly nodded knowing he was right.

Smoothing her hair, he said, "Not to spoil the mood, but I have to get up in the morning. Are you ready to ride back?"

She heaved out a breath.

It would seem the British government was impeding on their relationship.

CHAPTER EIGHT

Yet another report.
Ridley scanned the documents, almost numb.

Hundreds of sepoys of the Native Infantry grabbed their swords and rifles and rode through bazaars, burning and slashing at every white face, including countless women and children. British officers in Meerut, a town forty miles north of Delhi, were too stunned to contain the outbreak given the sepoys had been part of the Third Cavalry for eight years, annually paid for by the British government. Gutted bungalows, slaughtered livestock and the estimated corpses have yet to be determined, but all were shot, mutilated, stabbed, and burned beyond skeletal recognition making it impossible for magistrates to issue any death certificates. Orders by Meerut's British Commander-in-Chief were sent to bury all bodies and any other evidence relating to the incident lest panic over widespread revolts overtake all units.

It was only the beginning.
This was the India Britain had created.
Too many more were going to die.

Too many more were going to be erased.

And for what? Spices, jewels and textiles? Fuck.

A knock on the main door of the map room made him pause.

"*Mr. Ridley?*" a youthful male British voice inquired through the closed door.

Grabbing his cane, Ridley walked over to the door and unlatched it, pulling it open. He towered over the youth standing on the other side. "Yes?"

A lanky cadet with a freckled face snapped to attention with the thud of leather boots, setting a rigid hand to his cap in formal greeting. He veered his gaze upward. "Cadet Dunning, sir. I was tasked to deliver this parcel into your hands." Retrieving a wax sealed parcel from his oversized, undecorated uniform pocket, he held it out. "It arrived through courier twenty minutes ago and was marked as being of unmitigated importance out of London. To be read at once."

Big brown eyes, freckles and barely shaving with a fading bruise curving below his throat.

In his opinion, the boy was too young to be involved with the military.

Ridley tugged the parcel out of the youth's hand and set the parcel onto the side table beside the door. "Cadet Dunning." He squinted. "You look familiar. Have I seen you before?"

The cadet fidgeted. "Uh… yes, sir. That night you— Captain Thorbur. I… I was there."

"Ah." He eyed him. "I was a bit rough with him, wasn't I?"

The cadet cringed. "A bit? He had an inch of thread pulled through the skin of his forehead by the time you were done. Everyone knows you…" He fidgeted. "I'm not saying he didn't deserve it, sir. I… I would never judge you or…" His features flickered as if readying for a blow.

Ridley heaved out a breath. His reputation proceeded him. "Given my line of work and everything I have seen, overcompensation is necessary. Do you understand?"

Dunning over-nodded. "Yes, sir."

Stepping back, Ridley skimmed the youth's appearance, noting there were fresh dirt marks on the arms and knees of that beige uniform. The belt was crooked and the mark on one of the knees hinted at a tear. All done today. "Are you all right? What happened?"

Dunning averted his gaze. "A scuffle, sir. Nothing I'm not used to."

These military compounds and their idea of manning up a boy annoyed him. "How often does it occur?"

"Every day."

Ridley lowered his chin. "*Every day*? And you've been on the compound for how long?"

"Three months, sir."

Not good. Ridley tucked the sealed parchment into his waistcoat, pointing at the youth's bruised face with his cane. "Once in a while is understandable and will happen given pricks abound, but every day hints you've become a favorite pastime. Why is that?"

Dunning averted his gaze.

There it was.

The boy was overly submissive in nature. "You and I are going to ensure these officers and cadets respect you. What are your hours off?"

Brown eyes veered up in dread. "I would rather you not complicate my life, Mr. Ridley."

Jesus Christ. Why did everyone always think he was complicated everything? Merely because he had a mind to help? "You appear to be complicating your own life, Dunning. Set aside what you think you know about me. If you never address this problem, it will always *be* a problem."

Stepping toward the young man, Ridley leaned down against the stiffness of his own leg and dusted off that uniform with hard, solid brushes, ensuring the boy felt every thud against his flesh as he removed the dirt and dust from it. "Take pride in your appearance. Even after a scuffle. You should have cleaned up. Why didn't you?"

"I…"

Adjusting the boy's belt on those hips with a firm tug, Ridley used the head of the cane to prop that chin up and up. "Why do you think these men treat you with such disrespect?"

Dunning miserably held his gaze. "Because I let them."

"*Applaudissements*. Here is some advice from a man who has seen it all. Men overuse one organ: their cock. But one organ too many *never* master: the mind." Ridley drifted Chaucer's beak to the boy's forehead and tapped it. "It's as powerful as it is dangerous.

It's a weapon that can make a man either run into the fire to save others or dart the other way. Your superiors will insist upon the mastery of weaponry and that its mastery will enable you to survive. That isn't true. Weaponry will ensure you don't die, yes, but it won't keep you from holding onto your weapon once you realize you're *going* to die. Without *this*—" He gently tapped Dunning's head. "You're useless to yourself and the world. So don't let these pricks rule over you. Rule over them by letting them know they can't touch your mind. The moment they see you have no fear, it becomes *their* fear. For they are unable to hold anything over you."

The cadet blinked rapidly.

Lowering the cane, Ridley stepped back. "What are your hours every afternoon?"

"Gate duty ends for me at two. I don't return again until five."

"Do you play tennis?"

Dunning eyed him. "I… on occasion. Yes, sir. Though I'm not very good at it." He fidgeted.

"Meet me at the tennis courts tomorrow afternoon at three. Bring a racket and a basket of good leather balls filled with wool." Ridley pointed. "Your first assignment is to stop fidgeting."

Dunning gripped the ends of his coat until his knuckles went white, still fidgeting.

"Stop. *Fidgeting*." Ridley swung the cane at the boy's head hard, stopping it before it touched his ear, making the boy flinch. "It announces to the world you have no self-confidence. The next time you grip your coat like that or fidget in my presence, this cane *will* hit your head and it will remind you that having no self-confidence *hurts*. Are we understood in this?"

The youth stilled. "Yes, sir."

"I didn't hear you."

"*Yes, sir!*" Dunning boomed.

"Good. Use more force when speaking. There is no need to yell, but *never* mutter." Whirling the cane, Ridley thudded it into the floor. "How old are you?"

"I'll be nineteen soon."

The boy would see more than his eyes needed to. It was the one thing he himself regretted about his life. A mind could never unsee horrors and in his case, he sought to better understand it thinking it was the only way to stop it. All he understood now was that he had erased any chance of giving himself a normal life. "Why did you sign up for the military?"

"My father. He…" A breath escaped Dunning. "I was hoping to attend a university but he refused to pay for it."

Typical. "How long is your contract?"

"Ten years, sir."

It was going to erase not only this boy's life but his dreams. That is… if he lived long enough given was happening all over India. Ridley knew he himself couldn't erase the path he had long chosen, but he could erase it for this boy. "Did you want out of your contract and your university paid for?"

Dunning's lips parted. "More than you would ever know."

Ridley nodded. "I'll speak to the Field Marshal about reducing your years to something more attainable and ensure you have a stipend waiting for you."

Those brown eyes widened. "I… why?"

"The world needs more educated men. Go to Cambridge. They know what they're doing."

A tremor of a smile touched Dunning's lips. "I heard the officers say you were arrested twenty-four times."

"They do nothing but lie. It's fifty-three times. *C'est la vie.*"

Dunning grinned sheepishly. "I wouldn't mind getting arrested once."

Ridley pointed. "I wouldn't recommend it. There is no access to cigars or champagne." The military clock chimed. Ridley paused, his gaze snapping toward it. *Jemdanee.* "Do you have time to deliver a message to Miss Kumar for me over at Spence's?"

Dunning brightened. "Yes and with pleasure, sir. I know Miss Kumar."

"Good. Inform her that I will be late given I have a few other case files to organize, but that I will meet her at the Garden House this evening. She and I are attending a gathering the Field Marshal is hosting for his soldiers. Inform her to arrive on time and that I will join her shortly therefore when I am able."

"Yes, sir."

"Thank you. Now if you will excuse me…" Ridley turned.

Dunning gestured toward the parcel. "Do ensure you address it, sir."

Ridley nodded, waving him off. "I will, thank you. I will see you tomorrow at three over at the tennis courts. You and me."

"Yes, sir!" Hitting his four fingers to his cap, the cadet swiveled on his boot and marched down the corridor, calling, "No fidgeting be my name, tennis be the game!" He wiggled.

The boy was going to need every minute of his day.

Ridley set his cane against the wall and picked up the parcel bundled in twine to keep all of the folded parchments in place.

He paused, noting the seal binding the string together was marked with Scotland Yard's emblem. Breaking it, he quickly unfolded the top parchment, his gaze settling on Finkle's sloped writing.

Ridley,

I am detailing what has turned into a city-wide search and regret to inform you of the gruesome murder of our finest: Parker. The details of his death have already found its way into every newspaper and there is no silencing the panic. I have included facsimiles related to everything recovered from the cellar Parker was found in. His wife insists he had been missing for three days. The cellar belongs to a dram-shop on Birken Road where he was known to frequent. There are no witnesses and no arrests have been made. The facsimile pertaining to the rendering of the crime is included, along with the letter recovered from the scene itself. Take its meaning with due seriousness. Streets are being patrolled and residents on Basil Street are being warned. I have dispatched our best inspectors to your mother and your former wife and will continue to follow all leads. I trust you know what to do.

-Richard Mayne AKA Finkle

Staring at the words, Ridley's fingers gripped the parchment almost to crushing. It took four breaths before a lethal calm overtook his mind.

So much for retiring.

What the fuck was going on in London?

He methodically folded the letter back into its original state and unfolded every single facsimile Frederick had included, laying them out one by one.

Eleven. All related to Parker's murder.

Jesus. The man had a wife and three children.

Shifting his jaw, Ridley rifled through the parchments until a detailed charcoal sketching of the murder scene made him pause.

It was a dismembered, male body in a cellar surrounded by unmarked barrels. Bone and flesh scattered left, right, center, walls, floors, and the wood of the barrels. An ax was methodically propped beside the skull. Smeared against the wall in what he knew was the artist capturing blood, were the letters: HATCHLING.

Tucked into the gored mass of the sternum was a detailed sketch of a raven feather.

Ridley snapped up the parchment, bringing it to eye level.

It was staged.

He'd seen the original sketch of his father's murder. Hers was out of passion.

This was methodical.

Someone else was mocking his pain and wagging their fingers.

Someone else was bringing an ax to the skull of his past and swinging it.

Quickly searching for the duplication of the letter left at the scene, his gaze settled on the reproduction.

To the one who calls himself Mr. Evan Oswald Ridley,

By the time you travel back from a land full of heathens, an unlit ardor will blaze. Vidocq will be delivered in pieces wrapped in that flag of Blue, White, and Red. Your mother will scream in the same room your father did, holding a feather to her heart. Quincy will be missing more than a finger as a new client paints Mrs. Berkley's black door red, and razored into your arm will be more than a Hindu who will die from too many nicks. Your death or theirs. You decide their fate as forty-seven men await one word from my lips. Return by September and meet me at the crypt where your bones will lie alongside mine.

With blood pouring affection,
Chaucer who is back from the dead

His breath burned his throat.

Vidocq had once confided that every great inspector unearthed a notable Herculean nemesis.

A nemesis that made an inspector face everything he was in the eyes of the law while deciding what mattered most. He had called it the Mephistopheles Clause. When Faust had been forced to stand in the darkest part of the woods and wager his soul to a faceless demon whose fingers and lips and chin dripped with unending blood.

It had finally come for him.

After fourteen years of taking a shovel to the dirt, and just as he had decided to finally wash the muck from his hands, something had crawled out of the hole and grabbed his ankle.

Ridley numbly gathered the stacks of paper.

Death had never really held much power over him after he had spent his entire life holding a noose to criminals. Unfortunately… too much had changed.

He'd been blinded by a light too bright: Jemdanee.

She, who had forced him to be more than the devil.

Regrettably, only the devil knew how to slit the throat of darkness.

It was back to the battledore and shuttlecock.

Fuck.

"I'll right this for you, Parker." Yanking out his think rope, Ridley methodically knotted it twice, ensuring each knot reflected each thought. To save those he loved, he was going to have to play battledore with more than the villain.

He was going to have to play battledore with everyone he needed to keep safe.

Visit solicitor. Tight. *Last testament*. Tighter.

He had to take more than the ordinary precautions. Parker had already been spattered like paint across a canvas set on an easel by a master. It whispered of a demented darkness seeking to play with far more than pain.

It wanted acknowledgement.

And unlike most, this one was equally intelligent.

Forty-seven men await one word from my lips.

His father had died at the age of forty-seven.

It was no coincidence.

Someone had dug through old broadsheets from 1810 and was now writing a libretto.

"Who are you?" Ridley thudded his weight into the nearest wall, trying to think.

This one knew he was in India and knew he had marked his arm with Jemdanee's name. He'd only ever shown his bare arms and chest in one public place: *Jackson's Boxing Academy*.

It meant he'd been under surveillance for about nine months prior to coming to India.

So who would take that time? Why wait? Why now?

It was personal. Which meant… they had met.

Ridley felt himself drifting, his mind whizzing through every case his exhausted mind could sift through. Too many names. Too many cases. Piles of it.

Coca/limestone might and could and would speed it up.

What matters more? Your sense of justice or her faith in you?

Shifting his jaw, he flipped open the leather casing of his stash of cheroots from the side table lying beside Parker's file and stuck a cheroot into his mouth. Striking the flint of the match, he lit the end of the tobacco and dragged in several riled breaths, igniting it with a hiss. He eased out smoke between teeth, tossing the flint and matches.

Spreading out every last parchment, he dismantled the scene piece by piece.

His mind spiraled him into that inner-connected world of dissections he wedged together.

Skull downward.

Weapon belt gone.

Trouser flap unfastened.

Shattered porcelain chamber pot set in corner by barrel.

He'd been pissing. His back had been turned when—

Hack, hack, hack. At least fourteen times judging by the cleaved pieces.

Pool of blood with center swiped through. Body dragged.

Why? Not now. Back to the barrels.

Seven unmarked barrels set in no particular order.

One shifted to get to the wall to write a message meant for him.

Filled barrels impossible to move, indicating partially drained or empty.

HATCHLING.

This was personal. What hatched? Birds. A crow.

Chaucer had been hatched and purchased from the Zoological Society.

He would start there the moment he arrived into London.

After he…

Grabbing the side table with digging white knuckles, he jarred it into the wall violently, chanting to himself that he wouldn't pick it up or throw it. "Fuuuuuuuuuuuuuck!"

He swung away and dragged his hands through his hair before letting it drop.

Numb, he stared at the wall across from him, knowing what needed to be done.

He had to bury every weakness.

Ones this lunatic would expose, slaughter and gorge.

Welcome to the life you never wanted.

CHAPTER NINE

Later that evening
The Garden House Terrace

Draped in a very expensive jade sari she had purchased at the emporium with an all too devious smile, Jemdanee reveled in it being subtly sheer at the shoulders and at her midriff, giving the illusion she wore two pieces. She had even unraveled her black hair, letting it cascade down in thick waves past her waist and tucked and pinned a flamboya flower on each side.

She wasn't one to ever brag about her ability to make a man kneel, but she was doing it tonight.

Watching insects and moths veer toward the massive oil torches that singed them instantly to ash in the jutting smoke, it was a subtle reminder that she was merrily heading down that same path. Yes, life was the flame, and they were all eager moths, but love was the glass of the lantern that kept a moth from getting burned.

Arriving at the torch-lit terrace that was trellised to give the illusion of a dance hall tucked within the tropical grove of tamarind trees, Jemdanee dragged in a readying breath as if it were the first and only breath she had ever taken.

The muggy warmth of the night air was tinged with the heady scent of *raat-ki-rani*.

Its flowery, spice-ridden sweetness hinted of what the night would bring: Ridley.

With the flow of her veil, she breezed past gathered wives and daughters and mothers of officers who wore massive Western gowns that prevented them from even standing too close to each other.

Sweat trickled down their flushed faces and bejeweled throats, tarnishing the illusion of their unending sophistication.

Aside from Kalpita whom the Field Marshal *always* graciously permitted to attend for reasons everyone knew, Jemdanee was the only Hindu female in attendance.

Given she was in India, she found that rather amusing.

A flurry of low words from behind fluttering ostrich fans drifted toward her as she passed.

"I have yet to garner an introduction from him," Mrs. Jones stated, quickening her fan enough to cause her curl-frizzened hair to quiver. "Not that I am pining for one. Despite the level of intelligence he exudes, Mr. Ridley shows none in the social forum."

"Is he French or is he British?"

"Both. I heard—"

The two women fell into silence and eyed her.

Jemdanee tucked herself against the arch of the terrace.

To show their snubbing didn't bother her any more than their discussion of Ridley, Jemdanee leaned over to a tray-holding servant in a scarlet turban and pertly used her cupped hand to pile peeled oranges into it.

She paused. Oranges.

How fitting.

In between methodical chews of each sweet slice, she stared the two women down.

A thousand poisoned wedges to you.

They puckered their wrinkled lips and positioned themselves away.

A sudden flurry of words, whispers and the increased speed of countless wagging fans before female faces rouged from the heat, made women lean toward observing an arriving guest.

Pushing the last orange into her mouth, Jemdanee angled to see past pin-curled coifs.

Ridley strode past the torch-lit stone arches, his muscled frame dressed in all black.

Startled, Jemdanee choked on the segment of the orange in her mouth.

He looked like a Persian assassin.

Even his silk cravat and high collared linen shirt pressed beneath that form-fitted black embroidered waistcoat was black. Even his cuff links and the onyx cravat pin that gleamed against the torchlight as he turned to greet officers were black.

He was so imposing and so unconventional it was... *provocative*.

After coughing past the last of the orange and fully swallowing, with her eyes still watering, she veered out of sight and behind the farthest stone pillar, mentally preparing herself.

How did a woman seduce a man who had done more in his life than she had in her head?

It was intimidating.

On occasion, she peered out to see if he was looking for her.

With a widened stance of his hands locked at the wrists behind his broad back, Ridley remained by a group of officers on the far end of the terrace. Among all the red coats, he was the only one dressed in black.

He glanced around in between conversation with the officers.

Jemdanee pinched her lips knowing he was looking for her.

Turning away from him and the crowds, she offered up a chant to the gods, asking them for guidance in what she knew was a passion not even time had cured. Their passion had been born to smash the world into pieces and she was here to collect on it.

She removed her dance card from her wrist, unraveling the velvet string and using the small pencil, regally wrote onto each and every line, *Ridley, Ridley, Ridley*, *Ridley*, *Ridley*, *Ridley* and... *Ridley*.

She folded it against her sari, ready to collect every dance.

Captain Thornbur veered in, his bruised round face beaded with sweat, his dark eyes searching her face. "I came to apologize for my behavior toward you over these past few months."

Arrey. She knew why this whoreson was apologizing. Because of his fear of Ridley after he'd been pummeled. There was still blackened thread hanging from above his brow as if the edge of a table had clipped him to the skull. Uff.

She set her chin. "*Salla*. I have no interest in holding any discussions with you, *sahib*. You were never civil and therefore you have not earned a word from me."

He eyed her. "I brought a gift for you."

She snorted. "If you are attempting to socialize with me now after almost four months of treating me like an animal and terrorizing my respectability as a woman, you are sorely mistaken."

He cringed. "I don't usually converse with Hindus. 'Tis all very new to me."

She tightened her hold on the folded dance card, which her fingers crushed. "You have been in India for eleven months."

Thornbur adjusted his cap and dug into his other pocket. "I acknowledge that." He removed a gold bracelet and held it out. "For you."

Other women now peered in.

Shiva, Shiva. What an idiot.

Jemdanee tried to block others from seeing the bracelet, lest the gossip begin. "An apology was all I needed. What are you doing? People will assume you are attempting to woo me."

He eyed her. "Don't be ridiculous. Ridley had asked that I be genuine in my approach. So I… *here*." Thornbur leaned in and tried to wedge the bracelet onto her wrist.

She glared and jerked her hand away. "What are you—"

Ridley veered in, startling them both. "Are you all right?"

This was officially awkward.

Leaning in, Ridley searched her face and inclined his head in greeting. "Are you in need of a hero?" he offered in a husky, accented tone.

Her heart popped. One would think they had never met.

She crinkled the dance card.

Thornbur gestured with the bracelet. "I can assure you, Ridley, I was only—"

"Permit me to comment on your cumbersome, baseborn behavior, Thornbur." Ridley swung toward him and widened his stance. Holding the man's gaze, Ridley took the bracelet and tucked it into the man's coat pocket. "When I asked you to apologize to her, did I also ask you to give her jewelry and grab for her?"

Thornbur lingered. "I… no."

Women started to whisper.

People were gathering.

"Ridley… might you not…" Jemdanee held her dance card up to her nose in dread.

"I'm ensuring everyone knows you didn't invite this." Ridley glanced toward the gathering crowd and stepped toward the officer. "Thornbur," he rumbled out. "Your evening was going so well. What happened?"

Jemdanee cringed and felt like crawling away.

The young officer eyed him. "I was only—"

"Don't ever touch her or any woman without permission." Ridley looked down at the man who was a head shorter. "*Ever.*" Ridley adjusted Thornbur's lapels. "If I have to reprimand you again for misbehaving, my uneducated friend, I will puncture your subclavian artery. Find a medical book and locate where that particular artery is and how long it takes for it to flood out. Now be a dear and go dance. Twirl for me." He shoved Thornbur, twisting him by the shoulders.

Thornbur stumbled, turned and thudded into a pillar, sending a lantern crashing.

Flames where the oil spilled at Thornbur's feet flared. "Oh, shite!"

Jemdanee cringed, noting the flames were all too symbolic.

The devil was looking to strut.

Ridley pointed. "Fabulous twirl. Unending apologies about the fire."

The Field Marshal stalked toward them, his mustache twitching. "*Thorbur*! Are you annoying everyone again?"

Thornbur slid his cap down past his nose. "No, sir!" He saluted and darted past the crowds.

Servants hurried over and tossed water onto the burning oil lighting the floor, extinguishing it.

The Field Marshal veered toward Ridley. "Jesus, Mary and Joseph, must you turn everything into an opera? The boy was doing exactly what you asked him to do."

Ridley leaned in. "I didn't ask him to touch her."

The Field Marshal gave him a withering look. "Miss Kumar, marry this idiot and control him."

Jemdanee almost hooked the *pallu* of her sari over her head, her face burning. "How is Kalpita?"

The Field Marshal muttered something, edged back and departed, disappearing.

Jemdanee bit back a smile. "Trouble follows you everywhere, Ridley."

"Hold onto that thought." Quickly turning away, he grabbed a champagne glass off a passing tray, tossed it back and set it onto another passing tray. Swiveling back, he gave her a pointed look and paused.

His gaze dropped from her kajal smoked eyes to her breasts and exposed midriff.

A low whistle escaped him. "Why have we been avoiding each other?"

Jemdanee whirled the veil against herself. "I am here to answer that question."

He veered closer, towering. "*Cherchez la femme...* In other words, if a man is acting out of character, in order to stop it, it's important to find the woman who is the cause of it." His mouth quirked.

The heated scent of his peppery woodland cologne overtook her breaths. Something was different. He was almost... playful. "What has gotten into you?"

"Are you insinuating I have no right to be jocular?"

She met his gaze, sensing this was a decoy. "Out with it."

His amber eyes were unreadable. "I have a few things I need to do first." He snapped out his ungloved hand. "Dance with me and ignore the limp."

"What limp?"

"Exactly." Ridley set her hand onto the sleeve of his evening coat, pressing it into his forearm and led her to the floor with a cool, limping stride.

Her fingers and her palm and her knuckles pulsed beneath his, each juttering her heart into frantic beats as if she had just met him.

Joining the other couples on the vast terrace, they turned in unison toward each other as a breeze from the warm night rustled through, lifting the draped end of her sari up toward her face and between them.

Through the color of sheer azure, his hand caught the silk before she did and he gently draped it back down over her shoulder, his fingers skimming it down into place.

That touch was almost unbearable in its tenderness.

Taking her hand into his, he yanked her close, and firmly

positioned her against himself, setting a large hand on the sheer sari of her waist.

The searing heat of that hand penetrated her skin. There was only silk between them.

Holding her gaze, he pressed her against himself harder. "We go back ten years. This is me trying to be dashing for the only woman who will ever matter to me."

She lowered her gaze to his waistcoat, overwhelmed.

"Look at me."

Jemdanee snapped her gaze up to his.

He studied her. "Remember me in this moment and that I am capable of good."

She searched his face, feeling as if he were... saying good-bye. "Ridley?"

He held her gaze. "Not now."

They held their position, pressed against each other, waiting for the music to begin.

His cologne, his regimented breaths made her inwardly yearn for... *everything*. And more.

The music commenced and Ridley swept her effortlessly across the floor, turning them both with a quick ease and precision that was downright sensational.

Her breath hitched, realizing he knew far more about dancing than she did.

The limp impeded only in certain turns, but his strained face showed that he wanted to give her the dancing he had once told her he never would.

They danced in complete silence, but with each turning movement and each turning step, she secretly stole glances of his rugged face that hovered above hers and pressed her fingers into his coat tighter, wanting to burn the memory of him and those shifting muscles beneath the fabric into each breath she took.

It was a moment of forever that ended too soon.

When the music ended, Ridley brought them to a halt and twirling her once for effect, he released her. "Never say I didn't take you dancing."

She knew he was referring to their conversation back in London. Her heart squeezed. "I did not realize you knew how to dance so well."

He lifted a brow. "Hiccius doccius. I was raised by a French woman and shuffled off to Paris for nine years."

Hiccius doccius?

Who was this man?

She gave him a withering look. "Are you running out of words?"

"No. I am running out of time."

She lowered her chin. "What is that supposed to mean?"

His steady gaze bore into her. "You look beautiful."

Her fingers twitched.

Angling toward her, he removed one of the flamboya flowers pinned to her hair with a gentle tug, grazing her cheek. Holding her gaze, he tucked it into his pocket. "You have too many flowers in your hair. It's distracting."

"Too many? Last I knew, there were only *two*."

He quickly removed the other one. "Now there is none." He tucked it into his pocket, as well.

She eyed him. "Is this your attempt to... flirt with me?"

He released a breath through his nostrils. "Kumar?"

Oh, no. She was Kumar. "What is it, Ridley?"

"We have to talk."

Oh, no. "About what?"

His voice faded. "Are you listening?"

Despite his closed expression, she sensed his vulnerability. Something had changed. Something was wrong. She tried not to panic. "*Haan*. Yes. What is it?"

"Promise me you will cooperate with what I am about to ask."

She eyed him. "Hearing you say that does not sound very promising."

He shifted from boot to boot, then leaned in and lowered his voice. "A missive and a parcel arrived from London. I can't stay. I should leave tonight, but this time we have together is important to me and two days isn't going to change what awaits. I therefore will be leaving in two days and though it marks me to the bone, I'm leaving you here. I can't take you."

A heaviness centered in her chest. "I..."

He grazed her cheek. "Be the woman I need you to be. Stay here where you'll be safe."

Which meant... he was in danger. "Ridley... I... what is happening? What is it?"

"Everyone I ever associated with is in danger. It's why I'm wearing black."

Her pulse roared knowing *he* was danger.

After having seen him on that filth-ridden floor of an abandoned building bleeding from a seizure that had thrashed him into the chair and every board beneath him, she knew that had been the best scenario given his line of work. She couldn't have imagined what might have happened to him had that situation been handed over to dangerous men as opposed to an abandoned building.

Being part of his life she would have to accept living with that and the panic.

It was the price of loving him.

She slowly shook her head. "I barely survived what we went through back in London and you barely survived it yourself. You cannot go. Stay."

He glanced around as if everyone on the terrace annoyed him. "I'm not about to let my own mother and everyone else I know *die*. You needn't worry. I'm more than a limp."

She leaned in. "The limp was a warning. I will not let you define justice by holding only yourself to the flame. Given your mother is in danger, I am going with you."

He lowered his chin. "Absolutely not. One man is already dead because of me and there are enough pieces of him scattered for me to take this seriously."

Her stomach churned. "I am coming with you."

"No. I don't need to spend every fucking minute worrying about you."

"*Bas.*" She stared him down, ready to take him on. "I am going."

He squinted. "We have a problem."

"No. Not we. *You.* You have the problem. Learn to depend on more than yourself. I am far more lethal than I appear. You have yet to see me uncork jars that can make every man's eyes sizzle to liquid. For not every weapon has to be a blade or a lead ball. You are not alone in this. I am going."

A slow breath escaped him through straight white teeth. "Our minds are always at war despite our hearts wanting peace." He patted his pocket. "I take this night and your flowers with me." He tapped his forearm where her name was buried beneath his coat. "You are always with me. Always."

Her throat burned. "You are not leaving without me. I am going with you."

"No." He shook his head. "No, you aren't."

"*We do this together.*"

"You're not going."

She narrowed her gaze. "You cannot keep me from following."

"You do realize who the hell you are talking to, yes?"

All too well. "I thought we were equals."

"Not in this."

"If not in this then in what? Do not disrespect me merely because I am a woman."

Ridley unbuttoned his black evening coat one by one, exposing his black attire beneath. Holding her gaze, he dug out a band ring from his inner pocket and held it up, letting the gold glint against the torch-light. "Before I left London, I bought a ring for myself and had it etched." He tilted it out toward her. "Read what it says."

She dragged in a breath, leaned in and read *SHE BRINGS ME JUSTICE*.

Her heart flipped and then dropped. Her hands quaked, tears burning her eyes.

His features tightened. "Are you saying what I etched on it is a lie? Are you saying that when I ask you to do what is right by me, yourself and justice, you won't?"

"Justice is not something we can deliver to every part of the world as if we were gods, Ridley. We are human and humans die."

"Yes. They do. But if they must die, they die doing what is right." He held up the ring, his eyes clinging to hers. "When you receive this ring by parcel, it means you are to come to me." He slid the ring onto his own finger. "Whether I live or whether I die, the moment you receive this, come to London at 221 Basil Street. Not sooner. Do you understand me?"

She couldn't breathe, her eyes stinging. "Ridley, why are you doing this?" A tear rolled down her cheek knowing she was losing him. She swiped at it. "Why are you pushing me away when I am agreeing to stand alongside you? *I am here.*"

"Listen to me." He leaned in, smoothing her cheek. "Tomorrow late morning, you and I are getting married. It will ensure you are legally entitled to my estate should anything happen. I want you to be taken care of." Stepping back, he buttoned his evening coat as if he had finished a long day of work. "The day after you take my name, my trunks go with me and I depart. As your husband, I will do everything in my power to come back to you."

Unable to breathe, she whispered, "Whatever happened to my say and my equality?"

"I cannot possibly offer you equality when you're dead."

She glared. "Better I die than live knowing you are in peril."

He grabbed her face, startling her. "Don't forget who you're talking to," he growled, his fingers digging into her face. "I'm up against something that wants to make a cannibal look like a child with a lolly. I would sooner bury what we share then bury you in the ground. You're staying right here."

Despite a quiver running through the heaviness of her body, she felt eerily calm and ready for whatever following him into London would bring. Maybe it was the countless amputations she'd overseen or… her love for him. One even greater than she had imagined.

She held his gaze, digging his fingers even harder into her chin which he had already marked. "I can and will be your greatest weapon. Do not join in on the world's judgement by thinking I have no strength. Aside from my upbringing, I have attended more surgeries in these past three years than you have *in your head*."

Something dark flared within his eyes as he rattled her face. "I bet you fainted every time."

She shoved his hand away. "I only fainted once."

He tsked, not breaking their gaze. "You moths don't talk to each other. It's called the flame." He studied her for a long moment. "I have already visited a government solicitor and was advised, given your Hindu heritage, that having you written into my testament is not enough. If anyone, be it my mother or Vidocq, contests it for whatever reason, you won't see a farthing, but as my wife, your rights will be what I need them to be. Unbreakable. As such, we marry tomorrow morning at eleven at the Registration Office on Larkin's Lane. They permit the declaration of marriage outside of any one religion."

Her consciousness seemed to ebb. "You are asking me to

marry you for all the wrong reasons."

"How is it wrong that I want to protect you if I die?"

She swallowed. "I will not marry you for the sake of having access to your estate. You think that is what matters to me? *Do you*? I can financially oversee myself in this world."

"I need peace in this," he bit out, "and you will give me that peace, damn you. *Be there*."

"No. You will not force me to be a bride and then widow me by leaving."

A muscle in his jaw ticked. "Be at the Registration Office on Larkin's Lane. I will be there. I will be there waiting at exactly eleven. *Why*?" He leaned in and breathed out, "Because I love you."

Her heart popped.

He pointed and disappeared into the crowd.

Unfurling her trembling hands, she watched Ridley cross the expanse of the verandah, returning to a group of officers he had earlier been conversing with.

She lingered, unable to move or think or breathe or heave or anything.

How could he tell her of his love and then think he could leave her?

Kalpita bustled in with the flow of a pink veil and tsked from behind her ostrich fan, her dark eyes taunting. "Whatever was that about?"

Jemdanee tried to remain calm. "He means to leave to London and put himself in danger."

Kalpita paused and then patted her arm, the bangles on her wrist chiming. "She who cannot dance always blames the floor. You forget who is in my pocket: the Field Marshal. I will have my Charles put in an order that your Ridley cannot leave Calcutta or he will be arrested."

"That would have been brilliant except his mother is in danger and needs him."

Kalpita squinted and lowered her voice. "I will give you an amulet of a peacock bone dipped in gold. Wear it in his presence when the sun shines on the morrow so that it may glint and blind him into doing your will. Tie it around your wrist and secure the leather string to ensure it stays on. It will give you the outcome you seek."

Jemdanee gave the woman a withering look. "If peacock bones had that sort of power, all the peacocks in India would be dead."

"The power it holds is real. It was blessed by a *swami*," Kalpita insisted. "Use it."

Jemdanee paused at seeing Ridley grab two bottles of champagne from servers.

Because one was not enough.

He stalked past her and into the darkness of the night.

She almost grabbed Kalpita. Given the amulet *did* involve a bone, she wouldn't be surprised if it *did* hold power over Evan Oswald Ridley. "Where is it?"

"In my chamber."

CHAPTER TEN

2:14 a.m.
Spence's Hotel

Male shouts dug through the haze.

Startling awake, Jemdanee staggered up in her bed and drew in her limbs, realizing she had fallen asleep. She glanced toward the still closed door leading into Ridley's room.

He still hadn't come.

She flopped toward the shuttered window.

A sizable group of boisterous men beyond the shutters drunkenly bellowed out an off-key harmony. "*Come, come let us driiiink. Let us driiiink! Let us driiiink, let us driiiink, 'tis in vaaaaain to think like fooools on grief or saaadness. Let our money flyyyyyy and our sorrows diiiie! All worldly caaaare is maaadness. But wine, wine, wine, wine, wine, wiiiine and good cheeeeer, will spite our feeeear...*"

She grudgingly got up, adjusting the silk robe over her nude body that was sweltering in the stagnant heat of the night.

Damn the gods and the regiment and Ridley.

"*Come, come let us driiiink. Let us driiiink! Let us driiiink, let us driiiink!*"

She trudged over past the dark shapes of the room and found the massive window whose shutters were outlined by the moon and torchlights beyond it.

Pushing aside the shutters and the insect netting, she tightened her robe around her waist and was about to yell toward the drunken crowd gathered around torches when—

She paused, her breath hitching.

Ridley was… with them.

She recognized his large, muscled frame garbed in all black that was highlighted by the torches that illuminated the sheen of the fabric. His dark hair was heavily windblown and his black cravat had been removed and hanging around his exposed throat, as if announcing he belonged to no one.

Hidden in the darkness of her room, Jemdanee watched him.

Ridley swigged from what appeared to be a third bottle of champagne, talking loudly over the drunken singing of the others gathered.

Oyo, yes. Drink. You will need it.

He paused and jerked toward the direction of the massive gate behind them. He held out a rigid hand to the men around him, cutting it through the night air to command momentary silence.

Their voices all faded as they scrambled to their booted feet.

Jemdanee quickly pushed herself up against the sill to better see past the darkness of the terrace.

A half-naked woman lingered at the terrace gate, rattling the gates and calling and calling to them in Hindi.

The officers snorted.

One of them sat. "Christ. Every last one of these dots only ever want to get fucked. If I had *that* much money, I damn well wouldn't be an officer!"

The men roared with laughter.

Turning, Ridley whipped the bottle at one of them, shattering glass. "The only whores I see are the ones laughing." Thudding the head of the officer hard with a hand, Ridley adjusted his leather belt holding his pistol and turned. He limped over to the woman in the far distance, staggering against his weight and what appeared to be the drink.

Jemdanee's throat tightened knowing the justice seeker in him was in trouble.

The officers all leaned over and hooted in the darkness in between swigging brandy. "Why settle for one Hindu cunt, Ridley?

Stick it into *more*!"

Jemdanee almost gasped as she watched Ridley pass through the gate. He removed his coat and draped it over the woman's nudity whom he tugged up against himself.

He led the woman in his coat into the moonlit darkness.

She knew Ridley was the only gentleman left in India.

It riled her.

Shoving her bare feet into slippers, and not caring that she had nothing beneath her robe (this was India for vine sake!), she grabbed a leather satchel full of rupees for the girl. She eyed the machete Ridley had propped against the wall of her room a day earlier.

He was about to meet the girl who grew up on the streets.

Whirling it up, she swiveled off the ledge of the window, gauging the first floor fall. Easy. She tossed the machete, letting it clang onto the terrace and using the trellis, climbed down onto the ground floor of the terrace, landing with a thud.

The officers all paused and stared.

She tightened the belt on her robe ensuring her breasts weren't falling out past the fabric, snatched up her machete and stared down every officer as if she were the Field Marshal himself. "The only gentleman in India has clearly left. Therefore my Hindu *cunt* will join him." She pointed the machete at each head. "You may all claim to be officers, but the only rank or right you wear are the ones you have yet to push out of your puckered arses."

They said nothing.

Positioning the machete, she bustled past them and across the expanse of the terrace toward the gate Ridley had disappeared past.

She worried that the woman was leading him to trouble.

Bengali gangs sent prostitutes to find white men all the time.

She tightened her hold on the machete, its weight reminding her all too much of its power, and quickly tucked the satchel of rupees into her robe pocket.

Jogging her way past the gate of the hotel, she paused, seeing Ridley and the woman disappear around a corner past the Government House. Her heart pounded to keep up, her breaths as uneven as her running steps that echoed through the darkness of the night.

When she finally did catch up, she soundlessly followed at a distance through narrow dirt pathway that wound them into the surrounding city of Calcutta. The stench of urine and the putrid rot of fruit from abandoned carts overtook her nostrils.

It was nothing compared to the fetor she'd known when she had been at the scene of that murder in London. A scene she could now easily barrel back into in the name of saving Ridley.

Eventually setting herself against the farthest darkened mud wall, Jemdanee watched as Ridley guided the half-naked woman toward her lantern-lit hovel.

The woman shoved him into a wall and frantically hitched up her sari above her waist, exposing herself completely to him despite his coat.

Jemdanee's throat tightened.

Ridley rattled the woman's grabbing hands, forcing her to release her uplifted sari, which he tugged downward. Digging into his inner waistcoat pocket, he placed a sizable amount of bank note rupees into those outstretched hands and squeezed them, offering in fluent Hindi, "You owe me nothing."

The dark-skinned woman paused at seeing the money being gifted, and glancing up at him, kissed his hands, then his chest, bowing to him repeatedly.

He put more money into her hands.

The woman peered up at him, startled.

She attempted to remove his coat to return it to him.

"Keep it." He buttoned the Indian woman back into it and propped up the collar on it, still speaking to her in Hindi.

The woman lingered, clinging to his coat.

He turned her and her shoulders toward the hovel. "Go."

The prostitute glanced back at him and after lingering, disappeared inside.

Jemdanee swallowed in a reverence she knew she would always be cursed to feel.

Ridley, save us from the only thing that will ever hurt us: you.

Her slippered foot shifted, causing a rock to tumble toward him. She scrambled back further into the shadows.

He swung toward her, his own features hidden in the shadows which the lantern from the hovel no longer reached. His hand jumped to his leather belt as he snapped out his pistol and pointed it, the metal click announcing all that was left was the pull of a trigger. "Announce yourself." He said it in Hindi.

She gripped the machete hard and almost dropped the leather satchel of rupees, her breaths panicked. "Ridley! 'Tis me *Jemdanee*." She said it in English in case he couldn't understand her accent. "Kumar!"

He slowly lowered his pistol, uncocking it and shoved it into the holster of his belt.

Yanking the curtain leading into the hovel firmly shut, he limped toward her in the darkness and then towered, his Parisian cologne penetrating the night air. "What the hell are you doing here?"

She held out the satchel toward him. "This is for her."

Ridley took the satchel, weighing it. He eyed her and disappeared to deliver it into the hovel.

Reappearing, he propped himself against the wall beside her in the shadows, lingering close. He leaned down and flicked the lapel of her robe. "You don't appear to be... wearing *anything* beneath that," he slurred with a champagne tinged breath.

Her heart pounded as she gripped his wrist. "I waited for you but apparently you were too busy being productive and getting soused."

"Getting soused is a far better alternative than engaging in other forms of reckless behavior," he breathed. "Too many evils came to mind given you riled me and I opted for... the lesser one."

She rolled her eyes.

He cornered her to the stone wall that was barely lit by the moon and surrounding hovels. He shifted the machete intentionally against her hand, tilting the blade toward himself. "Were you going to defend her or... *me with this*?"

"I would have used it."

"I'm fucking Ridley. You don't save me, I save you."

May the world save itself. "And that is why you have a limp. Kali forbid you admit that I can swing a machete whilst you watch."

He nudged her with his knee. "Did you... leave Chunmun alone at the hotel?"

She paused. "*Haan*. Why?"

"What sort of mother are you?" he slurred. "Leaving an unattended wild animal for any period of time is *not* fucking advisable and I will most likely be… *paying for damages.*"

She heaved out a breath. "He is soundly sleeping in his room of choice and has your overlord rope to keep him from thinking he has to destroy anything."

He gave her a withering look. "How is it *everyone* is playing with *my* rope but us?"

If she didn't guide this conversation, nothing would. "Why are you going to London? You did not tell me."

He staggered closer and draped his arm against the wall, surveying her. "Some prick wants to play with my blood. It comes with the territory of my field."

She swallowed. "Had I not found you in that building, you would have died. You need more than yourself to get you through this."

He leaned in and dragged his champagne tinted tongue across her cheek. "It's inarguably late. Come." He grabbed her arm hard, startling her, and directed her with the strength of his body back through the streets, turning corners.

She glanced up at him in between the harried steps he forced them to take. She jogged to keep up with his long-legged steps, letting him hold onto her without any resistance, despite the severe grip of his fingers digging into her arm and robe, pinching her skin beneath. "Might you loosen your hold? I find it a bit tight. I think of shackles and London."

He glanced toward her, his features wavering.

Loosening his hold, he released her. Turning toward her, he tossed the machete she was holding, letting it clatter against the cobblestone. "Come to me, *mon ange.*"

Leaning toward her, he tossed her up hard, draping her in his muscled arms. "I may have a limp but I won't *ever* abide by it."

The warm night air seemed unbearably hotter as he adjusted her rigidly in his arms.

Her hands jumped to cling to his shoulders, her intake of breaths making it impossible for her to think. "What are you doing?"

"Ensuring you get home safely." He moved faster, his hold tightening.

She searched his face, trying to deliberately shut out any awareness of him. An awareness that wanted him more than she was prepared to admit. Her fingers gripped the buried rope that bound his bicep beneath his linen shirt.

He said nothing. His features were strained as if every step were walking through fire.

She used his earlier words against him and drawled, "Ridley, think of what we could do for London."

"Let me be the rickshaw and you the passenger. I'm driving."

She only let him carry her because she knew his pride meant more to him than the pain.

They entered through the terrace gates of the hotel, her still in his arms, as he strode back into the vast candlelit marble corridors of Spence's, his heavy booted steps echoing.

He never once glanced at her or said a word.

She peered up at him as he went up the stairs and eventually turned the corner toward their vast row of quarters.

A muscle ticked in his shaven jaw as he brought them to a halt before her darkened bedchamber. He thudded the door further open with his boot and angled her inside.

In the silence, he released her, purposefully letting her drag down the entire front of his body as he set her slippered feet down onto the marble floor. He held her gaze. "I am not in any condition to be engaging you. As such… I'll see you tomorrow at eleven."

Astounded that he was capable of being *rational* even when *soused*, it made her realize this man's mind was beyond her own comprehension.

A knot rose in her throat. "I will not become your wife only to then be abandoned. If I marry you, it will be for the purpose of standing by your side. Is that not what marriage is?"

His gold-flecked eyes were hazy in the dim candlelight. Despite their haziness, there was still a lethal calmness, strength and a warning. "Opposing me is *not* advisable." His voice turned to steel. "I would *never* forgive you if you force me to choose between us and your safety. Is that what you want? For me to choose?"

This was a war he was waging.

Only he was going into battle without any armor.

Holding his gaze, she did what any woman who sought to take back control: use what the gods gave her. She unraveled her silk robe and let it whisper down to her feet around them in the corridor, revealing her nudity. "Who says you will want to leave me once you have had me?"

Except for the dragging in of a breath that notably raised his broad chest, he only looked at her. Not at her nudity but her face. Her eyes. Her lips. Her nose.

Her heart jolted, feeling strangely more vulnerable that he was looking at her face. "There is far more below the chin," she offered.

He squinted. "I drank a lot of champagne for a reason," his voice held an ominous quality. "To ensure I didn't engage you."

Her breaths grew all the more uneven knowing she stood before him entirely naked and he hadn't even looked once. "Men usually drink to release inhibitions, not contain them."

His hazy eyes remained focused on her face. "Men usually don't have my level of intelligence even whilst sober."

"I will not argue with you on that based on the men you were drinking with." She lifted the unraveled weight of her black locks and arranged it over her own breasts.

His rugged expression now bordered on barely checked tolerance.

Unfazed, she held his gaze. "I once watched you try to destroy yourself in the name of what you defined as justice and I will *not* watch you do it again. If you leave in two days, I will leave in three. Three is a very symbolic number frequently used by my people. Siva is the third in the Trinity. He has three eyes, a trident, has three braids of hair and is the knower of three things: the past, the present and the future. The past has already left us, Ridley. We cannot change it. Not even you can. The present is what I now give you and if you will it, the future with me standing alongside even in the darkest times awaits." She gestured toward herself, skimming her fingers down her breasts toward her thighs and up again. "Consider *this* your farewell honorarium."

He stared. "I am… *intoxicated*, Jemdanee. Whittled. Temulentious. Flagonal. *Rummied*."

"Even *rummied*, you still appear to have a highly functioning use of the dictionary."

A muscle twitched in his jaw.

She leaned in and tapped at his jaw. "Earlier, you accused me of being incapable of trusting you," she countered. "I am offering you the ultimate trust. Me in your arms when you have

169

no control. How is that for trust?"

Ridley nodded and skimmed her appearance intently. He nudged her hair back over her shoulders to expose her breasts. Still methodically perusing her nudity, he leaned back, staggering and slammed the door behind them as if to ensure Chunmun wouldn't see anything.

She jumped but set her chin to ensure he knew she wasn't intimidated.

The moonlight through the open window was the only thing illuminating the darkness.

Jerking her toward himself with digging fingers, he molded her nudity to himself. "Say it."

She melted, gripping his muscled body in an attempt to savor every breath she was taking. She slid the cravat still hanging around his throat from his neck and let it slip from her fingers. "What would you like me to say?"

"That you love me."

She dragged her fingers up over his broad shoulders. To say it would be to lose control over him. "Do I?"

A champagne-tinted breath escaped him. "Be there tomorrow," he rasped. "Give me peace."

She tightened her hold on his waistcoat. "Invite me to stand at your side and I will marry you, but not as a silent partner. I would never agree to that."

He leaned down and set his nose to her nose, half-staggering to do it. "You're not coming to London. You barely reach my fucking shoulder. It would be like putting a marble into the hand of a lunatic."

"Marbles roll fast," she assured him in between uneven breaths.

"Never fast enough. I have seen enough to know." His hands dragged down her bare shoulders, digging into her skin and nudity, while holding her gaze. He stepped back, thudding the wall. "Put your hands against the wall. Face it."

Her breath hitched. He was asking her to face the wall.

Like a criminal.

She swallowed hard, trying to remain calm knowing what he was asking of her.

"*Trust*," he said. "Face the wall, *mon dévot*."

Those words sent a tremor through her.

She edged around his towering frame, unable to breathe, and

trusting him completely, she slowly, slowly set her hands against the roughness of the wall, flattening her palms to keep them from quaking.

What was she doing? Why was she doing this?

For his soul?

"Widen your stance," he intoned.

Any normal woman in the nude would have fled the room by now.

She blamed the street urchin in her.

Edging her nude stance to a more widened position, she waited, demonstrating she was in his power. Demonstrating the wetness pulsing between her thighs was overtaking whatever common sense she had learned.

Ridley came up from behind. Reaching around her, he set each large hand beside hers against the wall she faced, his heat pulsing into every inch of her skin as he pressed his fully clothed muscled body into her nude backside.

His nearness was overwhelming.

The room swayed and she with it.

He didn't move.

Only his regimented breaths in her hair made her aware he really was there. He stayed behind her as if trying to make her aware that even without touching her she was his.

A shiver of desperate need flooded her with a wetness that she could feel dewing between her thighs. "At this pace, you won't be there at eleven, either," she choked out, her mind leaving her. The base of her throat throbbed along with her exposed skin as she waited for his response.

His large thumb traced one of her fingers still pressed against the wall. "Don't talk."

She inhaled sharply at the contact as if he'd penetrated her to the bone.

His finger traced and tingled her one finger, his calloused touch rough. "Don't move."

She breathed lightly, roused by his words and his nearness.

He set his lips against her hair nudging it, while keeping her contained to the wall. "What happens to you now? Do you know?" His mellow baritone was edged with control. His one hand left the wall, skimming her arm and shoulder, as his forefinger now traced down, down the back of her spine.

She almost stumbled into the wall.

"*I said don't move*," he bit out into her ear.

His hand struck her derriere hard, startling her into gasping against the sting.

She quaked, her breaths almost puffing out, half expecting to be struck again.

"*That* is for attempting to seduce me. Do you think your body means more to me than your fucking life?" His hand struck her derriere hard again, startling her into gasping again. "*Do you?*"

They hadn't even gotten to the penetration.

A part of her was frightened out of her unhinged mind.

His hand rubbed her derriere hard, digging his fingers into it and making her writhe as she stumbled to stay upright against the wall.

"Is pain your game? Is that it?" he asked hotly into her ear from behind, his hands unbuttoning his trousers and shoving down the flap. "Do you want it to be?"

She closed her eyes in riled yearning, her breaths audible and shaky. She tried to hold up equally quaking limbs, chanting to herself not to slide before he even got to her.

The velvet tip of his rigid cock traced and dragged across the area of the skin on her bum he had earlier struck.

She swallowed.

He lingered close behind her again, the open flap of his trousers grazing her rear and taunting her with its heat. "Don't move." He dipped his head toward her bare shoulder, letting the tip of his tongue slide across her skin and entire shoulder.

Her nails scraped the wall as she swayed.

Positioning himself behind her, he gently gripped her nub, holding it between his fingers. He flicked.

Her body rattled against the core jarring sensations. She gasped.

Leaning more heavily into her, he dug his head into the curve of her arm and fingered her hard without letting her breathe past each rising wave.

With legs quaking, she dug her nails hard into wall, writhing.

He slowly wedged his large finger into her wetness. "Breathe." He pressed his finger *deep* into her, thrusting it hard up to the hilt.

She choked against the sharp pinch.

He eased the depth of his hold and pumped her wetness gently, circling and dipping, as if simulating his cock. He introduced another finger and pumped, and another, working and working it in, angling against her nub so she could feel it.

She gasped, spurts of coiling pleasure rattling her.

Quaking breaths escaped her knowing three of his fingers were inside of her.

He removed them, sliding his well moistened fingers toward the crack of her rear and sucked her throat from behind. Tilting his hips into her, he now used his other hand to grab his exposed cock, tracing its thick, stiff velvet length up against her backside.

She instinctively pushed back against that length.

He tapped it twice against her rear as if to announce he understood her need, but shifted his hips away so that his cock was outside of reach. His hands now curved upward and toward her front, grazing her breasts. Circling her nipples. His two hands veered downward between the wetness of her thighs again and its heat that pulsed in need.

"Remember this," he rasped. His fingers spread her folds with one hand as his other hand, dipped his finger against her moisture and then rubbed her nub again and again. First slow, then intent, then faster, then frantically.

A tremor overtook her body that seized her breath. It was a tremor she knew that was going to make her yell far too soon, far too quickly and without any control on her part. He wasn't stopping. His fingers flicked her nub so fast, she was choking for air.

The pulsing knot within rose as she cried out against the waves assaulting her body, too strong for her to fight. She staggered, hands sliding against the wall as her closely nearing peak shook her limbs.

He flexed, his body tensing as he frigged her relentlessly. "What do you want? Say it."

"*You*," she gasped. Moaning in a desperate effort to remain upright against the sensations, she tossed back her head to ready herself for the swelling roar of release.

She staggered.

He caught her, his muscled arm jumping beneath her to keep her from falling. He removed his fingers and dug his teeth into her. Hard. Harder. *Too hard!*

She flinched, the pinch reminding her that he hadn't even mounted her.

He slowly released his pinching hold of her skin. "No."

Raising her upright, he molded her against the mass of his still clothed body, and dragged his hands down her throat and to her breasts whose nipples he grazed before cupping them both his digging fingers. "I'm denying you for not respecting me," he whispered, his lips buried into her hair. "I'm denying you for erasing my peace. Do you understand?"

She swallowed, his muscled body holding her tighter.

He kissed her head hard and released her. Buttoning his trousers, he towered behind her for a lingering moment. "Good night, my love."

With that, he turned away and stalk-limped through the moonlit darkness of her room. Opening the door that separated their rooms, he stepped past it and slammed it, leaving her alone in the darkness.

A click resounded, announcing he had even bolted the door between them.

In between heaving, disbelieving breaths that he had left and had denied them both, she slid onto her side on the floor like jelly being shaken from a spoon.

Her face blazed from the heat of knowing his fingers had been inside of her.

She heard his heavy steps cross his room.

Jemdanee sat up, nude, and edging forward, turned her hot cheek against the coolness of the wall and knowing he could hear her, said, "A part of me knew you were going to do that."

He paused and said through the wall in a low tone, "I'll breathe better knowing I didn't hurt you." Something hit the wall hard followed by a crash against the nearest wall, shattering and sending a tremor through the floor.

She stilled, knowing it had to do with his limp. "Ridley?"

"I'm drunk."

An exasperated breath escaped her lips. She awkwardly crawled across the marble floor naked to her robe and with quaking limbs barely managed to tug it on.

"*Bonne nuit*," he rasped. "I have to be out of the stables by seven to… oversee file cases for the Field Marshal. I'll see you at eleven."

She stood, after stumbling. "Good-night, Ridley."

He said nothing.

Blinking rapidly, she resorted to the one thing she thought she never would.

In the light of the moon that peered in through the open shutters, she dug through the banyan box that held the amulet Kalpita had given her.

Jemdanee dragged out the peacock bone dipped in gold, wound it around her wrist and secured the leather string to ensure it stayed in place. She kissed it knowing Ridley needed the magic her gods were known for. If he thought he knew the true meaning of passion, she was about to redefine it for him in a way no woman had ever dared.

I protect thee from harm by becoming the very bone lodged in your sternum.

For this was now a war to protect his life and she was waging it.

Well before the sun rose, Jemdanee dressed, chalked her teeth and braided her hair tight. Gathering Chunmun into her arms, she quietly left Spence's and crossed the dirt road past the gates to the Government House where she had left a key hidden in a nearby pot to permit access.

She used it and entered the back servant corridors, veering into the massive kitchens to do something she hadn't done in a long time.

Not since her days with *maa*.

Chunmun darted out and toward the direction of the gardens, as he always did.

She, on the other hand, made sour black bread.

Slapping and kneading dough on the stone slab, she eventually tossed the prepared dough onto the fire and thought of nothing but Ridley and the sort of father he would make.

He would offer that child the world.

Knowing time was fleeting, she gathered several more items from the kitchen, including the bread she had freshly made, and slipped the key back beneath the pot, then turned toward the vast gardens. "Chunmun!"

He darted toward her and climbed up her sari, making her smile. She cradled his head and murmured, "We have to ensure he knows he is loved."

Chunmun perked at the wrapped bread and mangoes she carried.

"This is not for you." She smoothed his head and crossed through the gates with him, back toward Spence's as the quiet of the morning settled.

Veering into the stables, Chunmun hopped off her shoulder and disappeared into a stack of hay.

She watched through the hinged door as the sun started to smear the vast copper sky with color and light beyond the tamarind trees.

The muggy heat of the day was already ebbing in with the warmth of the breeze.

Seating herself on a crate with her gathered items, she waited by Ridley's stallion.

She eventually rose.

Readying his saddle, she tucked the sour black bread she had made into his leather satchel, along with a few mangoes and a flask of water.

The quaking in her limbs and the feel of his hands and his lips in her hair and on her body surrounded her. It was bittersweet, for she knew it had only resulted in her pleasure but his pain.

A pain she swore to erase.

Hearing heavy steps approaching beyond the stables, she tapped her forehead and lips in a quick chant to the gods asking for strength.

With the whirl of a dagger he sheathed into the leather belt fastened around his waist, Ridley hefted his weight onto the cane and stalked into the shade of the mud-walled stable. Tucking a ledger beneath his arm, he adjusted the stiff sleeves of a uniform with the flexing bulge of his biceps.

Her mouth went dry, knowing she hadn't even seen any of him or that muscle or nudity last night. It had been dark and he had made her face the wall. "*Namaste*, Ridley."

He paused, his dark hair falling into eyes that were the eerie color of gold amber.

Jemdanee set her hands together, pressing the tied amulet on her right wrist momentarily between both wrists. To blind him with her light. She held his gaze for a long moment to show him his soul was hers to protect.

He adjusted the ledger beneath his arm. "I have to go." His husky voice was final.

Smoothing the mane of his horse, she offered, "You still owe me a lesson on your shadow language. You have not taught it to me. *Oleald Ekcle Surogou*. Freedom is mine. That is what you once told me. That is why I have the freedom to protect you and I will."

Ridley rounded the horse and veered in close, taking the reins. He said nothing.

"I will only marry you if you take me to London."

"Might we not do this right now?" he rasped. "I have a headache of the worst sort."

"That is what happens to a man who imbibes."

"I thank you for yet another useless lecture."

She sighed. "Are you in need of a restorative?"

"No." Turning away, he dug through his leather satchel attached to the saddle, inserting the ledger he held into it. He paused at seeing the wrapped black bread.

He eyed her. Surveying the amulet, he slowly shifted toward her and lowered his chin.

She dragged in a breath, sensing the peacock bone dipped in gold was already *thawing* and *molding* and *whispering* to him. In that moment, she felt like she was eight, waving her god-carved rod and chanting the world to kneel to her command. "I snuck into the kitchens of the Government House and made bread for you this morning."

She felt stupid saying it, but leaned in and pointed to the bread in case he didn't know what she was referring to. "I also packed a few mangoes and a flask of water. Be certain you eat."

"One would think we were already married." Pulling out the wrapped bread, he set it aside on the stall and retied his satchel, turning his horse away from it.

Jemdanee's lips parted. "Are you not going to eat it?"

Ridley leaned in, while holding her gaze. "Are you saying

177

you want to watch me eat it?"

She pulled in her chin. "A thank you would have been appreciated."

"I thank you in French: *merci*." Unravelling the bread, he tore a piece off, which he pushed into his mouth. He chewed and paused. Tearing off a bigger piece, he pushed that into his mouth, as well, and chewed more enthusiastically. "You made this?"

Sensing he liked it, she brightened. "*Haan. Maa* and I used to make it every Thursday morning and sold them to neighbors. We made it so often, the recipe has stayed with me."

He widened his muscled stance, stiffening against his leg. "It's good." In between chews, he held her gaze. "The breaking of actual bread between us is a bit of a cliché."

She bit back a smile.

He veered in close. "*You*, my dear, should *not* have given yourself to me last night. That was incredibly stupid. You could have gotten hurt."

She leaned in, not in the least bit intimidated. "What is stupid is leaving behind the other half of your soul known as me. You need me. Smashing glass in your name is only the beginning of what I will do."

He stepped back. "Don't do this. *Don't*."

Swinging a muscled leg up and over his saddled horse, to which he adjusted his leg with the grit of his teeth, he glanced toward the entrance of the stables, then down at her. "A peacock bone amulet. How utterly… pittoresque. Do you even know how to use it?"

She glanced toward her amulet and back up at him.

"Is it yours?" he asked.

She eyed him. "No. It is Kalpita's."

He rumbled out a laugh, startling her.

For him to laugh (a sound she'd never heard!) meant it truly *was* enchanted. His eyes had brightened and his face became doubly glorious. "Why are you laughing?"

Shaking his head as he rolled his tongue against the inside of his cheek, he smirked and slowly shook his from side to side. His amusement faded as he adjusted the reins in his hands. "I'll see you at eleven." His amber eyes captured hers. "May the gods love you for being what you have always been. Hope and humor and *c'est la vie.*" He glanced toward the stables and whistled, holding up bread. "Chunmun."

Scrambling out of the hay that scattered and clung to his fur, Chunmun peered up at them, then jumped up onto the wooden railing, landing onto Ridley's shoulder.

She blinked rapidly. "What are you doing?"

He held her gaze. "Say good-bye to him. He won't be coming back. It will hurt, but his life will hold more meaning. He will still love you."

Tears overwhelmed her, feeling as if she were saying good-bye to far more than Chunmun. A sob escaped her as she held out her arms. "Might I… hold him one last time?"

He nodded and leaned down, passing off a piece of bread to her fingers.

Chunum jumped toward her and nuzzled his furry head into her shoulder, yanking on her hair hard. She grazed his small hand which took the bread and watched him eat it. Cradling his warmth one last time, she whispered into his fur, "I will miss you, Chunmun. Name your children after me and tell them about all the fruit I gave you." Swallowing hard, she kissed him one last time and passed him back off to Ridley.

Ridley held out more bread to Chunmun, whose tail wrapped around his throat. Ridley smoothed that small head, still holding her gaze. "He knows the jungle. He survived it well before you ever came into his life. Don't forget that."

She dashed away the tears rolling down her cheeks. "Do you speak of him or yourself?"

"Both." His voice grew faint. "Be there at eleven at the Registration Office. 15 Larkin's Lane. If you are not there, Jemdanee, you are choosing to end what we share and that is for you to decide."

Fisting the leather reins, he turned the horse and kicked his boots into its sides, riding past her and out from the stable. With the trail of dust, he disappeared through the iron gates with a gallop into the already crowded street with Chunmun.

Sobbing, she almost fell against the stall and touched the amulet with trembling fingers.

It made… Ridley laugh. That, in and of itself, had been magic.

She never thought it possible.

Eyeing the empty stable, she hurried out into the heat of the sun and back toward the grounds of the Government House to find Kalpita whom she knew was somewhere outside. She'd seen her.

Kalpita was always out this time of morning.

She eventually found her twenty minutes later sitting beside one of the fountains with her bare feet in the water, her sari hitched up to her knees and a bowl of sliced papaya at her fingertips. Her face was upturned to the shade of the trees and the wind that rustled through, her eyes regally closed.

One would think she wasn't a servant but a queen.

With a miserable breath, Jemdanee hitched up her own sari to her knees and splashed the cool water, spraying her.

Kalpita gasped, opening her eyes, and seeing her, tsked.

Grabbing a piece of papaya and pushing it into her mouth, Jemdanee seated herself on the sandstone ledge of the fountain. In between chews that were soft and melty sweet, she leaned in toward Kalpita and held up the peacock amulet, rattling it. "You told me to use this to command him, but you never actually told me what it is for. Might you tell me?"

Kalpita paused, seeing the amulet on Jemdanee's wrist. She eyed her and then primly took Jemdanee's hand, positioning it toward herself. With a quick fluttering of fingers, Kalpita unraveled the leather string and tied it on her own wrist, patting it into place. "I had too much *hariya* last night. I was supposed to give you the one with the three leather strings, not two."

Jemdanee lowered her chin. "*Kalpita*. That did not answer my question. Ridley *laughed* when I told him it was yours. He never laughs. Ever. Why did he laugh?"

The woman pertly adjusted the gold amulet, then glanced around, as if to ensure there wasn't a soldier or another servant in site, then leaned in and said in a flurry of Hindi, "I will give you the other one. That one has not been marked."

She blinked. "Marked?"

"*Haan.* Our modern people snub their noses to the ancient ways of India, but it holds great power. All things tantric leads to the root of life that rests within the pleasure of one's soul."

Oyo. "I am asking you to define its power."

"It is said the moment a man rubs his seed onto it, his soul is bound to its wearer for eternity. And… the Field Marshal and I

180

are bound."

Jemdanee choked and repeatedly plunged her bare wrist into the water, frantically scrubbing it until it stung at the thought that the Field Marshal's seed had—

Kalpita puckered her lips. "I will give you the one that was not rubbed by him."

Jemdanee flicked her wrists and swiped it against her sari, shuddering.

That head wobbled. "You were desperate and the rest was *hariya*." Kalpita leaned in and with a tapping finger to her hand, said in a sultry tone, "It works. I have been unable to get rid of the Field Marshal since. All he wants is me and *mmmmm*. Beware the golden bone of a peacock." She nudged her.

One good thing came out of it.

It amused Ridley enough to make him laugh. That was magic at its finest. "Kalpita?"

"Jee?"

"Ridley asked me to marry him. Am I wrong to deny him given he flings himself at danger?"

Those dark eyes met hers, growing serious. "Life bound to a white man who dedicates his life to danger is too much of a hardship. 'Tis why I will never wed my Charles despite my love. For we will suffer, as will our children."

Jemdanee sniffed hard and nodded.

Kalpita sighed and rubbed her arm. "Assist me in the kitchens today. Might you?"

Anything to prevent her from thinking about the pain she was about to deliver to Ridley. That pain, however, was going to remind him that what they shared would never be reduced to a piece of parchment he wanted her to sign for all the wrong reasons.

As his wife, he could legally demand and prevent her from abiding by his command.

But as his Hindu *bibi…* he had no say. None. At. All.

11:23 a.m.—15 Larkin's Lane, Registration Office

Her absence bespoke of a childish insubordination that made him want to smash every window out of every building on the block.

She thought she was loving him.

She wasn't.

What she was doing was murdering what little peace he had left in his head and in his heart.

"I think it is fairly obvious she isn't coming," the Field Marshal confided.

In the silence of the stuffy registrar room, Ridley half-nodded, numb.

Rounding the desk, Ridley set aside the folder he had brought with him, containing his will, and commenced systematically organizing the entire registrar desk.

The Field Marshal eyed him, his heavily tanned face wary. "What are you doing?"

"Giving her seven minutes." Ridley aligned the ledgers, corked the inkwells, set the quills back into their holders, using his fingers to smooth each end of the feather, and even closed the registrar book, setting it back onto its designated silver tray. "Were you able to look into any ships?"

"Yes. Four officers can escort you however far you need them to." The Field Marshal trooped. "There are no ships departing out of Calcutta for another month, given the last fleet of merchants left this week, but from my understanding there is a naval ship departing in five days out of Bombay. If you leave by tomorrow night, you'll be there on time. I can issue you a government signature missive to get you on board."

A ragged breath escaped Ridley, knowing he had four months of travel ahead of him, not including the coach taking him into Bombay. "I will take it." Removing the handkerchief bearing Jemdanee's smeared red lip rouge from the pocket of his morning attire, Ridley grazed his finger against it and stared at the linen.

He might as well be looking at her blood.

He'd always known that involving any woman in his life would put her in peril.

That was the price of letting the world know that he refused to kneel to injustice. Only now that injustice was bleeding across the hands of everyone.

It was like being married to Elizabeth all over again.

For he was back to loving a woman beyond his control. Beyond his reach.

Jemdanee was trying to dominate a very dangerous game she didn't understand. A game she had never played. In his name, she was reaching her hand for a pair of dice without realizing an ax would fall the moment her fingers grazed the ivory.

It was up to him to end her reach.

With the tightening of his shaven jaw, he walked around the entire desk and whipped and snapped the rouge-smeared linen so hard across its wood surface, thick dust plumed into the air around them.

The Field Marshal coughed and winced against the dust, waving a gloved hand while sending the shoulder tassels on his uniform swaying. "Whatever are you… *doing*?" He coughed.

"It needed dusting." Ridley shook his head in grudging annoyance. "If they cannot take pride in their registrars, what *can* they take pride in? Their funerals?" Trying to further distract himself from thinking about the fact that Jemdanee wasn't coming, he folded the handkerchief down to a perfect small square, then tucked it back into his waistcoat.

Why did he let Jemdanee into his heart knowing he wouldn't be able to keep her?

He quickly dug into the other pocket and removed a wad of rupee bank notes. He unfolded it and thumbed through its hundreds.

The Field Marshal lifted a brow. "You count them as if they were fives."

"I sold an entire room of books before I left London." He tossed over a thousand into the payment basket. "Based off the dust, they fucking need it."

Ridley grudgingly folded the remaining wad of rupees and tucked it away. He adjusted the gold ring on his finger, mentally preparing himself for the game he knew he had to play. "We have waited long enough." It hurt. How could she do this? How could she do this to his need to protect her in the only way he knew how? If he died, she would have nothing.

The Field Marshal lingered. "What do you want me to do?"

"I don't leave until tomorrow night. I will ensure my will reflects the decision she has made. I cannot very well do more than that." Rounding the desk again, he dragged his hair out of his eyes, then methodically opened drawers, scanning the contents of each one. He closed one. He closed two.

"What are you doing now?"

Ridley thudded a sander out onto the desk from one of the drawers, rattling the inkwells.

Holding the Field Marshal's gaze, Ridley patted the desk. "Everything is in place and ready for the next happy couple. It simply won't be me or you. Our careers ensured that."

The man's mouth twitched.

Leaning toward the desk, Ridley grabbed the folder he had brought with him and removed his watch. Flicking open the gold casing, he glanced at it. "Whoever thought I would ever see the day when women rule over men with the same disregard we rule over them." Riled, he tucked his pocket watch back into his waistcoat. "She decided. It's over."

The Field Marshal sighed. "Shall we proceed as planned?"

Rounding the desk with his folder, Ridley pointed at him. "Yes. Arrest her the moment she tries to leave Calcutta. No shackles, please."

"I wasn't planning on it."

They stalked out and down the aisle beyond, falling into stride with each other's regimented, stalking steps.

They left the building as if *they* had gotten married.

CHAPTER ELEVEN

L ong after everything had grown still, save the call of koels in the distance beyond the windows, a click made her pause.

A knock on their adjoining door made her glance up in astonishment from the book she was reading. She set her knuckles against her teeth as if the dead had creaked open their caskets, knowing Ridley was finally done being miffed.

Heart pounding, she crawled out of her bed, shoving aside her phytology book. Clasping a hand over her mouth to keep herself from breathing too loud, she quickly crossed the room and unlatched the door leading to his bedchamber.

She swung it open, ensuring the unmarked gold-dipped peacock bone wrapped on her wrist was ready to control this entire situation.

Peering into his *diya* lit room, her lips parted.

His broad back still to her, Ridley was shirtless and smoking a cheroot. With the shifting of taut, bunched muscles, he shook out the linen of his bed that had almost blown off the mattress due to the open window and mounting wind.

He smoothed the linen with the rigid sweep of his scarred hand, the hemp rope bundled around his shifting bicep.

She lingered, unable to even wheeze.

Leaning over the bed, he closed the window enough to keep the wind from disturbing the net and sheets. "Were you reading?" he asked matter-of-factly over his shoulder as if he were fully dressed.

She fingered the doorframe she leaned against for support. "*Haan*," she breathed out.

Taking a drag of the cheroot, he blew out the smoke. "Are you coming in or not?"

She entered his room and closed their adjoining door behind herself.

Turning back toward him, she eased out a steadying breath, feeling as if she were finally meeting the real Ridley.

He removed his boots, letting them thud onto the marble floor. "Latch the door," he offered past the cheroot dangling from his masculine lips.

She hesitated but… latched it. "Why are you asking me to latch it?"

Easing out smoke, he removed the cheroot from his lips. "Because I wanted to see if you would do it. And guess what? You did. You obey some orders."

She crinkled her nose. "Based off that mocking tone, do you want me to leave?"

"No." He tapped the ash off the cheroot and searched her face. "How was your day?"

She pressed a hand to her cheek in an effort to remain calm and drifted toward him. "Long."

The hiss of the tobacco glowed as he glanced down at her with brooding features. "Mine, too. Aside from being jilted, I had to cancel on Dunning, which made me feel like an even bigger prick. Not to prioritize, but I'm giving the boy my afternoon tomorrow. It's not like you need me."

She lowered her chin. "I did not realize you had it in you to be a father."

He stared her down. "I did not realize you had it in you to jilt me." He reached down and tapped at the peacock bone, holding her gaze. "Don't insult yourself or me. You aren't going to need that."

"Then why invite me into your room?" she countered. "What did you want?"

Looking toward the net-draped open window before them,

he eased out smoke through his teeth into the night air around them. "Back in the land of England, we call this talking. In France, we call it something else given my shirt is off. Choose whichever suits you."

She lingered, awed by the candlelight illuminating the squared tanned muscles of his chest and every band of sinew that defined a stomach that did not even look real. The overly defined bulk of his arms showed scars.

He was… *beautiful.*

A god.

Seven of them. Maybe even another hundred.

He tapped more ash off his cheroot. "How about we get to the point of this evening?" Sticking the cheroot into his mouth, he stepped toward her and yanked her up and into his muscled arms hard, just before her knees collapsed.

He swung her back to the bed.

Jemdanee clung to him, her pulse roaring. Her chest quaked.

"Are you all right?" It was mocking. He tightened his hold around her body and the lower half of her sari that was beginning to unravel. "The look on your face might as well be a scream heard in the middle of the night."

She held his gaze and remolded her lips, nose and eyes. "How is that?"

The cheroot twitched against his lips. "Worse." He set her onto the softness of the bed past the mosquito net. "You've survived this long. Relax."

Her arms thudded into the mattress hard enough to make the linen billow. "You make relaxing impossible." She sank deeper into the mattress like fruit wobbling in gelatin.

Ridley continued to smoke what little remained of the cheroot and eyed her from where he stood at the side of the bed. "We're going to talk about what happens tomorrow night." Shifting forward and toward her, he stretched himself alongside her and propped his dark head against his hand. "I leave at exactly ten at night."

Jemdanee turned toward him against the pillow. "Why not wait until morning?"

He searched her face. "Traveling at night has its perils, but it's less straining without the heat. I rise early tomorrow morning. My trunks depart with me into the barracks and then into a

187

military coach from there in the evening. The hotel is already paid for throughout these next ten months. The owner has instructions to ensure this entire floor remains yours. You're across the street from the compound which will further ensure your safety should you need anything from the Field Marshal. Tomorrow night, meet me at the old banyan tree of the Government House at nine o'clock. That gives us an hour to say *adieu*. Be there at exactly nine. If you're late by even a minute, I'll leave without saying good-bye at all. Do you understand?"

It would not keep her from following. "I understand."

"Good." Taking up a section of her unbound hair, he brought it to his lips. "No peach oil?"

She lowered her chin. "Are you attempting to seduce me, Mr. Ridley?"

He held out the still glowing cheroot between two large fingers, observing it. "No." His low voice matched the disquiet in his amber eyes. "I'm attempting to enjoy this. You. Me. *Joie de vivre*. Equanimity. Quintessence."

If Casanova had a very well-educated nemesis, Ridley would be it.

She stared him down. "I would reach for the dictionary but at the moment, you are in the way."

He rolled the cheroot. "I *am* the way, Jemdanee. Never forget it."

She gave him a withering look.

He tapped her cheek. "What did you do today aside from break my heart?"

She set her chin. "I assisted Kalpita in the kitchens."

"Were your hands weighed by too much dough at eleven this morning?"

A soft breath escaped her. "If I legally bind myself to you, Ridley, you will have more say over me than I do myself. That is the way of the law and marriage. And given your decision to go into London without me, I prefer you not own me."

He said nothing.

"The decision I made this morning was not based off of how I feel for you."

He said nothing.

"Are you angry?" she pressed.

He stared her down, nodding. "Very. But I am choosing to

set that aside in this moment knowing we won't see each other for some time. Maybe even never again if things go badly."

Her throat tightened. She held up her black diamond ring. "So much for eternal commitment."

Edging closer, he held out the cheroot. "Take this."

Jemdanee took what remained of the cheroot he offered, her fingers grazing his. She brought the last of the cheroot to her lips as he watched.

They held each other's gaze in silence.

He leaned over her, searching her face, and then lowered his head, hovering the heat of his mouth close to hers. "Keep it between your lips. Don't move."

She stilled, the cheroot tilting out of her mouth and almost touching his shaven chin.

Holding her gaze, he lowered his mouth until the burning end of the cheroot singed his lip.

She winced for him, startling back as hot ash fell from its end and onto her chest. She coughed and blinked, swatting away the ash. She glared at him and his mouth that now had a mark flaring red on his upper lip. "Why did you—"

"*My*. Look at that unending concern." He squinted, his mouth took on an unpleasant twist. "She did the same to my heart this morning, but for some reason is more startled by the blister on my lip." Snatching the cheroot from her, he leaned back in agitation, reaching out a muscled arm and set the stub of the cheroot into the pan on the nightstand.

Rolling back toward her, he remained propped on his hand. "Learn to better appropriate your concern, because right now… I'm not fucking impressed."

She eyed the burn mark on his lip. "There is something wrong with you."

"Or maybe I have reached a level of intelligence others have yet to understand. An ordinary life is for ordinary men, Jemdanee, which I will never be. You seem to forget that. So stop treating me like other men." He sat up and swung off the bed with a thud.

Walking over to the sideboard, he tossed up a tin and removing its lid, brought it over to her. Sitting on the edge of the bed, he held out the open jar of the thick scarlet substance.

Bloodroot. London.

She swallowed. "To have carried that from London insinuates you expected to be burned."

He rattled the tin. "No jargon. I knew you would end up burning me in one form or another. I therefore brought this as a peace offering and am asking you tend to my lip in the way I once tended to your wrists. Or did you forget all that I have done for you?"

May a thousand peacocks peck him in the penis for attempting to lay on the guilt.

Grudgingly sitting up and leaning toward him, their gazes locked. She dipped some of the cool substance onto her finger and slowly and gently streaked the salve on his upper lip.

Leaning away, he thudded the lid back onto the tin and tossed it onto the bed. His amber eyes clung to hers. "If you don't want what is about to happen next, leave. Go. Now."

She held his gaze, her skin on fire. "I thought you wanted me alive."

He leaned in. "You changed this game the moment you didn't show up at Larkin's Lane. So how about we become what you reduced us to and fuck?"

It was obvious he was miffed.

That made two of them.

She glared, pushing past him and off the bed. "You will not end what we share by reducing it to what you men always do: *your ego*."

Ridley stepped in front of her, bumping her to a halt. "My ego was never stabbed. Try again. It lays beneath the fucking sternum, has four chambers and two ventricles. Name it."

Jemdanee angled in. "*Ego*. E-G-O."

He tugged her loosened braid down hard, forcing her face and chin to jerk up to his. "You appear to have a lot more of it than I do." He hovered over her mouth with his own. "This is where you admit that your greatest fear is losing the only man you will ever love. But guess what? He wants you to live no matter what happens. And you will. I've lived my life. You haven't."

She swallowed.

He still hovered over her mouth. "Don't think you fucking understand the game you're playing. *You don't*."

Her heart fluttered.

Tilting toward her ear, he breathed hotly, "Are we doing this?"

She grabbed his arm hard to keep herself from falling, a quaking breath escaping her as she drifted her hands down the smoothness of his taut velvet skin, to his waist. "You cannot make love to me and then leave," she choked out.

"Why not?" His voice broke with huskiness. "It will give us both something to live for."

Unable to breathe, her hands frantically jumped to his shaven face in an effort to capture what was so close yet so far away. No longer thinking but feeling, she jerked his head down toward her lips, wanting to *show* him that he was all that mattered.

He resisted, holding her gaze.

She dug her fingers into him. "I will follow you."

"I'm fourteen steps ahead of you and those bare feet. Try to remember that."

"No. Nothing will keep me from—"

"I will." He seized her lips and forcefully worked his tongue against hers, the acrid taste of the bloodroot tinting their tongues. "I'm erasing that you broke my heart," he said against her mouth.

She staggered as she gripped his thick hair hard in an effort to keep him bent down toward herself, their mouths working against each other faster and harder, tongues biting, needing.

Her chest heaved in an effort to keep up with the storm that was him.

Ridley rigidly swept her up into the muscled bulk of his arms and turned them back to the bed. He draped them both onto the mattress. He ground his erection into her while tonguing her deep and deeper.

She melted, wanting this moment to last beyond a lifetime.

Ridley broke their kiss and hovered above her, his flexing heat penetrating every inch of her skin through the silk of her sari. His hair fell into his eyes, making him look like the wilderness he was daring them both to enter.

He rolled off to the side and stretched out, tucking his large hands behind his head. "How often do you masturbate?"

She sat up, her breaths uneven. "You *cannot* be serious. You interrupted our lovemaking to ask *about* lovemaking?"

"I'm trying to get to know you."

She eyed him. "Not to disappoint you, but masturbation is a very small part of who I am."

"Yet a very big part of what defines your pleasure. Answer. How often?"

She flopped back onto the pillow beside him. "Once a week."

He paused. "Is that all?"

Ouch. "Not all of us are interested in entertaining ourselves on the hour."

"You appear to be repressed."

She gasped. "How am I..." She shoved him. "If I am so repressed, why are *you* the one on this bed wanting to talk about it instead of actually doing it?"

He shifted his jaw. "There is more to sex than actually doing it. Fucking creates bonds and I want this bond created properly."

She blinked, trying to understand him. "You overthink everything."

"It's better than not thinking at all." He shifted toward her. "Where do you usually masturbate?"

It was going to be a long night. "Where else? In my bed."

"Never anywhere else?"

"*Nahin.*"

He eyed her as if disappointed. "What do you usually think about when you do it?"

This was... "*You*," she admitted out of the corner of her mouth.

"How nice. Am I doing anything to you?"

Her face was hot. "Why are we...?"

"It's my hope you'll disclose enough for me to give you what you want."

Oh.

"Am I doing anything to you?" he repeated.

"*Haan.* Penetrating me."

He heaved out a breath. "That will be happening regardless. How? Am I above, below, behind..."

He certainly made everything entertaining. "Above."

"Why above?"

She gave him a withering look. "I never really thought about why. You simply are."

"Am I *always* above?"

She snorted. "Yes. Always."

He nudged her. "You need to start putting more effort into your fantasies."

She couldn't believe she was getting lectured over how poorly she masturbated! "What about you, o Hades? When do the flames take you and how hot do they burn?"

"Sometimes as much as four times a day. Never planned. Never the same fantasy. Ever. In my mind, you and I have more or less fucked creatively enough times for me to know exactly what I want out of you once your body is less virginal."

She choked. "Four times a day? How do you make time for that?"

His voice grew husky. "It's never about time. It about leveling one's body and one's mood and one's mind to be what it needs to be: *calm*." He unbuttoned his trousers, drawing attention to a visible and sizable erection buried beneath the fabric. He shifted his hips and rubbed it, but left the flap fastened. "Have you ever touched a prick before?"

Jemdanee veered her gaze to his from where she lay on the pillow, her face hot. He was certainly making her first time memorable. "No."

He grazed her arm. "Unwrap your sari for a moment."

If he thought he could make her writhe due to his level of experience, she could double it.

Unwrapping her sari, she shoved it down to her waist, exposing her breasts. She felt stupid.

He veered his gaze to the expanse of her breasts. He shifted toward her, his hand drifting and curving around each one, his thumb hardening each nipple. "I want you to be comfortable around me. No matter what I'm doing to you or how I'm looking at you."

She swallowed, her breaths uneven. "That may be a bit difficult. In truth, I am beginning to believe I am in anatomy class not in bed with a lover."

He smirked and took back his hand, propping himself on his elbow so he could keep looking at her breasts. "I admire your honesty and your breasts are gorgeous."

Her nipples tingled without even being touched. The cooling breeze of the night from beyond the green net tightened her skin. "These are coming with you to London."

"Your rear is about to hurt. Turn around. I'll fuck it."

She quickly yanked her sari back over herself, self-conscious. As always, he was a bit too casual about everything. She shifted toward him. "Might I ask how many women you have entertained in this manner throughout your life?"

He squinted. "Nineteen."

She gasped. "Are you including the furniture you took them on?" She sat up and shoved him to inform him it was excessive. "No wonder you appear to be so casual about… *sexual congress.*"

He tugged her down and against the mattress. "No need to get huffy. Only one of them ever meant anything to me and that was my first wife. Everything else was me being stupid."

"At least you admit to being stupid." She squinted up at him. "Are you even clean?"

He pinched her. "*Ey.* Insult the cock if you must, but not my level of intelligence. I invested in the best condoms Paris and London had to offer."

"Because, naturally, why stop at Paris?"

"Someone is jealous," he burred. "That hints at emotional attachment which would have been nice to have seen at eleven this morning." He turned toward her, searching her face. "Are you in love with me?"

To admit it would give him too much power. "Why do you want to know?"

He settled back onto the pillow beside her. "I already know. It would simply be nice to hear it." He buttoned his trousers and adjusted them against his erection. "Why not say it?"

"That would be like telling a dog where the bone is at. I prefer not to disclose its location."

He quickly rolled onto her and pinned her to the mattress with his size and weight. "This dog already knows where to dig." He slid down her length and lowered his mouth to her thighs, grazing his hot tongue and his open mouth to them.

A shaky breath escaped her.

Rising, he held her gaze and tugged and pulled back her sari, exposing her breasts. Lifting her hips, he unraveled the rest, whipped it off to the side, leaving her completely naked.

She gripped the linen, wanting more than this night.

He leaned down and laved his hot tongue across each dark nipple, until they hardened and pointed. "We could have been doing this legally." He outlined the curves of her breasts with his fingers and then spread her thighs. He slid his whole palm on the lips of her cunt, using his entire wrist to methodically rub her clitoris and his middle finger to curve up into her vagina.

Her eyes almost rolled to the back of her head in an effort to remain sane. "Since when do you… care about… legalities? Justice, yes. The law? Only when… it suits you."

Ridley skimmed his hands down her legs, folding them upward so he could curve his palms around her toes and then skimmed his hands back up to her thighs, before curving up her belly, breasts and her throat. "Touching you suits me. This and you and your skin reminds me of everything I am sworn to protect." He leaned down and sucked her throat hard.

Gasping, she slid her hands down between them, trying to undo his trousers, but unable to.

His feral gaze held hers. "Allow me." He tugged the linen flap of his trousers *hard*, ripping the buttons and presented his heavy thick length. He knelt, towering above her and brought her hands to it. "Get to know my body," he murmured.

He waited, kneeling with towering, tense muscles.

In disbelieving breaths, she slowly dragged her quaking hands up his toned, muscled thighs to his jutting, thick length that rested below a beautifully defined abdomen. She slid her fingers over the long velvet hardness of his cock, her hands appearing small in an attempt to round it from root to tip. Swallowing, she slid one hand beneath his sac and the other she slid back and forth over the tip of his cock, her face on fire and her body aching.

He slowly wet his lips but otherwise only watched her from above.

He spread her legs wider with his knees and lowering his gaze to her opening, watched his own thumb slide from her clitoris down her slit. "Remember us like this."

A shuddering jolt of pleasure made her frig his cock.

His nostrils flared. He lowered himself onto her. "We'll erase one of your longstanding fantasies. I'll stay on top. Afterward… you'll be forced to get more creative. Agreed?"

"Y-hes." She dragged him down and gripped his waist, waiting.

His heated breaths fanned her cheek as he slowly gripped her hair with both hands, cradling her. He set his forehead to hers. "It will hurt," he rasped.

She swallowed. "I know."

His mouth grazed her earlobe. "Breathe." His hands skimmed her body as his tone grew strained. "Take control of your pain. Guide it in."

She yielded to her own riled need. Gripping his thick length, she guided it between her moist thighs, nudging the head of him into the opening of her womb. The pressure of that sizable tip hinted of the amount of stretching needed.

He shifted his jaw. "Look at me."

She held his gaze and gripped his waist harder, bracing herself for loving him.

Edging it into her, he mounted and pushed down and in.

The searing pain made her stiffen, but she refused to show it. Out of pride. Out of need.

She gripped his back harder, determined to prove that in his name she would take on everything.

Watching her face, he fisted her hair and slowly rode his cock into her, stretching her orifice with a steady, patient pressure. "Breathe."

"I am... trying."

He captured her mouth, working his hot tongue deep against hers. Slowly, his cock pumped into her, increasing in its steady need, but still gentle and not overly deep.

She clung to him, writhing close to bone-clenching tears knowing he was being gentle, while letting him take what the world refused to give him: pleasure. For this was love. Being able to take and hold pain for another. Especially when needed most.

He buried his head into her hair, edging in and out of her with deep strokes. "Jemdanee," he rasped, his hot breath brushing her cheek. "Everything I do is for you. Always. Remember that." He gently stroked in and out of her, the weight and massive width of his muscled body burying her in his heat, his dampening skin and heavy breaths mingling with hers.

Her entire body burned as she forced her mind to drift but his warm mouth against hers and his tongue between her lips, grazing her own tongue, dragged her back to him and that he needed her.

Her heartbeat throbbed in her ears as she sank into the sliver of pleasure she took from the tip of his hot tongue tracing her upper lip, then her lower lip. His entire mouth was soon molded against hers, his tongue delving deeper, toward the back of her mouth, twining and flicking.

Pressing his lips harder into hers, his mouth widened, forcing her tongue further into the wetness of his mouth. She feverishly pushed her mouth, her lips, her tongue against him, determined to fight through fire to get to him.

His hot hands gripped each of her wrists, dragging both of her arms above her head. He shifted against her, still buried deep within her womb. "Now we can fuck." His hands gripped her as he dug his prick more fiercely and harder into hers. Deep push. Then circle.

The searing heat of his body became her own.

Her body writhed, arched and trembled.

His mouth pressed against hers, his tongue roaming. His broad muscled chest expanded in a deep tremble. The fabric of his trousers slid down his thighs, exposing more of him to her as his large hands trailed up her spread thighs. "You're so beautiful." He stroked into her, each stroke emphasizing each word. "So... fucking... beautiful."

Exploding sensations possessed every nerve ending of her body.

He slowed his pace and rolled. Upward. Against her nub.

Roll. Upward. Into her nub.

She panted, the heightened sensations of pleasure making it worth the earlier grit of pain.

His thick length dug deeper making her gasp. Roll. Upward. Into her nub. Again. Again. Again.

Pressure welled.

She moaned, drawing in disbelieving shaky breaths as his sun-bronzed, broad shoulders shifted against her body, his tongue tracing in and out of her mouth. His fingers trailed downward and pushed into her thighs as he spread her legs farther apart and pumped into her rhythmically.

Rapture rose in the pit of her stomach with each pulsing push—push—push.

Her breaths hitched as her fingers slid up his throat and grabbed hold of his thick hair. She held him against herself more savagely, wanting and needing to remember the beauty of knowing he was hers.

She climaxed and cried out. Tensing, she spiraled in and out of bliss to a skin-moistened calm.

Ridley smoothed her hair, trailing his hands down to her throat. "I'm taking you two more times tonight."

She swallowed against his trailing fingers in exasperation. "You are not even done."

"I warned you about opening the door," he rasped, hovering over her mouth. "In this moment, you're only seeing a sliver of me. As I told you before, my way is the rope."

Her lips parted.

He dragged her hand to the rope binding his arm. "Hold it." She swallowed and gripped it.

No longer meeting her gaze, he stroked into her. "Tighter." She tightened her grip.

"Nails. Harder. Make me feel it. Make me believe we can erase every divide between us."

To prove that she could and would take on anything in his name, she dug her nails into the rope and him and his skin, feeling a piece of leather bending out from beneath it.

Withdrawing, he knelt and grabbed her wrist, bringing the peacock bone to the swollen and stiff thickness of his veined cock. Holding her gaze, he gritted his straight white teeth, his muscled broad chest quaking as he pumped his hand over his cock, jerking his hips into forced pleasure.

He shuddered, groaning, spilling the warmth of his seed onto the gold-dipped bone on her wrist. He seethed through his nostrils and masculine mouth, letting more and more spurt down over his knuckles until the last of his seed dripped, which he rolled with his thumb to push from the tip of his cock. He spread the entire pooled semen into the expanse of the bone from one end to the other, holding her gaze. "Is this what you wanted? To have complete control over me and my soul?"

She felt the sticking warmth of his seed as a shaky breath escaped her, seeing every inch of his tan, sinewed and muscled body flexing. "I only want to ensure you never drift into the darkness you once fell into."

Leaning downward and toward her, he dug his fingers into her hair and bit her bottom lip. "It's too late for that. My path was set well before you ever blessed me with a smile." The tension in his face faded as did the grip of his fingers. He searched her face.

She kissed his chin. "No path is ever set."

"That is your optimism speaking. Reality always has different plans." Easing away, he rolled them both over, tugging her against himself hard as he laid himself on his back. "For a moment, I was yours."

Mashing her cheek against his chest, she swallowed in angst and traced a finger against its velvet heat. "For a moment, I believed it."

His hands roamed over her naked curves. "I miss hearing you laugh. You did a lot more of it back in London."

She traced her lips against the curve of tensing muscles on his chest. "Hearing you laugh this morning was worth a peacock giving up his bone."

They held each other in silence for a long time, the net around the bed flowing against the incoming wind as jackals barked in the far distance.

He dug his lips into her hair. "I waited a half hour for you at the Registration Office."

She closed her eyes, not wanting to think about it or argue. One night of peace. One night of nothing but this. Him. Her. Them. She pretended to sleep.

"Jemdanee," he whispered. "Understand that any goodness I have left within me would cease to exist if anything happened to you. I would turn into the very thing I'm fighting."

She pretended to sleep.

Kissing her head, he murmured, "Welcome to the life you never wanted." He smoothed her cheek and hair.

Those words burned into wanting to hold onto a future she vowed to make real: them.

Despite what he thought, there was no changing what she wanted: him.

Not to say that the words he'd once spoken to her in London didn't still haunt her mind. It did.

What you do now will affect the rest of your life and will stay with you. Always. Like a knot. Only you'll never get it out. When you're older, you'll find your place and your stronghold. When you're older, you'll find a man worthy of you. Unfortunately, that man won't ever be me. Aside from the age difference, it's very difficult for me to belong to anyone. For they will always belong to my profession first and to me last.

And she, despite the cursed love she had for him, knew she was still last.

For he thought he could leave her and face evil on his own.

No. Not while she was breathing.

"Jemdanee?" he whispered.

She said nothing. Because damn him into hell she was going to London.

With or without his permission.

CHAPTER TWELVE

Ridley watched the green net around the four poster bed flow and ripple against the incoming wind. Jackals barked in the far distance.

He knew she was pretending to sleep.

Her breaths were still forced and uneven.

It annoyed him.

It meant she planned to oppose him and follow him to London.

An arrest was the only thing that was going to knock some sense into her. The Field Marshal had already agreed to keep her in confinement until he sent word.

He slipped out from holding her and rose from the bed.

Fastening his trousers, he leaned toward the teak bedside table and grabbed a book. He blankly opened it and paged through it.

Life certainly knew how to rape him. Losing a father wasn't enough. Losing the goodness of his soul to the criminal world that was determined to destroy the last of him, wasn't enough. The world now wanted her.

At least he would always have this.

His mind had already accepted what lay ahead.

Two months by coach and two months by boat. Then however long it would take to track this prick down in the name of a game. A game. As if that was all he, Evan Oswald Ridley, was. As if his pain was a deck of cards to be shuffled.

Ridley closed the book, wishing he could erase who he was.

Setting aside the book, he glanced back at her bronzed nudity, her long black hair scattered across the pillow and her closed eyes attempting to play the scheme of stillness despite their occasional movement beneath lids.

It miffed him off.

Everyone treated him as if he were an animal waiting to rip through throats and go wild.

"I know you're not sleeping," he rumbled out in agitation. He jerked the linen away from her nude body. "And I also know what you're thinking." His hand quaked as he gripped the linen hard to calm himself and his thoughts. "If you oppose me in this, there are orders in place and you'll only have yourself to blame. So don't follow me out of the city, do you understand me?"

Her eyes popped open, revealing astounded bright blue eyes. She sat up, dragging back the linen over her nudity and the sari that had pooled around her waist. "You need me."

Ridley shifted toward her on the bed, taking hold of her long black hair. He raveled it around his hand and held her gaze. "Come here, *mon chou*. Knee to knee. Eye to eye."

She hesitated and then scooted toward him across the linen.

When they were knee to knee, he wove both of his hands in her hair and tugged her close. "If you follow me to London, Jemdanee," he warned in a low tone to ensure he was as serious as the blood running within him, "you will be arrested and kept in confinement. For I would sooner strip you of your dignity and end what we share then let you think you can kill yourself, and in turn, kill me. You will *not* murder us both."

Tears welled in her eyes. "Ridley, I am scared for you."

His chest tightened. Though she refused to say it, the love she had for him was pure. More than he deserved. More than he could have hoped for.

Setting his head against hers, he softened his voice. "One day, *mon dévot*, we will find a way to be together again. It simply won't be anytime soon."

She hesitated, searching his face. "You assemble your weapons and I will assemble mine. Permit me to protect you as you protect me."

He wasn't a man known to melt often, but in that moment, he damn well did.

Capturing her lips, he lowered her back onto the mattress, his mind and his body wanting to remember every moment of her and this. His cock thickened and hardened.

There was only one other way to ensure she would stay.

The devil whispered that it was up to him to ensure it.

Working his mouth slowly against hers, he shifted his weight onto her. He wrapped her legs around himself and still tonguing her, positioned his length against her wetness and softness. He guided himself into her and with the jerk of hips, penetrated her tightness to the hilt.

She gasped, stiffening beneath him.

He gently rolled into her, attempting to retain control over her body that was adjusting to his.

This wasn't about pleasure.

It was about containing her heart. Her breaths. Her womb. Her soul. Her blood. Her life.

He buried his head into the softness of her throat and needing to unleash the depth of everything she made him feel, he pushed into her tightness, stretching it so it never forgot the feel of him. Deeper. More. Burn. The tightness of that cunt was intoxicating. Hot. Wet.

His prick grew stiffer and thicker, pressing and stretching against her squeezing vaginal lips.

Fuck.

His prick grew unmanageable, his sac overly tight.

In between steel-controlled breaths, he jerk-jerk-jerked into her tightness, ensuring her he was hitting her clit every time, while working through mind-numbing, core-tightening sensations, frigging out the primal need to spill.

Their gaze locked.

She panted, gripping his shoulders. "Ah! Ah!"

Her quim. Tight. Too tight. He gritted his teeth.

Pumping his throbbing prick, and in between pained, ragged breaths that blurred his reality, his skin overheated he thudded three years of need into her. "Do it. Let me hear you."

"Ridley!" She cried out and shuddered, her nails digging into him.

He imagined every inch of her bronzed writhing body

bound, with her hemp-covered knees spread wide to him so she couldn't *ever* close her slit to him.

He thudded his swollen cock into her, no longer aware of anything but a need to—

"*Fuck.*" Intelligent words usually fleeted even from a cultivated mind like his, for he still was at the foundation of his soul what he refused to acknowledge: a man in need of being wanted by a woman who had drowned out his common sense.

His mind spun and careened on its axis knowing that by filling this moment of physical desire, he was tearing apart his soul in her name.

Sweat drenched him as he worked into her relentlessly, smearing his lips across her cheek in an effort to taste the bronze of her skin. "Bite my shoulder. Show me your love."

She gasped, her teeth punishing him as she dug them into his shoulder.

He was not losing her to what waited in London.

There was only one way of ensuring she didn't follow.

Beyond prison. He was taking her soul.

Gritting his own teeth, he pushed the length and thickness of his rigid cock hard and harder into her wet tightness, digging deep enough to feel the resistance of her womb. "I may be leaving," he growled, "but this part of me will stay. You will always be mine."

She rolled her hips upward, informing him her womb was his.

Pumping through the coiling need of his core that erased his mind with blinding bliss, it rocked him and his entire body forward. His prick erupted, pulsing in time with his swollen sac and his seething breaths that tried to keep up. He hissed out breath after burning breath between bared teeth as he held her gaze.

Groaning, he jutted and staggered.

His ragged breaths filled the room as sweat traced its way down his face and throat.

He savagely held onto her. His breath and body still tight against the crashing waves of pleasure that jarred him further into her. He was… still… climaxing.

He seethed out breaths as his semen spurted into her womb in pulses that rattled him in the longest lasting fuck he'd ever had. He poured his pleasure and every last drop of semen into her sucking wetness to ensure she knew of his love.

There was no taking it back and he didn't regret it.

Her ragged breaths and his mingled.

She smoothed her hands against his entire back. "What if I end up with a child?" she whispered.

He hoped. "Then it becomes your duty to protect our babe," he rasped. "You are the shield to its life. That is why you will stay."

She was quiet for a long moment. "Is that why you did it?"

Ridley swallowed hard, smoothing her hair. "I cannot make promises, but I will do everything within my power to come back and hold you both."

Jemdanee buried herself against him. "Ridley, you are making me hate you."

"Better to hate me than to love me and die for it. I can earn your love again when I return."

She glared. "Giving birth doesn't come without some risks, *phaujee*."

He kissed her. "If you mean to lecture me, I suggest you lecture yourself. Penetration always involves the possibility of offspring whether I spill into you or not."

She tried to break their hold.

"No." Rolling them onto the mattress he eased out a breath, holding her tight and tighter. "I have to be in the barracks in the morning and throughout most of the day, so I won't see you again until tomorrow night when I leave. This is the only time we will have." He molded her against himself.

She tried to push him away.

He gripped her. "Tomorrow night, I will ensure you receive ten thousand rupees to see you through the next year. Your residence will be heavily guarded by the military to ensure you remain safe at all times."

Her voice cooled. "There is not much equality in what you are doing. You are binding my hands and expecting me to accept it." She shoved him and pushed hard. "*Release me!*"

He unfurled his arms, numb.

She scooted off the bed, dragging her sari off with it.

Ridley watched her tug up her sari over her full bronzed breasts, covering what he already missed. *Stay calm.* "I'll be at the tennis courts with Dunning tomorrow at three. Join us."

She walked over to the adjoining door and unlatched it. "I will be packing my entire inventory of flora all day and will see you tomorrow evening at nine. I depart when you do."

Anger coiled and singed and scraped the corners of his mind. He sat up. "Ey. Don't think you can oppose me *and* treat me like this."

She opened the door, glaring. "You used my own body against me. How could you?!"

Unbelievable. "I told you what I was doing. You could have stopped me. Why didn't you?"

Her features twisted. "Maybe a part of me fears it will be all I have left of you."

Ridley's heart squeezed with... *regret*. A bleeding regret that ripped through his mind.

He didn't regret that maybe her belly would stretch with his child. His regret was knowing he might never see either of them again. There were only so many passes in life that he, as an inspector, was going to get and he knew in his gut that this was it.

He was Faust standing in the darkest part of the woods and it was over. But at least for a few glimmering, incredible breaths, he saw what the future might have been: her.

His soul burned, wishing he could have given her more. It had been wasted on coca/limestone and the three years they had lost. He tapped the mattress, softening his voice. "Stay with me. Sleep with me. Come."

She glared, her blue eyes flaring. "I have tried to talk to you and you do nothing but play god with both our lives. What if I end up with a babe and you die?"

"Cease being overly dramatic. You might not even end up pregnant."

"*Might* is not the same as *not*. Nor are you addressing the possibility of your death, which obviously does not scare you, but it does scare me!"

Jesus. "Can you permit me a moment of peace I have never known?" He hit the mattress with a fist. "You. Here. Now. Why? Because this sort of love deserves more respect. Are you saying you don't love me? Show me your love and your respect. Come here. Lay down."

She tossed her hands into the air and let them flop to her sides. "For as intelligent as you think you are, you are an idiot."

He pointed. "How does insulting the man you love progress this conversation?"

She rolled her eyes. "Nothing else seems to. Stubborn as you are, you think you deserve nothing but death and off you go to play with it and lalala. No wonder you rifled through nineteen women and could not make your first marriage last!"

Ridley lowered his chin, the sting of that comment slashing far too deep for him to ignore. He rolled off the mattress and thudded his bare feet onto the floor, buttoning his trousers. "Pardon me?"

She paused.

He stalk-limped toward her, towering. "Say it again. Only slower. Something about my inability to be a man to any woman and... *Elizabeth*? Are you saying you know her? Are you saying you talked to her extensively about the sort of marriage she and I had?" He glared. "All I did was suffer and she enjoyed every fucking moment of it. So go visit that madhouse I divorced and the amount of people she loves to hurt with a smile, because guess what? This son of a bitch that wants her dead, too. So consider yourselves all equally privileged for having ever known me."

She blinked up at him, then averted her gaze.

Taking her arm, he guided her into her own room. "Insult me if it will permit you to breathe, but we don't always get to choose how we go in this life. That *is* life. Do you think my father chose to go by the way of the ax at the age of forty-seven? Sometimes the dirt on the path before us is exactly that: dirt. It's time you acknowledge what you and your giggles refuse to: *the dirt is real*."

Knowing he might not see her again if anything went wrong, he swallowed past that pain and tried to remain calm. "I will see you tomorrow at nine." He pointed rigidly at her, chanting to himself that he wouldn't yell at her for taking their only night away from them. For this was not how he wanted their last moments to be spent. "If, in the end, you still prefer to hold an ax over a baby, Kumar, then I have to say, you're an even bigger loon than I am."

With that, he slammed the door, tremoring the wall, and

locked it.

Everything disappeared into a single pinprick that reminded him of the moment he had been told he couldn't see his father's body.

Numb, he damned himself for having love yet another woman.

Without the usual organizational time he took, Ridley started blindly gathering everything in his room and shoving it into trunks.

Books. Clothing. Uniforms. Ledgers. Books. More books. Too many books. His shaving razor. His cane. Everything.

He crushed everything in, trunk by trunk by trunk and strapped all three with the grit of teeth. Hefting it up, he tossed each trunk out the window so he didn't have to go through the corridor.

He then hopped on the ledge of the window and joined the trunks.

It was his way of saying goodbye to what he refused to feel.

The following afternoon
Officer Sanctioned Tennis Courts

Although everything was unraveling, the rope master in him always had a plan.

Ridley rolled up his linen sleeves to his biceps, exposing JEMDANEE to the world. He rounded the youth, reached into the basket set beside his boots and snatched up one of the leather balls stuffed with wool. "We begin."

Dunning, who fingered his wooden racket, eyed the razored lettering. "That there is true devotion, sir. I have never seen a man do that to himself."

He liked this boy. He offered his mind freely. Few did.

Ridley tapped at the lettering with the leather ball. "Women don't always appreciate the length men go through in their name. Not even spelling it out to them is enough."

"She didn't like it?"

"She accused me of being a loon."

Dunning turned the racket but said nothing.

Ridley pointed at the boy's head. "You are thinking it, too. Aren't you?"

Shaking his head violently, Dunning blurted, "I would… no. I would never, sir."

Veering in and towering over the boy, he bit out, "You fold your hands at cards too quickly. Don't ever let me or others intimidate you or… guess what?" Ridley shoved him hard, sending the boy stumbling backward. "You lose. Every. Fucking. Time."

Dunning stiffened, his fingers and knuckles whitening against the racket he held.

Ridley veered in again close. "Are you going to stand there? You have a weapon. It's called a racket and it's in your hand. Make use of your environment." He thudded that shoulder. "Do you have a sister?"

Dunning stumbled and eyed him. "Four."

"Any brothers?"

"No."

"Any male cousins?"

"Only female ones."

"Who are you closest to? Your father or your mother?"

He hesitated. "My mother."

Ridley sighed. "That explains everything." He thudded his shoulder again. "Learn to be soft when it matters most, but never always. Always isn't going to protect you. Who cares if you offend the world? The world doesn't care if it offends you." Ridley shoved him. "*Swing at me.*"

Dunning's features wavered.

"I'm the tennis ball, Dunning. Swing. Let that racket fly and hit me. You have permission."

The youth hesitated then whipped back his arm and swung.

Catching his arm hard, Ridley effortlessly held it in place. "Try again. Use the racket despite me holding it. Use it."

Dunning gritted his teeth and wrestled against him, trying to move the racket. "I… I'm trying to— You won't let me!" He flopped his arm. "I'm not good at this."

Keeping that arm and racket between them, Ridley held his gaze. "You give up too easily. Just because you're weaker, Dunning, doesn't mean you can't outsmart me. We only have these next few hours and it isn't much time to give you much of anything, but it's enough to get you started. After we finish, I'm leaving you to continue with one-on-one special training I arranged with Brigadier Brinkworth. He will ensure you push through the ranks within a few months."

Dunning's lips parted. "Brigadier Brinkworth is a legend."

"Damn right. I'm hiring him to train you and in return, you can peer in on Jemdanee for me. Keep her out of trouble. I already have things in place for her, but an extra skull is always nice. Will you do that for me?"

Searching his face, Dunning hesitated. "Is she not leaving with you?"

Ridley released his arm. "If she does, she could end up dead. An ax straight through her. And if you think I'm exaggerating, I can show you some facsimiles of what could happen to her."

Dunning eyed him. "You don't have to say anything more, sir. I'll look after her as best I can."

He knew he liked this boy. "Your contract was reduced to a year by the Field Marshal."

Dunning choked. "He... reduced it for me?"

"You have four sisters and a mother. You have other wars to fight." Turning, Ridley muscled the leather ball against the wall, thudding it. "Go up against that wall."

"Yes, sir!" Dunning jogged over to the wall and faced him.

Ridley pointed. "That wall behind you is your future. It will always be there even once you leave this tennis court. That wall is the woman you love. That wall is everything you ever believed in. What are you going to do to protect it knowing I plan to destroy it?"

Glancing toward it, Dunning whirled the racket and squinted. "Pummel anything that comes near it."

"Bravo." Ridley picked up another leather ball and whipped it.

Dunning roared and swung at the ball with the racket, missing the leather ball.

It thudded the wall behind him.

Dunning eyed it. "Does this mean I have no future?"

Ridley tsked. "Wait until Brinkworth is done with you. That wall behind you will become a reality and you will learn to protect that reality *without* a racket." He pointed. "Again."

Dunning whirled the racket.

Picking up another ball, Ridley gritted his teeth at the thought of Jemdanee and whipped it so *hard*, the leather seam popped when it hit the wall.

Dunning eyed him. "Am I going to live through this?"

"Barely." He tossed up another ball. "*Again.*"

CHAPTER THIRTEEN

The coach was waiting.

Her trunks and the massive medicinal chest were already long strapped within that coach.

Perusing the room one last time, Jemdanee paused.

Something gleamed against the light of the *diya*. Drifting toward it, she dragged aside the green netting of the four poster bed and peered at a necklace set with a dark green stone speckled with red. It had been set on her pillow, announcing Ridley had visited the room in the past hour without her knowing.

She could smell his cologne.

She gathered the weight of the necklace, her lips parting.

It was unusual in its gleam and red inclusions.

She'd never seen anything like it.

Slowly, she pulled it over her head and set it around her throat, its weight reminding her of the association she would always share with him. Heavy. Weighing. Refusing to let her breathe. Much like the black diamond ring that weighed her finger.

She clung to the pendant, kissing it hard.

It was time to step off the cliff and forget there was a bottom.

Her man needed her.

Peering into the mirror one last time, she smoothed her moonstone sari against her curves, and eased out a shaky breath, deciding to keep her hair in a braid.

It was a rope. And Ridley had already tied her in knots.

Steadying her mind, she quietly left Spence's and crossed the dirt road past the gates to enter the grounds of the Government House where she once again used the key in a nearby pot to access the kitchens.

She entered the back servant corridors, veering into the massive kitchens.

She decided to bring a peace offering in the guise of food.

With a stack of mangoes she peeled and sliced by the light of a single candle in the silence of the kitchen, she sucked the stickiness from her fingers and then carried the bowl of peeled and sliced mangoes outside into the darkness of the warm night.

Trying to even her breathing, she made her way through the torch-lit grounds shrouded by night.

In the far distance, toward the Banyan tree grove just past her greenhouse whose glass gleamed from surrounding torches, she spotted the old massive banyan tree.

A flickering lantern illuminated the silhouette of Ridley with a satchel and a stack of books beside him. He sat, casually propped against the trunk. His good knee was bent to allow for his muscled arm to drape it as he continued to read a book, his gaze intent.

It meant he was thinking.

When wasn't he?

She was beginning to realize that was his problem.

Weaving her way through the low hanging branches of the banyan, she seated herself beside him on the ground and nestled close. She set the bowl of mangoes between them to create a very visible line neither of them were allowed to cross. "A peace offering."

Ridley continued reading. "You are late."

"By a minute."

"By seven." He didn't look up from the book. "Where were you?"

At least he was talking to her. She didn't even expect that much. "I was peeling mangoes." She tapped at the bowl. "Did you want one?"

He shifted his jaw. "No."

She sighed and tilted over to read the gold lettering on the leather bound book. The title was longer than the book. "*Experimenta circa effectum conflictus elecrici in acum magneticam?*" She eyed him. "Whatever are you reading?"

"I am studying electromagnetism."

"Dear Kali. Why?"

"It's a branch of physics that will one day rule the world."

She wasn't even going to try to understand his mind.

He continued to read.

She blamed herself for their argument. She shouldn't have left his bed last night. Nor should she have brought up his former wife. It had slipped out like an eel.

The tongue, the tongue, always the tongue. "I wish to apologize for the words I said."

"It won't give us back the night you took from us."

Her throat tightened knowing he hadn't looked at her once. "The necklace is beautiful."

His voice grew distant. "Heliotrope. I bought for you in Bombay."

"Does it hold any meaning?"

He turned a page and continued reading for a long moment. "It has a long history. The red inclusions, however, gives it the name it is most known for: bloodstone. I thought it fitting. I am the stone and you are the one attempting to squeeze the blood out of me."

She heaved out a breath. "Is this what our remaining moments will be? You grouching?"

"I'm not angry with you, Jemdanee. I was last night and throughout most of the day, but not in this moment. I'm far angrier with what life has given me. One would think I would be used to it by now, but it never hurts any less." Without meeting her gaze, he gestured to the pile of books. "Pick one. Read."

She nudged the pile of books. "I prefer to talk."

He flipped a page hard. "I know about the coach, Kumar. Having it sit in front of the hotel all day is anything but discreet."

"I am not attempting to be discreet. The moment you leave, I leave."

"The moment your little foot touches the floor of that coach, you will regret it." He picked up a book and set it on her knee, tapping it. "It's a translation of *Les Bijoux Indiscrets* by Diderot."

Picking up the book, she paged through it. "I am bored with it already."

"It will fetch you a price of four hundred pounds. Don't take any less for it and only sell it if you need more than what is in the satchel."

She noted its rather slim spine in disbelief. "Four hundred? For this? *Why?*"

"1748. Its popularity has remained constant." He eyed her. "It's the story of a sultan who possesses a magic ring which makes the genitals of his ladies at court speak."

She rolled her head toward him. "What level of absurdity do you think I would believe in?"

"Page forty, bottom sentence going into page forty one."

Realizing he was serious, she quickly flipped to forty and read, "*His ring was instantly leveled at her…*" Her brows went up. "*…Panting for breath was heard… Ah! Ah! Pray stop… you melt me excessively…*" She slapped the book shut. "Why do you even have this book?"

"What book don't I have? Despite its level of *absurdity*, it is exactly what you and I have reduced ourselves to intellectually in the name of passion. It's quite fitting."

She tsked, imagining him as a boy of nine sternly seated at the table and pointing at his parents to sit down. "Did you raise your parents or did they raise you?"

He returned to reading. "Try not to dig for compliments in our last moments together. If you get bored, feel free to leave anytime. I won't keep you from boarding your coach, but don't say I didn't warn you. You will be under close surveillance from this night forth."

Jemdanee eyed him, the shadows of the lantern light illuminated his rugged features, blurring his dark hair into the darkness that surrounded them. It was obvious he was attempting to dominate and muscle her into submitting to what he wanted.

Setting aside the bowl of mangoes on the other side of herself, she scooted closer to him, nestling knee to knee beside him. She propped her chin against his muscled arm and nudged him in the hopes of softening him. "Read to me."

He shifted his jaw and tapped at the page. "It's in Latin."

Of course it was.

She dragged her bare foot gently against his trouser-clad leg. His injured one. "I love you."

He paused, his rugged features softening. "Do you?" He gripped her foot tightly, his thumb tracing it.

She smiled. It was amazing how three seemingly simple words could soften a gruff man with a million. She smoothed a hand down his muscled calf, her fingers grazing the marred knots of skin beneath the fabric of his trousers. "I love you very much."

He gave her a withering look. "Whilst I am enjoying this," he rumbled out, "don't think I'm about to change my mind because you're purring."

She nestled closer. "What happened between us last night is not the end, but the beginning. I am asking you to believe that. Take me with you."

He said nothing.

"Your life is worth far more than the price you are putting on it." Tossing the book from his hand, she grabbed up a sliced mango from the wooden bowl and wedged it past those lips until her finger slid it against the side of his cheek. "With this mango, I thee wed."

In between the slowest chews she had ever seen any human take, he stared at the bowl between them. He dug through the entire bowl, crushing each and every one until not even juice remain before tossing it.

She veered her gaze to the bowl, watching him crush and throw out more and more as if it were his right. She gave him a withering look.

He held up a hand, the mango juice dripping. "With all of these, I thee wed. Why the hell didn't you marry me? Hm? What was the point of being stubborn?"

She softened her voice. "I will marry you when you choose to live for love, not die for it."

He tossed his wrist, sending the juice and stickiness away from himself.

She grabbed his hand and using the end of her sari, wiped it. "You see? I am useful."

A ragged breath escaped him. Leaning in, he pressed his forehead into hers.

She smoothed his face, trying to remain calm. "Do not let this loon take what is ours."

"He already has," he rasped, "but that doesn't mean I won't make him regret it." Dragging over the wooden bowl, he tilted it. He held up one of the few mangoes remaining and brought it to her lips. "We say *adieu*, my love."

Tears overwhelmed her. "I will not chew to that."

"Yes, you will. Honor me by keeping yourself safe. That is all I ask." He slid the mango past her lips hard until his large finger wedged it against the side of her cheek. "The moment you're done chewing, I leave."

Jemdanee let the sweetness of that mango soak in her mouth, shifting it to sit stubbornly against the inside her cheek. "You have put too much power into my mouth." She waggled the mango. "I will not chew or swallow. Which means you will never be able to leave."

She waggled the mango at him again.

He smoothed her cheek. "Stop making me regret what I cannot change."

She chewed the mango grudgingly.

He leaned in and pressed his masculine lips gently to hers, lingering with his velvet heat but not doing more.

In angst, she focused on every half breath of that moment knowing it was one they would both have to make last.

His lips traced to hers.

After the way they had parted last night, they needed a better ending.

She swallowed and whispered, "Make love to me. Make us both believe it will last."

Something intense flared through his entrancement. "As you wish." With the grit of teeth, he gripped her sari at the hem and *ripped* the fabric to her navel with the jerk of muscles.

She choked, the mango falling out of her mouth and flopping off to the side.

Capturing her mouth hard, he shoved her between the gnarled roots of the ground.

The world splashed away as if she had been submerged into a molten river as his digging mouth and his rigid tongue pushed against hers faster.

Ridley flung her ripped sari apart, his calloused fingers digging into her legs, her skin. "I worship your need to be with me." He tongued her until she could barely hold him or breathe.

217

"I worship your strength in *wanting* to be with me."

Pushing open her exposed thighs, he brought the coolness of a mango to her nub.

She choked, gasped, giggled and writhed as he flicked the ripened fruit against her. "What are you—"

"Who worships you?" he breathed against her throat.

"The mango," she gargled out with a laugh.

He bit her shoulder in reprimand. "*No*. I do."

She gasped and clung to him in exasperation woven with mind erasing ecstasy, digging her nails into his broad shoulders to return the deliverance of his punishment.

"Who worships you?" he insisted, frigging the mango faster against her nub.

"You do," she choked out, unable to think.

Blinding bliss was beginning to take over the last of her body and mind, rippling sensations through every inch of her. The swaying of the banyan branches against the cooling wind above them matched the trembling of her heated, straining her thighs as he frantically masturbated her and bit her throat hard.

Her eyes almost rolled back with her.

Holding up the mango between them, he guided it to her mouth.

She shoved it away, snapping back to reality. "Do *not* feed that to me."

He held her gaze and slowly inserted it into his own mouth. "Mmmmm."

Cringing, she pushed at his face. "*Salla*."

"And you think you're ready to be my hero?" he breathed. "*You're too squeamish*." He quickly straddled her and undid the buttons on his trousers, letting his erection fall into his hand as he positioned himself between her thighs. "I'm not holding back. You're going to take it."

Their gazes locked between heavy breaths.

With the grit of teeth and savage jerk of his hips, he penetrated her so fast and so deep, the pulsing thick length of his cock hit her core hard, blurring her reality with agony.

Fully buried to the hilt in her womb, he wrapped her legs around his waist and dug in rougher.

She bit past pain, gasping to take in air against the weight of his body and the ache of her thighs.

Tucking the remaining half of the mango from his own mouth into hers with the push of his tongue, he stilled. "Now you know how I feel when I'm with you," he whispered. "In pain. Always."

The stretching of his deeply buried cock pinched her too deep.

He tongued her. "You're not fucking me." He kissed her deeply. "Move more."

She couldn't breathe. Everything about him blurred her reality and her heart.

He dragged his lips across hers. "I'm waiting."

She tried to roll her hips up against him, quivering to find the pleasure he was denying her.

"Harder. So our bodies remember it."

"It hurts."

"I know. Take it. For me."

A tear rolled down her cheek and mixed with the juice of the mango streaming from her lips as the root of his cock repositioned in her cunt and hit and rubbed, hit and rubbed her nub. She moaned and gave into the ecstasy of extreme pleasure that was now piercing past the extreme discomfort.

He dragged his tongue across her mouth in an attempt to soothe her, thrusting faster until he thudded into her tightness without restraint.

She panted to keep up with the demand of pleasure that smeared her mind. She swallowed hard and was rewarded with the tingling sweetness of fruit that was almost gone.

"I love you," he rasped against her throat, between heavy breaths, still fucking her.

"*I love you*." She gasped and pushed up and into him, nearing her peak. There. There!

His heated breaths fanned her mouth faster and faster as he thudded into her with his prick.

She flinched, clinging to him as her core unraveled in gloried agony. She trembled, her body erasing everything she had ever known until finally... she spiraled into the climax she didn't think she would touch against the pain.

Ridley dragged himself out to the tip, then rammed it back in and in an anguished groan against her throat, let seed wash into her in warm jets she could feel. "Take it." He pumped and pumped and rammed and rammed through it, groaning. "Take it." He eventually stilled.

Forehead to forehead, they breathed their way back to a chest heaving calm as sweat trickled against their pressed bodies.

The world swayed and fell into the silence of night as the sway of the banyan tree branches rustled overhead.

Dragging his lips across her cheek, he rasped into her ear, "Never forget me, *ma femme dorée*."

Tears overwhelmed her as she dug her fingers into him and kissed and kissed his face and his throat and his lips and his chest, refusing to let him go. "Do not speak as if you are already dead to me."

"Be prepared for the worst and be surprised by the best." He pulled out, buttoning his flap and covered her nudity with her sari, dragging her *pallu* from her shoulder and draping it downward and over the ripped slit he had made. Kissing her lips hard, he whispered, "The satchel has all the money you need."

She swallowed.

He skimmed her braid from its beginning to end, his features growing anguished and tapped at his ring. "Wait for it to find you." His husky voice cracked. "I love you."

She tried to grab for his face but he already jumped to his booted feet, tossing up one of his books.

"Let me walk away or I never will." He turned and quickly strode off into the silence of the vast garden, gripping the book as if he had no need for anything else to keep him company.

Jemdanee laid her cheek against the ground and eased out shaky breaths, listening to the call of nightjars. The same nightjars that had sang the night she had first arrived to the Government House.

She wasn't staying.

Scrambling up, she winced against the soreness of her own body. "Ow."

How did women walk straight in the world?

None of it had even been with his rope. Uff.

Knowing she didn't have much time, she frantically grabbed up the satchel and shoved his books into it. Leaving the bowl, she folded and tucked her *pallu* better around herself to cover the exposed section of her thighs and jogged after the far distant shadowy figure of Ridley that was almost at the gate.

She sprinted against the now cool wind, refusing to let the

heaviness of the satchel or the soreness of her body slow her down. Stumbling past the gates, she swung out and upon seeing Ridley, scrambled back.

She set herself against the stone arch of the gate, her heart pounding and waited, her angst making it impossible for her to breathe. Listening to his heavy steps fading, she edged back out and watched as Ridley hoisted himself into a lantern-lit military coach.

He paused, glancing toward her.

She remained in the shadows and counted out each breath, tears streaming down her face.

He stood on the step of the military coach, still looking toward her.

She knew he knew.

She pressed her fingers to her trembling lips and held them up.

He pressed his fingers to his lips and held them up.

It was good-bye. For now.

But not forever.

Ridley ducked inside.

A sob escaped her.

Once he was in the vehicle and the thudding of hooves penetrated the dirt road with the swaying of lantern lights that went in the opposite direction of where she stood at the gate, she dashed across the nearly empty shadow-strewn street.

Running faster and faster, until plumes of dust surrounded her as if she were rising from hell to be with Ridley, she found the strength to finally shout in Hindi to her waiting coachman, "*Challo!* Follow the military coach!"

She jerked to a halt, between heaving breaths, realizing the Indian driver was not in the box.

She frantically ran past the shadows toward the lanterns of the coach.

A figure stepped out from behind the coach. "*Miss Kumar.*"

She froze.

The Field Marshal whirled a wooden baton, tapping it against shackles he held, and pointed at her head. "It appears you are attempting to leave the city. Are you?"

She hissed out a disbelieving breath. "No, *sahib*. No. I was only…"

"Satchel down, please."

She decided to play the part of a memsahib. "It will get dirty if I set it down."

He glared. "You and Kalpita might as well be the same woman. Satchel down and hands up."

Jemdanee gripped the satchel tighter, her knuckles whitening. "You cannot permit Ridley to face this alone. What if he dies and tonight is the last I ever see of him? *Are you that unfeeling*?"

The Field Marshal's tone hardened. "I wouldn't recommend using female tears. I've seen enough to be immune to everything." He veered in, the iron shackles clanging as he stood over her with the grip of the baton he lifted. "Satchel down and hands up or a haversack *will* go over your head."

She knew the man well enough to know that the baton would hit her head if she resisted.

Numb, Jemdanee dropped the satchel with a thud and set both of her hands against her head.

This is what loving a man led to. This.

Being humiliated.

Being helpless.

Being shackled.

Being fucked.

She paused.

The towering, muscled figure of a man emerged from the shadows and with the grit of teeth, used the back of his rosewood musket to dash the Field Marshal's skull.

Eyes rolling to the back of his head, the Field Marshall collapsed, limp.

She choked, scrambling back as the Field Marshal's hands were each latched with shackles.

Finished with bolting the shackles, Lieutenant Bradley thudded a large leather boot onto the back of the Field Marshal and inclined his head, never once breaking her gaze. "Ridley placed you on a military list of passengers who aren't allowed to board any ship in any port. That means London is out of the question unless you and I come to some sort of agreement. Name your price, cherub, and I'll name mine. Be forewarned, it's hefty."

The unwelcome tension stretched even tighter between them.

There were worse things than bargaining with a fallen angel.

Ridley needed her and whatever price she had to pay to ensure he lived, was the face of the coin she would hold up.

THE END OF BOOK 2

The Whipping Society Saga

FEATURING MR. RIDLEY & JEMDANEE KUMAR
throughout all three books

BOOK 1, MR. RIDLEY
BOOK 2, THE DEVIL IS FRENCH
BOOK 3, REBORN

ABOUT THE AUTHOR

USA TODAY best-selling author Delilah Marvelle is the winner of the *RT Book Reviews* Reviewer's Choice for Best Sensual Historical Romance of the Year and had *Booklist* name *Forever and a Day* one of the Top 10 Romances of 2012. She loves researching the grittier side of history that gets omitted by too many historians and collects vintage and out-of-print books that allow her to delve into the underbelly of forgotten history. Aside from writing, she is also the co-founder of the Historical Romance Retreat, which brings the world of history and romance alive for readers! You can visit her website at www.DelilahMarvelle.com or visit the Historical Romance Retreat at www.HistoricalRomanceRetreat.com.

CPSIA information can be obtained
at www.ICGtesting.com
Printed in the USA
BVHW032205140323
660475BV00003B/117